EXILE
FROM
EDEN

Also by Andrew Smith

Grasshopper Jungle
The Alex Crow
Rabbit & Robot

EXILE FROM EDEN

OR, AFTER THE HOLE

ANDREW SMITH

First published in the USA by Simon & Schuster BFYR, an imprint of Simon & Schuster Children's
Publishing Division, 1230 Avenue of the Americas, New York, New York 10020

First published in Great Britain in 2019 by by Electric Monkey, an imprint of Egmont UK Limited
The Yellow Building, 1 Nicholas Road, London W11 4AN

ISBN 978 1 4052 9396 9

A CIP catalogue record for this title is available from the British Library

63042/001

Printed and bound in Great Britain by CPI Group

Typeset by Avon DataSet Ltd; Bidford on Avon, Warwickshire

For Trevin and Chiara.
From the surface, I have dragged down bits and pieces for you.

CONTENTS

Part One: A Model of the World

Part Two: All Stories Are True

Part Three: After the Hole

PART ONE

A Model of the World

"The jury is undecided on humanity," I said.
"How so?" the wild boy asked.

What matters is real love for things of the world outside
us and for the deep secrets within us.

—Max Beckmann

All stories are true the moment they are told.

Whether or not they continue to be true is up to the listener.

Like all self-portraits, this is a true story.

This is where I assemble, as a unit, everything I know.

It is filthy art, and pure as water; it is a model of all things that ever came before me, without end, constructed by the broken hands of someone who'd never been a firsthand witness to anything at all, to be honest, in his life.

It is all so futile, isn't it?

The Breakfast Papers

I am my father's son.

If there is one thing he gave me, it is this: Like my father, I have an endless fascination with putting things together.

One time—this happened about two months ago—he brought home a kind of puzzle for me. The puzzle had been sealed inside a large colorful box. The box said this on it:

THE VISIBLE MAN

SCIENCE ASSEMBLY PROJECT

After I put the puzzle together, I decided to name my visible man science assembly project Breakfast.

My grandmother, whose name is Wendy, was unhappy with the way I'd put together Breakfast, my visible man science assembly project.

Wendy was always so regimented and constrained.

She said, "Why don't you follow the instructions?"

"You don't need instructions if you know how to think" was my answer.

I didn't even bother to consult the image of the visible man that had been printed on the cover of the box Breakfast came in. No matter. He wasn't much of a man—visible or otherwise. He was missing some key parts, and anyone could see that, whether you looked at the instructions or not.

My father told me that science frequently regards modesty as being superior to truth.

But Wendy was angry because I'd glued Breakfast's brain on top of his see-through head, as opposed to inside his skull, which is where anyone—instructions or not—would have naturally concluded a brain belonged. I also painted an extra set of eyes on Breakfast's brain and affixed his lungs to his shoulders as though they were a pair of chubby pink wings.

Breakfast was arguably ugly, but he was mine.

Also, he infuriated Wendy, my grandmother, who was eternally attached to elaborate lists of rules and protocols.

I might explain the name I'd given my modestly edited visible man science assembly project. Breakfast was a real person, and he was out there somewhere. In many ways, I was obsessed with the idea that one day I would meet the real person named Breakfast. I frequently tried to imagine the feeling of meeting anyone else, especially a young person—a boy, someone like me—which is what my father and I concluded the real Breakfast was. I had never seen another human being—visible or otherwise—besides the people I'd lived with for my entire life.

Think about that!

Because it had been my understanding that everything people had decided for themselves to be real—and this was supported by accounts, without end, in stories, books (true and otherwise), paintings, and music—had all been a result of stitching together the collected experiences and emotions of the people around them, even if they were lies. And among the many things my father had brought home to me over the last few months was an odd assortment of artifacts he'd used in compiling a presumed history of this boy who was named Breakfast.

Father called these artifacts our Breakfast Papers, and, like me, Father wanted to find this person, if for no other reason than to validate Breakfast's existence and to put to the test our assumptions about the boy's life.

Maybe it was just a game—something my father made up to keep me entertained. Who knows?

Perhaps none of it was real, but, like the visible man science assembly project I named Breakfast, putting things together was something my father and I were both driven to do.

We lived inside a hole.

Naturally, I had nothing to compare our hole to. I had only on one occasion been anywhere else that wasn't within very short walking—or sprinting—distance from the hole. But growing up here, and hearing the others talk about our hole as they did, I pieced together a picture that it was pretty nice and concluded that we were all very lucky, which is what my father liked to call me: Lucky.

Robby, my other dad, called me Arek, which is my real name.

So, after sixteen years and some days, I crawled up from our hole in the snow-covered ground. I was like one of those bugs—a cicada, which I have only seen in books from our library.

The books tell me that cicadas live for about seventeen years underground, and then, after they come up, they only live another month or so. Knowing that the upstairs part of their lives will only last a few weeks is probably what keeps them underground so long. In any event, it was not my intent that Mel and I would expire in a matter of weeks, but what can you do?

I grew up with Mel. She's the only other person I know who's basically been a human cicada. Mel and I were born in the hole. I also had powerful, unexplainable feelings about her—feelings that caused a sensation like something was growing inside my rib cage, trying to crawl out of me, like the plastic parts inside Breakfast, every time I even thought about her. Like now. But I would never have told Mel about that.

It would have been too weird.

I asked my father about the way Mel made me feel, how sometimes I couldn't sleep thinking about her. It was times like these, when we would talk—especially about things that happen to boys when they are fifteen or sixteen—that my father's eyes would turn into different kinds of eyes (I can't explain this, having no context), and he would tell me about BEFORE THE HOLE and AFTER THE HOLE as though some clear demarcation existed, but it was invisible to me. I could only see the after.

My father could straddle time.

Near this place where we live there are three holes in the

ground, surrounded by an immense accumulation of other artifacts from which I have constructed an understanding of the way things were before we got here. Before the hole.

The holes are in a field, flat and wide, located about two thousand steps from a house whose roof, according to my father's account, had been sheared away by a tornado that struck just months after I was born. My father says the house is "historic," but he says that about everything, without end.

He is probably right.

Everything is historic when you think about it—even things nobody would ever care about.

I ate pancakes this morning.

My socks tend to get dirty on the bottom, on account of the fact that I rarely wear shoes inside our hole.

My hair is the color of pale tea—just like my mother's.

And the three holes look like this:

I have two fathers, one mother, and a grandmother.

I only pretend to remember who Johnny and Ingrid were—based on the things my family told me about them. I can't remember a thing about Johnny and Ingrid, but sometimes, when I think about the holes, I make up my own stories about them.

The Sinking of the Titanic

In the library, with walls covered in layer upon layer of my father's drawings, there is a painting called *The Sinking of the* Titanic.

The painting is enormous.

My father, who took the work from a museum in St. Louis, had cut the painting from its frame and rolled it up in order to get it down inside our hole.

There have been times when I sat and looked at that painting for hours, as though I were actually watching a terrifying story play out in front of my eyes.

The painting is the work of a man named Max Beckmann.

There is one other Beckmann painting in the library. I can't describe it yet.

At times, it was all nearly too much for me: a place called St. Louis, museums, an ocean, and dozens and dozens of people struggling to save themselves against an unrelenting and unforgiving nature, without end. Think about it—all that chaos and disorder, everything without end being made all the more real by the experiences of the people huddled in small boats and others in the water. There was so much in that one painting for me to learn about the world before the hole. It was the things like Max Beckmann's painting—all the art, the music, the books and books and books, without end, inside our hole—that made me feel like I needed to get out, away from my home.

My father, whose name is Austin, said this to me: "This picture shows everything about the way things have always been in the world."

"Okay."

"It says it all. You really don't need anything else."

"Oh." I nodded as though I agreed—or at least understood—despite the fact that I'd never seen water deeper than could be held in the steel sink in our kitchen, where Amelie and I used to bathe together.

I believed that, in bringing all these things inside the hole, my father was attempting to make me feel as though I could see the outside, that I would be happy for the completeness of my world belowground—for not dealing with all the terrible things other humans had eternally suffered.

I think my father was like that; he only wanted to protect me from the way things had always been and keep me safe inside my jar, where nothing ever happened, and ships never sank. My mother carried her anger like a broken grand piano growing out from her chest.

If I ever constructed a visible mother science assembly project, that is how I would build her.

But even the painting of the sinking ship made me long to go out. Because no matter what my father told me, I could not believe that *everything* was in Beckmann's painting. And this bothered me too, because I had come to realize, at sixteen years old, that I had crossed a point in my life where I no longer believed all of what my father told me, as though his words were no longer proof enough for me.

I needed to see things with my own eyes and touch them with my own hands.

I was sad about this. It was just before the last time he and Robby, my other father, left. I felt as though I was taking from my father, even though there was no such thing as stealing in our hole. Why would anyone steal from anyone here?

But I *was* stealing part of his world from him—the parts I would not allow him to put together for me, whether he had accurately followed instructions or not. I didn't say anything about it to him, but he could tell. All fathers can tell these things about their sons; I am certain of it. I could see his eyes change, after all. I'm sure he saw mine change too.

And I was convinced that I should try my hardest to never be a father to a son.

"What's wrong, Lucky?" my father asked me. It was the morning of the day when he and Robby were going to go outside to get things and bring them back, so they could continue assembling the world inside our hole.

We sat in the library together, in front of the big painting of the sinking ship and the terrible ocean.

My father smoked a cigarette.

Every time he would leave with Robby, my father's eyes transformed into his *before* eyes. I can't explain it, other than to conclude that all sons watch their fathers straddle time.

I think Max Beckmann went into a hole.

I think Max Beckmann painted *The Sinking of the* Titanic with his *before* eyes.

Ingrid's Bloody Nose

Breakfast, the boy, was born in a place called Kansas City, which was inside another place called Missouri, that was inside another place, and another place, and another place, without end.

It was difficult for me to comprehend, despite the maps and drawings my father offered me. After all, the only place I had ever known was the hole. I could draw a map of how to get from the theater to my room, from the showers to the bowling alley, or to where Louis kept the chickens, but nothing bigger than this could accurately construct a model of my understanding of the actual world, or what the world was located inside of, which would be inside something else, and something else without end.

One time my other father, Robby, went up to the top at night. It was summer, which was not a good time to go outside.

Outside the hole, there were monsters. And Iowa.

Robby could be so daring and fearless at times, like nothing mattered.

If he had been on the *Titanic*, I think Robby would have sung and told jokes to the shivering people in the small, crowded lifeboats.

Robby brought me down a miracle.

This happened when I was thirteen, just around the same time things began changing inside me, and my chest, without warning, would ache for Mel. Thirteen was a bad year for me. My mother's sadness and anger became a stormy ocean inside the hole, drowning me, and I think Robby was only trying to make me happy.

Robby had trapped two insects in a jar, and when we brought

them into my bedroom and shut the door so everything was dark, the insects floated in the air inside the jar and made little lights, like dancing balls of fire.

Robby told me the lights I saw there in the blackness of my bedroom were the ghosts of Johnny and Ingrid. He laughed.

And I constructed an episode from the past, before the hole, about Johnny and Ingrid. Of course accuracy was not an issue, since anything I put together would stand as the way things are, just like my visible man science assembly project.

Every story is true at the moment of its telling.

"Johnny and Ingrid were passengers aboard the *Titanic*," I said. I pointed up, toward the ceiling of my room, as the two little blobs of light bounced like lifeboats on the sea. "Naturally, they survived the ordeal. Otherwise they would not be up there in those other holes."

"Naturally," Robby agreed.

"Ingrid was the star of the cruise. She had just come from Europe, where her cakes, pastries, and delicate cookies delighted royal families, militarists, radicals, writers, musicians, painters, and spies. Everyone on the ship wanted to be seen in her company, because Ingrid was so beautiful and charming, but Johnny wore Ingrid on his arm like dazzling human jewelry. They were inseparable, and also madly in love."

"What does being in love feel like?" Robby asked.

I shrugged. "I don't know. Nobody explains it very well, not in any of the books I've read."

"It's because you should never use a word in its own definition," Robby pointed out.

Robby was the smartest person I knew.

I continued. "Ingrid was prone to getting terrible bloody noses. She'd gotten one the night the *Titanic* ran into the iceberg that would end up sinking her. Ingrid thought it was very funny—the bloody-nose part, not the sinking and all the terror and stuff—but Johnny was embarrassed and mortified. Ingrid's gown was streaked with slashing rakes of blood. If Johnny hadn't taken her outside for air, and to escape the puzzled glances of the other passengers who were eating in the ship's elegant restaurant, both of them might have gone to the bottom of the sea with the ship and so many other passengers. As it was, Ingrid's bloody nose ended up being a sort of life preserver—as well as a ticket to a place called Iowa."

The lights inside the jar, which was inside my dark bedroom, which was inside our hole, without end, winked and danced.

You Man in the Sky

Breakfast and Olive stayed on the sixth floor of an otherwise empty hotel that overlooked the river in a place called St. Louis.

They had been living there for three months through a very cold winter, having crossed from one side of the state of Missouri to the other. But St. Louis was not a good place to find food, or much of anything. Like so many other big cities, St. Louis had been torn apart and picked clean long before Breakfast and Olive got there, probably before Breakfast was born.

Breakfast told Olive that he felt it was time for them to leave again.

Olive didn't talk. She never said a word, even if Breakfast, at times, imagined she did.

Breakfast was completely wild.

"You have to be wild to survive," he told Olive. "Just look at me, wouldja? There's no denying I'm wild. Who's got money? Me. I've got money. Wild."

Breakfast wrote his name everywhere he went and frequently scrawled messages that he called "instructions," too. Some of these he'd leave behind, pinned to walls or doors, scribbled on old paper currency, which Breakfast didn't like to abandon, but there was only so much of the stuff he could carry.

"If I could make people believe in this stuff, do you know how rich we'd be, Olive?"

Olive understood Breakfast; she just couldn't talk.

"Richer than anyone," Breakfast said. "Of course, we'd have to find someone, first, and then get them to believe it, second."

Breakfast waved a fan of hundred-dollar bills in the air between them.

Breakfast didn't wear any clothes in summertime. But it was February, if that mattered, and Breakfast wore snowboarder's boots with wool socks, long underwear, bib overalls made for skiing, a parka that was adult-size, so the sleeves dangled beyond the length of the twelve-year-old boy's arms, and mirrored aviator goggles. But the boy hated wearing clothes.

He was wild.

To get in and out of their hotel, Breakfast and Olive had to climb down the dark stairwell to the second floor, where someone before them had constructed a rope elevator on a pulley system that hung from the rail of a fake balcony in a filthy room whose plate-glass windows had been smashed out.

The hotel offered protection from the monsters, who didn't come out much when it was cold. Olive kept Breakfast safe during warmer times of the year. For reasons Breakfast couldn't guess, the monsters were terrified of Olive. So it was a lucky thing he'd found her, alone and hiding in a dilapidated gas station two days after the monsters had driven him away from the farm.

As far as he knew, Breakfast was the only survivor. The wild boy had not stayed around to be certain, but he had been certain it was time for him to run. He was just ten then, and Olive had kept him alive for two years.

Sergeant Stuart and the others on the farm—his army— had tried every manner of ways to scare off, and even kill, the monsters. Nothing they tried ever succeeded. A man named Old Everett had been convinced he could mesmerize and pacify the monsters by dancing naked in front of them and singing a song.

The song Old Everett sang went like this:

Todeli-ho-ho-ho, good-bye
Kalamazoo-o-o, good-bye
Mr. Engineer, be sure the track is clear
We're going all the way from Kalamazoo to
Timbuktu

And it worked the first time. But the second time Old Everett tried it, he didn't make it to the first "good-bye" before being eaten, headfirst.

Good-bye.

People on the farm had tried shooting the monsters, but that was pointless. The army tried setting fires but only managed to burn down every house they'd lived in. They tried concoctions of poisons and even leaving out sacrifices of cattle or sheep, but the monsters were unstoppable, and they only wanted to eat one thing: people.

At least they had been unstoppable until Breakfast found Olive. But they were alone now, and Breakfast was convinced that if they could keep moving, they would eventually find someone else. Or someone else might find them, which was why Breakfast left so many messages wherever he and Olive went.

And the monsters, many of whom stood ten feet tall, looked like this:

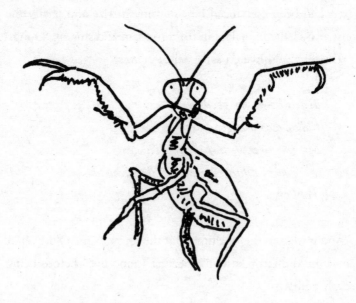

The first piece of Breakfast Paper my father found was a note written by the boy on the back of a political campaign yard sign in a place called Keokuk, which he and Robby had driven through in one of their many automobiles one winter. Think about all the things my father Austin had to explain to me: politics, campaigning, Keokuk, and what *yards* were.

The front of the sign, printed in red, white, and blue, said this:

VOTE KRONENWETTER

CITY ATTORNEY

I had no idea what any of all this had to do with me, how it all came together.

But the back of the sign said this:

you man in the sky i saw you shouting and singing
on your wings and motor up above us here and
you never looked down and saw me and olive
waving and yelling back at you can you help us
please and i have lots of money we need to go some
place safe now its getting to warm i will give you
some money and my name is breakfast

Adam and Eve's Drive-In Movie Theater

I have seen photographs and works of art.

I have read books in which awkward and fumbling, desperate males make attempts without end to defend and win the most beautiful women in their world. I don't know what any of this means. I have only seen four women in my world: Wendy McKeon, my grandmother; my mom, whose name is Shannon Collins; Connie Brees, who is Robby's mother; and Robby's young sister, Amelie Sing Brees.

I call her Mel.

I read poetry, much of which makes no sense to me, but I find it beautiful nonetheless.

A man named John Keats wrote, "Beauty is truth, truth beauty." I have spent a great deal of time thinking about those words. I see all the truth in Mel Brees, and despite the ugliness of the situation in his painting, Max Beckmann must have been telling the truth when he painted the sinking ship, because the beauty of the work is striking.

When Amelie and I were younger, Wendy or Connie used to give us baths together in the big stainless-steel sink in the kitchen where Louis, Amelie's father, cooked meals for everyone. I didn't know the exact reason my grandmother made us stop bathing together shortly after I turned eleven years old, because Mel and I certainly hadn't outgrown the sink, which was big enough to float a small boat in. At that time, I was told by Wendy, who was in many ways the SPEAKER OF LAWS in the hole, that I was now big enough to start taking showers alone, or only with *the boys*, with my father or Robby, who was just like a father to me anyway.

Wendy told me that it had become inappropriate for me to continue taking baths with Amelie. I didn't know what she meant by that, so I asked my father, whose name is Austin.

"Well, son, the way things were in Iowa, most people believed in a very strict separate-when-naked doctrine when it came to dealing with boys and girls. Wendy has pretty much always been like that. Before the hole, all the people up there were different," my father explained.

"How so?"

"Johnny used to say that when we moved down here, we all started to act like a bunch of *dang hippies*. Well, except for your mother and Wendy, who was Johnny's wife."

Not only did I not remember who Johnny was, outside of the things I had filled in about him on my own, but I didn't know what "dang hippies" were either. Eventually, my father and Robby found some movies, which they showed me in our theater. We watched them alone, without anyone else from the hole in attendance, so I could learn about things like hippies and, potentially, their belief systems when it came to being naked around other people. The movies were called *Easy Rider* and *Alice's Restaurant*. It was all very confusing to me—Iowans, hippies, taking baths, whatever.

My father explained that before the hole, people—especially American people—were *inhibited* about so many things.

"Oh. What does that mean?"

"Inhibited means when you're afraid of what other people are thinking about, so you think there's something wrong with you, and you go out of your way to appear lifeless and dull, like a curtain rod or something. People used to think there was something wrong with just about everything that there was nothing really wrong about, because they worried so much about things like sex and wars, and being overweight, and shit like that. The thing is, the way things used to be, you were supposed to be embarrassed about things like taking baths with other people. Your grandmother still is embarrassed about things like that."

Wendy was quite possibly the last Iowan in the universe.

I did not think I'd ever been embarrassed about taking a bath, or not having any clothes on in front of people in my life, but now I felt bad.

"So, people used to have wars against other people, and, simultaneously, they used to be embarrassed if they were naked in front of somebody?"

I found it hard to believe—like my father was just making everything up again, to play tricks on me.

My father said, "Yes."

I nodded. "That sounds fucked."

"It was, Lucky."

"I'll try to always keep my clothes on around Wendy from now on. I wouldn't want her to go to war or anything."

"Nobody wants to go to war against Wendy, son."

"Or, especially, go to war naked with her."

I think about taking baths with Mel every day, and now I also understand why Wendy is so opposed to the idea. Rules are dumb when you are not allowed to participate in their drafting.

I wonder if Mel thinks about taking baths with me.

I would ask her if she still would like to take a bath with me sometime, but I'm too afraid. And I know we could still comfortably fit in that enormous steel sink, but someone would catch us, and no matter how big a hole is, being in one is never pleasant when someone is mad at you for breaking rules, whether you're invested in them or not.

Our sink, where Mel and I used to take baths together, looks like this:

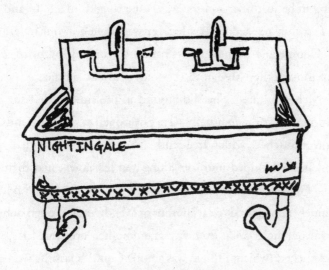

I am not as good at drawing as my father is.

One time—this was the last bath we'd taken together before the termination of our bathing rights—everything in our hole shut down. The hole suddenly became very, very dark, and very, very quiet. I imagine something similarly dark and quiet likely happened aboard the *Titanic*.

The blackness and silence smothered us, without end, like too many heavy blankets. And Mel and I were in the warm water together, inside our gigantic steel sink.

Although Robby and my father had told us all we should expect such a thing as a power failure, the expectation did little to alleviate the panic we felt. In a matter of seconds I could hear the faint cries of my mother, who shouted my father's name from somewhere far away in the darkness of our hole. And Connie, who had been our bath attendant on that particular day, gasped and told us to stay put and not to move, because everything was going to be just fine, and she was going to go find a light and tell *the boys* they needed to fix whatever was broken in our hole.

Connie and Wendy always called Austin and Robby *the boys*, even though they were both very old, if you asked me.

Mel was scared. She slid around in the sink so that she was right next to me. We usually were positioned at opposite ends, so our feet touched, which frequently made both of us laugh.

Connie bumped into something and fell down, and then she said, "Fuckbucket!" which was a word I never understood and was definitely not allowed to say in front of Wendy, even though nobody else in our hole, aside from my grandmother, ever cared if I said "fuckbucket," which, I think, was among Connie's favorite words.

I laughed.

"It's not funny," Mel said.

She was so close to me, the entire lengths of our bodies connected. This was the moment, at the age of eleven, when I became aware there was something electric between Amelie and me. I didn't understand it, could never explain it, but it felt wonderful, being there in the warmth and dark with our skin touching like this. In many ways, looking back on the moment now, it felt like the beginning of my life. I stretched my legs out and rubbed Mel's feet with mine. I wrapped my arm around her.

I whispered, "No. I think it's funny when your mom says 'fuckbucket.'"

"It's a good word," Mel agreed.

Mel had good taste in profanities.

"My father always tells me that you and I are like Adam and Eve," I said. I felt a droplet of water fall from Mel's hair onto my shoulder. She moved her thigh very slightly against mine. I wondered if she felt that same *thing* that I was feeling too. I wondered if *the boys* could simply attach wires to us, and in doing so generate all the power our hole would ever need, without end.

And I hoped it would stay dark like this.

"I don't know who that is—Adam and Eve," Mel told me.

I shrugged. Distant, panicked voices swirled around us. But other than that, and the clanging of cupboards and drawers as the others inevitably fumbled for sources of light, the hole was so quiet. I hadn't realized how invisible the constant buzzing of all the everythings we relied on had been to me throughout my life. Maybe it was the absence of the buzz that made me suddenly aware of the other buzz I'd never noticed until that moment, sitting naked in the bath next to Amelie Sing Brees.

"I think Adam and Eve were terrific friends of Johnny and Ingrid's," I said. "Adam and Eve ran a drive-in movie theater in a place called Iowa City, and during the daytime, when it was too bright to project a motion picture on the outdoor screen, they gave people licenses to drive cars, which was something my father told me people had to have in order to operate an automobile, although, according to my father, only Robby had ever bothered to get one—a driver's license, I mean. Has your brother ever shown you his driver's license?"

Mel shook her head. I could feel the movement in the dark, a wordless answer. I could feel her heart beating, a wordless question, and I held her tighter.

"It has a picture of him, when he was sixteen years old. You look like him. He was very nice-looking on his driver's license."

"What if you didn't get a driver's license?"

"Well, I imagine you would never be able to watch a movie at Adam and Eve's drive-in movie theater," I said.

And Mel said, "Is all that true?"

"Every story is true when it's being told. Whether or not it will continue to be true is up to the people who hear it," I said.

"Then I believe you," Mel said.

A light bobbed through the darkness of the kitchen toward us. Connie was back, carrying a thick candle.

She said, "One of the chickens got stuck inside the generator panel. It's a real mess."

"I hope they fix it soon, so we can watch a movie in the theater," I said.

Connie put the candle down on the long flat surface where we'd pile dishes for drying. She held up a towel for me and said, "Okay, come on, Arek."

But I didn't want to move away from Mel.

Connie repeated, "Come *on*."

I stood up. The water came to just above my knees.

"Oh my," Connie said.

She was looking directly at my penis, which was acting willful and unmanageable.

And I shrugged and said, "Fuckbucket."

That night, Louis cooked chicken for dinner.

Things Like This Are Bound to Happen When You Put Poultry in Control

Two weeks after my sixteenth birthday, my father and Robby left again.

They had never been gone longer than twenty days—not that I could remember in my entire life. When three weeks began nudging closer to four, I became worried and angry. The others in the hole seemed to be carrying on as usual, as though they expected Robby and my father to simply climb down the ladder at any moment, but I had this overwhelming sense of dread and impotent anger.

I don't exactly know who it was I was mad at. I was probably mad at the hole. I was probably mad at the hatch that kept us shut inside. I was probably mad at the number 16.

I was impossible to live with. The others, perhaps with the exception of Mel, avoided me as though I had some kind of enormous protective bubble around me, warning them off, ordering them to keep their distance. Even my mother seemed to want nothing to do with me.

Let me tell you about what happened when I was thirteen years old, something about my mother, Shannon Collins.

The complexity of her sadness was unsolvable to me. I suppose it's simply one of those things about grown-ups that you can never understand until you arrive at a certain point in your life—maybe a place where you can straddle time, as my father can.

At thirteen years old, I was not there yet.

My mother's sadness, I think, was an artifact, a relic from *before the hole*, from before Arek Andrzej Szczerba, which is my full name. It weighed me down. And although I don't really understand what it was, I think my mother disconnected herself from love after the hole.

She used to be in love with my father. I didn't know if he was still in love with her. Like I said, these things are unsolvable, without end.

And she and my father fought bitterly the day he and Robby took me out and taught me how to drive an automobile. It was winter, and everything was covered in an impossible glaze of heavy ice, so we were fairly confident the monsters—the Unstoppable Soldiers—would be nowhere in sight. Still, as always, Robby and my father brought along the special guns they kept loaded with small pellets containing some of Robby's blood, which was the only way we knew of to kill the monsters, since they had all developed, somehow, from a sample of my other father's blood.

I was thirteen years old the day I learned how to drive, but I was as tall as my father and could easily manage the controls on the vehicle. I did end up crashing the car twice, which made Robby and my father laugh very much. We had plenty of automobiles, so it didn't matter that I'd crashed the car more than it may have mattered if we'd all had to walk back to our hole.

And it was nobody's intent that I learn how to drive that day, either. My father and Robby didn't even tell anyone that we were leaving; they'd hoped nobody would notice, which was not likely when the population in the hole suddenly declined by about forty percent. The original plan was to take me fishing through a hole in the ice at a place called Clear Lake.

It was all very confusing to me—fishing through a hole. I had never seen an actual fish in my life, much less a lake. To be truthful, I did not see a lake that day either, because Clear Lake, frozen over as it was, looked exactly like a barren, treeless field covered in white.

We left before sunrise. My father and Robby woke me up. I had been sleeping in the bed next to my father's, which is where I usually slept, especially ever since Wendy made rules about segregating boys and girls—or, more accurately, *the* boy and *the* girl. They leaned over my bed, dressed in heavy clothing—jackets, overalls, long underwear, hats, gloves—which made me think they were coming to tell me good-bye before leaving on one of their runs where they'd scavenge supplies and other unnecessary things, like puzzles of visible men for me.

My father put his hand on the side of my face, which was damp from sleep sweat.

"Hey, Luck. Get up," my father said.

I opened my eyes, and he said, "Let's get you dressed. We boys are going on a secret mission."

I thought about everything secret we could ever do. I thought about being on the *Titanic*, in the middle of an ocean. I thought about shouting and running, wild, as fast as we all could, without end, away from the hole.

All boys dream of going on secret missions with their fathers.

They dressed me in an outfit similar to theirs: thick wool socks and red, button-up long underwear that came inside a plastic bag, frozen in time from an Iowa crowded with humans, before the hole. I pulled on some stiff, dark-tan-colored overalls that said CARHARTT on them. Then I had gloves, a flannel shirt that I tucked down inside the bib on my overalls before hooking the suspender straps over my shoulders, a heavy jacket, and boots that laced up to my ankles and felt strangely weighted on my usually shoeless feet. But my favorite thing they gave me was the hat. There was a bill on the hat, and it was lined with soft yellow fur. It had flaps that could cover my ears and fasten together under my chin. And everything was older than me, but was also new, which was hard for me to imagine. All these clothes had never been worn by any other human being until I'd put them on down here inside our hole. It made me feel different and somehow disconnected from the hole.

In the hole, when I wore anything besides just underwear, it was the thin white-and-blue jumpsuits that said EDEN on them— the ones I hated, the same suits everyone else in the hole always wore. Putting on all those clothes Robby and my father brought for me made me feel free, despite their confining heaviness.

It's hard to explain.

"You look like a real dynamo," Robby told me after I finished dressing.

I didn't know what he meant.

"What's that mean?" I asked.

"A boy from Iowa," my father explained.

"I'm a boy from *under* Iowa," I said.

We stole out into the bitter-cold darkness of an Iowan winter's morning.

When Robby turned our truck north onto Highway 65, the edge of the world to the east of us was just beginning to glow with pale light. My father and Robby smoked cigarettes and played music, which Robby sang along with. The morning was spectacular, wonderful, and magic, and I believed that if I had died at that moment, I would have been happier than I'd ever been in my life.

I understood—at least partially—why Robby and my father—*the boys*—always went away from us. It was so thrilling that I was afraid I couldn't take it all in and keep it with me. If I had been Max Beckmann, I would have painted a big blue swirling image of the three of us crowded together in the front seat of a four-wheel-drive Ford truck going north on the ice-covered highway while frozen stars twinkled above like the ghosts of everyone who had ever been here before I was born.

"This is the best thing I've ever done since I was sixteen years old," my father said.

He put his arm around me.

I sat in the middle, watching the miracle of the Ford's headlamps skimming over the glaze on the roadway as we rushed forward.

Robby put his arm around me too. He said, "What do you think, Arek?"

I said, "I never want to go back."

Robby squeezed me, and my father told me he loved me, then leaned over and kissed the side of my face. The truck slowed down, and drifted diagonally forward a few seconds before stopping in the middle of the highway. Then Robby opened his door and got out.

He dropped his cigarette in the road. "Come on, Arek. Let's trade places. I want to show you how to drive. You need to be able to do it. Don't be afraid. There's no way on earth you could possibly be worse at it than your dad is."

My heart raced. I forgot about everything that had ever happened in my entire life up to that moment. I forgot about the hole. I forgot about my mother's sadness. I even forgot about Mel—how I used to take baths with her, and even sleep next to her, holding her close in the same bed when we were children. All there was now was this endless day just beginning, the road in front of us without end, being here with Robby and my father in the freezing dawn, dressed like a human being, and nearly—nearly—straddling time.

When Robby told me to press down on the long pedal beneath my right foot, the back end of the truck spun counterclockwise down the highway in front of us, which was now in back of us.

I pressed too hard, and our truck whirled around twice before ending up in the shallow ditch on the east side of the road.

Robby and Dad thought it was funny.

I was scared and embarrassed. Also, I crashed into a sign that looked like this:

It looked like that, except it was flattened down and pointing up at the sky, as opposed to down the highway behind us, which was how it was facing before I made the truck spin around.

"Maybe you should drive again, Robby," I said.

"Don't be silly!" Robby said.

"I am trying not to be silly, which is why I think I should stop driving now."

"Just hang in there," Robby told me.

But in twenty minutes, when I had to turn left near a place called Mason City, we crashed into another sign that said:

ENTERING POULTRY CONTROLLED AREA

The truck was a mess.

Part of the bumper hung down in front of the right wheel. It scraped the roadway and made a terrible racket. Also, the headlamp and one of the mirrors on the side of the passenger door were missing.

"Things like this are bound to happen when you put poultry in control," my father said.

"Exactly," Robby agreed. Then he exhaled an impressive cloud of cigarette smoke and said to me, "Drive on, Arek. We are almost there."

Why Don't We Do It in the Road?

We made it to Clear Lake—alive—just after sunrise.

I watched as Robby, a cigarette dangling from his lips, cut a perfectly round hole in the white field we stood on using something that looked like a motorized wine opener for a giant. There was indeed a lake beneath our feet.

"What if the ice breaks?" I said.

"It won't," my dad answered.

I looked back at where I'd parked the broken-up truck, and then at my boots, worried about the integrity of the ground. "At least the *Titanic* had lifeboats."

"Don't worry so much," my father said. "Fishing with your dad is a rite of boyhood."

"Did you ever fish with your dad?"

My father didn't answer. He didn't need to. I saw his eyes turn to *before* eyes.

Robby dragged an ice chest out from the back of the truck and parked it beside the little hole in the frozen lake. He and my dad sat on the chest next to each other and instructed me on how to use the small pole and line. They told me I had to twitch the bait until I felt something tug at it. I made certain the ice hole was too small for me to fit through. I had no idea what might be down there, pulling on the opposite end of the line I held on to.

They lit a fire in a small steel tub, and my dad cooked us a breakfast of eggs and warmed biscuits he'd brought from our kitchen inside the hole.

It was a spectacular morning—so blue and bright that it hurt my eyes and the muscles in my cheeks. I was not used to such beauty. I wished I could paint like Max Beckmann. The day swelled inside my chest, the same way Amelie did.

"Why have you never taken me outside like this before?" I asked.

My father shook his head. "Your mother and grandmother would never stand for it."

Robby nodded. "There will be hell to pay when we get home, Porcupine."

Robby called my dad Porcupine. I didn't know why, but I thought it was funny.

"What do you pay in hell?" I asked.

My dad said, "Missed opportunities for days like this, I guess."

The line jerked. The tip of the pole stabbed downward. I screamed a little.

Something angry and alive was on the end of my line.

I caught a bucketful of yellow bass that day. It was an amazing thing.

They weren't actually *yellow*, in my opinion—Dad explained that was just their name. They were in truth more of a dirty-brown color, like honey, and they had thin, black horizontal stripes running along their sides. And inside their mouths, behind the opening of their gills was the most brilliant color of red I'd ever seen. It's hard to explain, but I also thought the fish had extremely disappointed expressions on their faces.

I couldn't decide whether they were disappointed for spending their lives in a hole, or disappointed for having to leave it.

My father told me we were going to take the fish home, that we'd eat them for dinner that night, and maybe Mom and Wendy wouldn't be so angry about how the three of us *boys* ran away from home for a day.

If bringing home a bucket of fish softened their anger at all, it would have been terrifying to see what things would have been like had we come home empty-handed.

Robby and Dad had brought a bottle of whiskey with us to Clear Lake. They both got extremely drunk while I stood over the little hole in the ice and caught fish. I thought it was funny. They wrestled in the snow and ice, laughing, pretending to fight, and each one alternately letting the other play as though he'd won. They kissed, too—not the kind of kiss like when Dad would put his lips to my forehead at night before bedtime and tell me he loved me and how I was the best thing that had ever happened to him; they kissed like people did in some of the movies we'd watch together in the theater in our hole. They kissed the way nobody else in the hole ever kissed—the way I wanted to kiss Mel, only I was too afraid to try, and too scared of Wendy, besides.

It wasn't as though I'd never seen my two fathers kiss like that before. They were definitely not *inhibited* around me. My mother had asked me at times if I'd ever seen Dad and Robby kiss, or if they ever slept in the same bed together, and I'd always lie to her or change the subject, because it didn't really matter, and it would only add to the complexity of her sadness. I told Dad about it. I told him I'd said, "I don't know," and my father said "I don't know" is teenage-boy speak for "Leave me alone." Still, it was something Dad and Robby never did around anyone else, and they knew I'd never say anything about it, anyway.

It didn't matter.

In many ways, I was simultaneously happy about it and jealous, too.

"Hey!" I said. "I caught another fish! I thought we came on this secret mission so we could all fish together."

Robby and my dad got up from the frozen lake surface. Robby brushed powdery ice crystals off Dad's shoulders and back. Robby's hat fell off. There were sparkling diamonds of snow in his hair. They laughed and wobbled a bit when they stood. I could see how happy they were, and I could almost feel the heat radiating from their red cheeks.

"Sorry, Lucky," my dad said.

"It's okay. I thought you guys forgot I was even here."

They sat down on the ice chest and passed the whiskey bottle back and forth between them. Then they lit their inevitable cigarettes.

I put the fishing pole down and sat beside them in the snow, next to our little fire.

On that day, after thirteen years in the hole, I believed I had found something I'd never known was there. What I found, I think, was my father.

I would lose him again that night.

I drove the entire way back to our hole without crashing once.

I felt powerful and in charge. I'd never had any idea what being so far outside the hole could do for a thirteen-year-old boy.

Let me make a few things clear about that trip:

Robby and Dad sat beside me in the front seat, smoking cigarettes and passing the bottle of whiskey back and forth from time to time. Even though the trip back to the hole consisted of one right turn and one left turn, with a bunch of nothing but ruler-straight, ice-covered roadway in between, we would have definitely gotten lost if either of *the boys* had attempted to drive.

And when we were heading east on Highway 20, I nearly did crash the truck, because there was something massive and black standing in the middle of the road. Whatever it was had not been there when we had passed this way in the morning.

Dad and Robby didn't notice anything until I stopped the truck about two hundred feet away from the thing.

I said, "Fish in a fuckbucket!"

That was the first time in my life I had ever seen one of the things—one of the monsters that had been responsible for our life in the hole—an Unstoppable Soldier. I had seen my father's drawings, and he'd shown me photographs of insects called praying mantises, telling me, "Imagine this thing, towering over you, nine or ten feet tall."

And he'd explained that in the summers, when it was warm, the things were usually green or the color of dry straw, but in winter the ones that survived—because they'd frequently die off in massive numbers—turned a dull, ashy black.

My dad took another drink, then puffed his cigarette and said, "Yep."

Robby nodded. "Uh-huh."

Then my dad said, "Pull up a little closer, son."

And I had never said this to my father before, nor since, but I asked him this: "Dad, are you out of your fucking mind?"

I was shaking, about to vomit, and I needed to pee worse than I'd ever needed to pee in memory. I clenched my penis with my left hand to stop myself from urinating all over inside my new Iowa-boy outfit. Thirteen is too old to pee yourself in front of your dad.

My right hand was paralyzed, cemented to the steering wheel.

Robby casually reached into the backseat and grabbed one of the paintball rifles.

He said, "It's okay, Arek. Just stay put."

Staying put at that moment was the only thing I possibly could do.

The thing in the road saw us. It opened its spiked arms and raised them above its head, but I could see the thing was weighed down and sluggish from the cold. I had never seen anything so horrifying in my life.

Robby opened his door and got out of the truck.

And I thought, *What the fuck are you doing? What the fuck are you doing?*

I wanted to turn the truck around and go as far and as fast as I could away from here.

Then my dad got out, without the other rifle. He was still smoking and holding on to the whiskey bottle. And then I actually did say, "What the fuck are you doing?"

Robby walked forward. He sang, *"Why don't we duh-do it in the road . . ."*

Dad followed him. "Let's do this, Rob."

They'd left their door open.

Robby had gotten about halfway between the truck and the giant salivating insect. My dad took a swig of whiskey. Robby kept singing, *"No one will be watching us . . ."*

I said, "Fuck you both!" and unfroze my right hand so I could reach across and slam shut the passenger door. Then I locked it.

Then I thought, *Why am I locking my dads out there with that fucking monster?*

I was terrified, and very confused.

Pop!

Robby squeezed off just one shot, and that was it. Then my two fathers fell down in the road, laughing like lunatics and kicking their feet in the air.

And I left a substantial amount of vomit and piss in the middle of Iowa Highway 20 behind the rear gate of our battered Ford truck.

A Very Short Chapter About Fish and the Sea

This all will stand as a sort of explanation for why it was that my mother, Shannon Collins, rarely said anything to my father, and ultimately to me as well, after that day when I was thirteen years old and climbed down the ladder beneath the hatch, dressed like a before-the-hole Iowa boy, proudly carrying a bucket of dead fish.

I think Mom knew something about the desire we boys felt to run away from the hole.

It made me wonder sometimes about Louis—if he felt the urge as well. But he was always so unexcitedly content with everything about the hole, especially with his role as our little society's chef; and he and Connie were so obviously in love with each other, even if I'd never seen them kiss the way I'd seen Robby and Dad do it.

And when Robby and Dad—my two fathers—followed me down into the hole and secured the hatch behind them, red faced, zigzagging all crooked legged, smiling, my mom silently stared at each of them for a long time, then said to my father, "Austin, are you and Robby *drunk*?"

Dad laughed.

Then Mom looked at me for a long time, wordlessly asking the same question of me.

I knew that was what she'd been thinking—that maybe all three of us boys had gotten drunk together that day, away from the hole.

So I just shook my head and said, "I drove."

And then I lifted my bucket slightly and added, "Look. Fish."

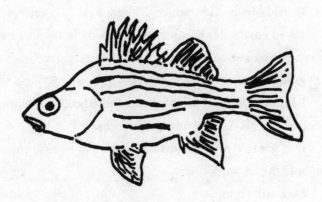

My mother was very, very angry at us.

Listen, I won't say much more about that night except to say that it reminded me of a Max-Beckmann-after-the-hole painting.

The fish dinner was delicious. Most of our food came from jars—preserved meats and vegetables from the greenhouse *the boys* had constructed above the hole and that Louis worked on without end, year after year.

It made me proud that I had brought something so satisfying back to the hole.

Mel told me she thought I was very brave and strong, and that she loved the fish, and also my hat, which I wore, along with my new red long underwear—and nothing else—at our dinner table.

Wendy frowned and told me I should put on clothes.

My mother and father argued after dinner. She told him she would never allow me to leave the hole with him and Robby again. Never.

Never.

Then she slapped my father.

Outside of movies, which I knew were all pretend, I had never seen anyone hit another human being in my life. I started to cry. Robby started to cry too.

I didn't want to see anything else.

I went to Dad's room and climbed into bed. In a minute Dad came in too. He did not turn on the light.

Dad got into my bed next to me and put his arm around me and told me he was sorry.

I was still crying.

I put my face on his chest and listened to his heart trying to tell me a wordless apology, without end, for everything that wasn't Dad's fault. I thought about *The Sinking of the* Titanic, and how similar we all were to those people in the small, crowded boats and in the raging, cold ocean that swirled, without end, in every imaginable shade of blue in that beautiful painting.

And I said, "The most beautiful prison is still just a prison."

Crazy People Should Never Be Allowed to Give Things Names

I never left the hole again like that until I was sixteen years old. Mother would not tolerate it.

But Dad and Robby had gone away, and they did not come back.

I'd been thinking about this moment since the day Robby and Dad took me ice fishing at Clear Lake. In truth, I will always believe they intended to come back to the hole, but something had happened to prevent their return, because my two fathers would never leave me like that.

On the other hand, I also realized that the trip we'd taken when I was thirteen years old, when they'd taught me to drive, and how to fish, and how to kill an Unstoppable Soldier, and maybe even what it looks like when two people love each other—I realized there was more to it than that, that it was some sort of preparatory test for me, so they could see if one day I would be able to look after the others in the hole.

I selfishly did not want to look after the others in the hole. As with Wendy's rules, I resented having no say in the forced imposition of growing up.

Although I could drive a car and fish and even kill an Unstoppable Soldier if I needed to do these things, I also hated myself for my inability to put into words that I had fallen in love with Amelie Sing Brees.

So I needed to run away from the hole.

I needed to find my father.

It was in the third week that Robby and Dad had been away that Mel and I were doing chores together—cleaning the kitchen, which was one of the tasks our Saturday job, according to Wendy, always involved.

Mel and I spoke in near whispers while we worked. My mother, or Wendy, was always just around the corner from us. I believed they were afraid of what had been happening to me.

I was afraid of what had been happening to me.

"I've decided that I need to leave," I said.

Mel had been drying dishes and stacking them on the steel shelves on the wall above the counter. I couldn't help but think about how we used to take baths together here. I couldn't stop wondering if Mel thought about it too.

"What do you mean? Leave the kitchen?" Mel asked.

"No. I mean leave the hole. I'm leaving, and I'm going to take that black Mercedes motorhome Dad and Robby brought back."

Everyone else called the hole Eden. I could never call it that. It was just "the hole." The guy who created it, who was in some weird way like a great-uncle to me, should never have named the place Eden. But we all knew he'd been insane, anyway.

Crazy people should never be allowed to give things names.

Mel was silent for a long time. When she finally spoke, her voice came very softly.

She said, "Why would you do that?"

"I have to find my father. And your brother, too."

I looked directly at her, but I could tell she was willing herself not to look back at me. She was mad at me or something. Everyone was mad at me, except, maybe, for Louis.

Mel looked like she was talking to the stack of plates in front of her. "You should wait for them. They will come back."

"No," I said. "I'm not going to wait anymore."

"Your mom and Wendy will tell you no," Mel said.

"Of course they will. But how can they possibly stop me? They can't keep me prisoner here," I said.

Then she looked at me. It was like she was sizing me up, maybe realizing for the first time in her life that at sixteen years old, there really was no way my mother or Wendy—or anyone— could make me do anything I didn't want to do.

"What will I do if you don't come back?"

"I'll come back. I promise."

Mel turned away from me. She put her hand up to her face. I knew she was starting to cry, and I wanted to hug her so badly. I wanted to take our clothes off and get in the bath together. I wanted to do everything I'd ever dreamed about doing with Mel.

"Arek, what did you do? What did you say to her?"

Wendy, my grandmother, had been standing just inside the passageway to the dining area. She'd been watching me and Mel do our chores.

She was probably getting ready to make a rule about whispering.

I shook my head and said, "I don't know."

No Wonder We Came Down Here

Max Beckmann was a degenerate.

I mean, that was what they called him after the hole he went through.

"They" were the Nazis, and the hole Max Beckmann went through was called World War I.

That night, after I told Mel I was going to leave, I sat in the library alone and stared at my father's drawings and the Max Beckmann paintings he'd brought down into our hole. I was trying to make up my mind about saying good-bye to Mel. Although I'd made a promise to her, I honestly did not know if I would come back.

I wanted to see things. I wanted to put my feet into a river. I wanted to pick leaves from a tree. I wanted to throw a rock at a window.

And I'd get caught if I went to Mel's room to say all this to her.

The other Max Beckmann painting in our library came from a place called Germany, which is on the other side of the world from our hole. My father never told me how it came to be here, and I never asked him. I was always afraid of the painting, and now, as I sat in our library among all our useless books and artwork and artifacts from before the hole, our Breakfast Papers, while I thought about the clothes I would wear in making my escape and what I would steal before leaving, I found myself staring at the Beckmann painting to the point that it almost began to move, to speak to me.

It's a horrifying image.

The painting, I think, shows a family that has been living inside a hole, just like us.

Where do I begin?

Where do I begin? With the choking man? The family's hole has been invaded by three strangers. One of them, his head bandaged, casually smoking a pipe, is breaking the father's arm, while a second man twists a knotted sheet around the father's neck and hangs him from a rafter. The woman—the mother—may be dead. Her hands are tied to some kind of post, and she has apparently been raped. There's another woman who is tied upside down. You can only see her legs and a portion of her dress, which is red. And there's a little boy—their son—wrapped in the folds of the third intruder's cloak. He is being abducted. The third man is going to do something terrible to the little boy, who looks on at the suffering of his parents with an odd, worried smile. Music is playing. There's a phonograph on the floor beneath the table where the father is being tortured. And behind it all is a woman in a red coat, silently watching the unfolding of the scene, like the rule giver. She's the Wendy of Max Beckmann's hole. At least, that's what I thought.

So they called Max Beckmann a degenerate, and he had to leave Germany before the Second World War. He must have been very, very smart, and also lucky.

One time, my father, staring at Max Beckmann's after-the-hole painting, said this to me: "This is exactly what the world was like, before we came here, Arek."

I sat there in the library that night.

I could almost hear my father's voice.

I could almost hear the music from the phonograph in Max Beckmann's painting.

I could almost hear the waves on the sea as the *Titanic* was being swallowed whole.

I thought this was exactly what my world was like now.

And I always thought, no wonder we came down here.

A Sure Sign of Spring

Winter tightened its fist around April and wouldn't let go.

Breakfast and Olive headed south, looking for somewhere warmer than St. Louis.

The boy drove a white Missouri State Highway Patrol car south to a place called Cape Girardeau, where it stopped working in the middle of Independence Street, next to an awful-looking building called Rush Hudson Limbaugh Sr. US Courthouse.

"I wonder if they keep money in there," Breakfast said.

Olive never talked.

That day, Breakfast could feel it was finally getting warmer. The Unstoppable Soldiers would soon be out in numbers.

Driving down from St. Louis, Breakfast and Olive had seen the empty husks of at least a dozen of the monsters who'd died from the cold, and in the woods along the highway outside a place called Perryville, they saw a living one, tall and green, its head pivoting as it watched the highway patrol car speed past it.

Breakfast liked police cars. Police cars went fast, and their flashing lights and sirens made him and Olive very happy.

They kept limited belongings in a black canvas duffel bag Breakfast stowed in the backseat of the patrol car—mostly Breakfast's horde of currency, a few articles of clothing, some food, a siphon hose for gasoline, a knife, and ammunition for the rifle the boy constantly carried.

The rifle was a Bushmaster AR-15 with a sixteen-inch barrel. The rifle's primary use was for hunting deer and rabbits, if they were big enough to withstand obliteration from the impact of the 3,200-foot-per-second rounds fired from the gun.

The weapon was useless against Unstoppable Soldiers, but that didn't matter as long as Breakfast was with Olive. Unstoppable Soldiers tripped over their own spindly legs trying to run away from her. Breakfast had even seen one leap from a bridge into the Meramec River just trying to get away from Olive.

Unstoppable Soldiers do not swim.

Olive and Breakfast watched the monster flutter and drown as the river carried him away.

"Ha! Damn! Look at that dumb bug, wouldja? I hope that doesn't hurt your feelings or nothing," Breakfast said. "Because I like you just fine, Olive."

Olive patted the back of Breakfast's hand.

The Unstoppable Soldier gurgled and gagged.

Breakfast scratched his balls and spat into the river.

Sitting behind the wheel of the patrol car in Cape Girardeau, Breakfast was barefoot and shirtless. Soon enough, when the weather became hot and humid, Breakfast would abandon clothing altogether. He was what some people would have called a New Human. He was the manifestation of the prediction men of science had made for what would become of any survivors after the plague they'd started from Iowa corn. Breakfast was born nearly five years into the event—the onslaught of the Unstoppable Soldiers—and therefore lacked any notion of what the *old humans* would have practiced as social conventions, like wearing clothes, for example.

Nothing was social or conventional anymore, and Breakfast, at twelve years old, was completely wild.

He got out of the car and peed on its front wheel.

"Come on, Olive. Let's get us a new car."

Olive slid across the front seat and climbed out on Breakfast's side.

"Did I ever tell you how wild I am? Ha! Maybe a thousand times, right? And rich! We're rich, Olive! We don't have a care in the world, as long as we stick together."

Olive nodded and held Breakfast's hand.

The boy scrawled a message on a stock certificate he'd found inside a kitchen cupboard in a collapsing house in Cahokia.

The stock had been issued in 1969 by Pan American World Airways, Incorporated. Breakfast took it because, like money, the stock certificate looked like something people would give you things for. If there were things to give. If there were people, aside from the men he had seen flying above him in the machine with wings.

There must be others, Breakfast thought. He would find them.

The certificate was stamped with a value of nineteen shares.

On the stock was a picture of a large eagle. The eagle perched on a branch that sat balanced on the north poles of two hemispheric maps of the world. On the outside of the two half worlds crouched naked men—one on the left holding a torch and one on the right lifting a staff with a snake coiled around it. The men were smiling, even the one on the right, who seemed to be on the brink of being eaten by the eagle, which was the same size as the naked guys holding things. Or maybe the eagle wanted the naked man's snake.

Breakfast liked snakes.

Breakfast used a red crayon to write his message on the Pan American World Airways, Incorporated stock certificate. The message said this:

> *breakfast and olive have lots of money more than*
> *this here and we are going south still looking for*
> *you anywhere you are are you looking for us if so*
> *go south because we are taking our money and*
> *going that way to i will leave the light on the*
> *car so you will look here and also we are going*
> *someplace warm but you dont need worry about*
> *the monsters since there scared of olive and run off*
> *whenever they see her also i am only twelve years*
> *old*
>
> *yours truly breakfast*

Breakfast scratched his balls and picked his nose. He left the patrol car's emergency lights flashing and tucked the stock certificate beneath the vehicle's windshield wiper.

"Come on, Olive. Well, keep your eye out for the monsters. It's getting warmer, girl. Warmer and warmer. Wild! We're wild as they come!"

Breakfast and Olive found a nice new red-and-white van that said CAPE COUNTY PRIVATE AMBULANCE on its sides.

Breakfast didn't really know what ambulances were used for, or police cars for that matter, but he especially liked the ambulance because it was big and fast, had lights and a siren, and even had a bed in the back where he and Olive could sleep if they needed to.

The ambulance was perfect for them, Breakfast thought.

Speeding down Interstate 55 with the ambulance's siren wailing and lights blazing, in the flat, green, middle of nowhere, Breakfast and Olive passed a chain-link-fenced lot with a peeling plywood sign that said:

KEMPLE MOBILE HOME SALES

"Wouldja look at that! Ha-ha!" Breakfast said.

Outside the lot, in waist-high grass that had long since gone as wild as Breakfast, sat a shiny green John Deere tractor with brilliant yellow wheels. And bent over the top of the front end of the tractor, his spiny arms tightly clamped to the rising air stack and spark arrester, was a six-foot-tall, man-eating Unstoppable Soldier, pumping his abdomen in wild thrusts against the slots on the John Deere's grille while his triangular head rocked from side to side and his useless wings buzzed like static electricity.

Breakfast slowed the ambulance, and then stopped so they could watch.

"I guess that's a sure sign of spring, right, Olive? Ha-ha!

Dang, that buck sure is making a mess all over those front tires, though! Ha-ha-ha!"

Breakfast scratched his balls and spat on the floorboard between his knees. He slapped the steering wheel, and laughed and laughed.

A Chance Encounter with Bigfoot

I had already decided which vehicle I was going to take.

I had also decided to try my best not to crash it.

The thing was a customized Mercedes military vehicle that had an entire living space built inside. It was four-wheel drive, so it could go almost anywhere, and all black, and the windows were so dark you couldn't see inside it at all. The machine was almost like a movable hole because it had everything: a bed, a shower, a toilet (which I decided to avoid using if I could), a small kitchen, and two televisions that played movies on discs. When Robby and Dad brought the Mercedes home to our hole, they stocked it up with every imaginable item it might need, even liquor, which is something I had never tried.

In truth, being alone and out of the hole felt terrifying.

Inside the hole, everything is cut up by walls and floors and ceilings. Inside the hole, there is a constant drone—the mechanics of the hole, the mechanics of our little society's interactions. But out here, everything goes on without end, and sounds peak and wane, a rising ocean under its own control. Light and dark escape all command.

I was so alone.

So, as I drove away from our field that had three holes in it—the one called Eden, and the other two for Johnny and Ingrid—I had to keep telling myself out loud to be brave, not to turn back. It was a struggle, without end. A big part of me wanted to turn around and go back to the hole. But if I did that, I knew I would never again be able to leave.

So I drove.

I turned the opposite direction on Highway 20 from where we'd gone that day I learned how to drive—away from Clear Lake. I knew where I wanted to look first, to try to find what I'd found that day three years earlier.

I wanted to find my father.

In the dark, I drove through the little town where Robby and my dad were boys—a place called Ealing. It was much as I had imagined, but many of the homes there had burned down or collapsed from weather and the weight of all that emptiness, I suppose.

It was just like they told me it would be.

I turned the van down a street called Kimber Drive. I had heard the name so many times throughout my life inside the hole. This was where my father had a job when he was sixteen years old, in a little store in a row of buildings whose windows were all broken out, all the doors smashed in. I didn't get out of the van. I didn't want to look around the town too much. It was a sad, dead place.

It made me feel like that other Max Beckmann painting.

It was just like they told me it would be.

Past the town, I started feeling too sleepy to drive. So I parked the van in the roadway, took off my shoes, my shirt, and pants, and climbed into the bed. I covered myself with two sleeping bags.

The dark and quiet were new kinds of dark and quiet that I must say possessed an endlessness, a depth, that I had never considered. It felt as though I were on the *Titanic*, staring down into the swirling sea, without end.

I turned on the television and put one of the discs into a slot on the player beside my bed.

A program about something called Bigfoot came on.

"Bigfoot" is the generic name for a monster that was rumored to live in several forested areas in what used to be the United States of America. The show seemed to imply that the monster actually did exist, but that human beings had generally been too ill prepared or stupid to accurately document its existence.

At one point in the program, eerie whistling noises howled from the speakers while the screen showed the jittery image of a dense pine forest at dusk.

Over the reverberating howls, the narrator said, "Whether or not you believe it, you are listening to true recordings of Bigfoot creatures in their natural environment. . . ."

It was very frightening.

I wanted to shut the program off, but I was afraid I would hear Bigfoot howling outside the van. I didn't know what to do.

So I let the program continue playing, but I covered my face beneath the sleeping bags. I kept telling myself, how could I ever find my father if I was too afraid to be out here only an hour or so after leaving the hole?

I tried to not think about going back, and how nobody would even know that I'd gone away if I returned before morning. But going back was all I could think about, until I heard something moving, and then all I could think about was Bigfoot getting inside my van.

A clicking sound, like a door opening.

I tried to remember if I'd locked all the doors—counting in my head how many ways in or out of the van there were—and I was certain I had not secured all of them. I didn't even know how many ways in or out there were.

Something that was not me moved inside the van.

"Arek?"

And hearing that, I screamed.

I had never screamed from fear in my life. The feeling was simultaneously exhilarating and profoundly sickening. Beneath it all, I held on to a glimmer of hope that Bigfoot would be as frightened by Arek Andrzej Szczerba's noises as Arek Andrzej Szczerba was of his.

Whether or not you believe it, you are listening to true recordings of Bigfoot creatures in their natural environment. . . .

And then I realized the voice that had called my name did not belong to a cryptozoological monster; it belonged to Mel. She had been hiding inside the Mercedes's small bathroom.

For a moment I couldn't say anything. My throat had frozen in fear.

"Arek?" Mel repeated.

Of course she couldn't see me. I was hiding beneath two sleeping bags.

Finally, I uncovered my face. "What are you doing here?"

I was a little bit angry, and embarrassed, too. But I was also overwhelmingly happy that I was not alone, and that Mel was not Bigfoot, and that she was here with me, away from the hole.

"I'm sorry if I scared you. I didn't know what to do, and I was tired of waiting for the right time to let you know I was here," Mel explained.

Amelie Sing Brees definitely did not pick the *right time* to let me know she was here, unless by "right time" she meant whenever it would most likely cause me to scream and nearly pee in my bed, which is something I hadn't done since I was maybe four years old.

Peeing in your bed is no way to start off your first night as an independent adult.

In truth, I did not want to be an independent adult.

"People—Wendy, my mother, your mom and dad—are going to be very mad about this," I said.

Mel stood in the doorway to the Mercedes's coffin-size bathroom. The light from the television made her seem like a shadow. Bigfoot stopped howling. The image on the screen was a grainy and quaking film clip of a Bigfoot monster walking through a forest.

"My parents won't be mad. But Wendy and Shannon will, for sure. They're going to be very mad at you, Arek," Mel pointed out.

She was probably right. Connie and Louis were not like Wendy and Shann. Mel's mom and dad didn't carry around their anger and disappointment like overstuffed suitcases they clunked into everyone else's shins. Connie and Louis were always happy, always okay with the way things were.

"We should go back," I said. "I should take you back home."

"You can't just *make* me go back," Mel said.

I thought about how I'd told her earlier that day that Wendy and my mother couldn't *make* me do anything unless I wanted to. And now here Mel was, saying the same thing to me.

Nobody should ever *make* anyone do something.

"Well, what are we going to do, then?" I said.

"We're going to find your dad and my brother. That's what we're going to do."

The Night

Memory is a funny thing. It tells the story over and over; it edits and reshapes the scene, color, angle, and sound.

It is not static, motionless, like a painting of a sinking ship.

It is a last glimpse I had of my father sitting in the passenger seat of an uninteresting white car as he and Robby pulled away from us in the frozen and jangling beauty of a brilliant blue Iowa afternoon. It was February—not that it mattered—a few days after I'd turned sixteen.

When I calculate such things, I estimate that my father taught me 95 percent of everything I know. Here is one thing I know, and I concluded it on my own: It was time for me to leave our home and look for him.

That second Max Beckmann painting Dad kept inside the library—the one with the family under assault at the hands of the three cruel intruders—is called *The Night*.

Let me tell you about the first night Mel and I spent away from the hole.

It was awful.

For me, it could easily have been a Max Beckmann after-the-hole painting.

First it began with my feeling *inhibited* and embarrassed in front of Mel. I had never felt inhibited or embarrassed about anything in my life. It was almost as though I were straddling time—like Dad could—and becoming a before-the-hole human being, with all the agonizing hang-ups and self-doubt.

I didn't know what to do.

I gulped a few times, and Mel and I just looked at each other dumbly. I was convinced each of us was trying to figure out what the next step in this awkward dance was going to be.

Let me tell you how frustrating this was. All my life there had never been anything I wanted more than to be somewhere alone—protected against intruders—with Mel. And now that I was in such a place, I was terrified. I felt weak, inadequate, and I wanted Mel to ask me to go back home to the hole, which I certainly would have done.

I began to sweat.

Mel said, "Are you all right, Arek? You're sweaty."

I mopped my palm through my hair and pushed aside the sleeping bags.

I got out of the bed.

On the television, a man was holding up plaster models of enormous footprints.

I was dressed in the red long underwear and wool socks Dad and Robby had given me when I was thirteen. It all still fit. I hadn't gotten much taller, and I generally resented wearing our in-the-hole white-and-blue outfits, which, naturally, made Wendy upset. My grandmother was afraid, I think, that as I got older I would challenge all the order she had crafted for everyone in the hole. This fear of hers was probably correct.

Now that I was out of the hole, I was never going to wear an Eden jumpsuit again.

We would need to search for new clothes for Mel, too, so I wouldn't have to look at her dressed up like she didn't belong here above the surface, so she could, like me, become something else.

We were cicadas—except I was the only sixteen-year-old.

Mel was fifteen when we left the hole.

I took a deep breath.

"I'll sleep over there," I said. "You can have the big bed."

I tossed one of my sleeping bags onto the smaller, narrow bed that served as a sofa, beneath the motorhome's side window.

Mel said, "No. You don't need to do that."

And I thought about all the possibilities that could result from not changing my sleeping place. I thought about Amelie Sing Brees *making* me sleep next to her in the big bed while we watched the program about Bigfoot together.

But Mel said, "I'll take the small bed."

The knot in my throat dropped like a sack full of bowling balls.

"Oh. Okay. Thanks. Um. Mel."

I watched as she slipped off her shoes and stretched out under the sleeping bag. I wanted to tell her she should take off that Eden jumpsuit but was not prepared to honestly tell her why.

And she said, "Good night, Arek. What are you watching?"

The Question Superheroes Never Ask

We watched the entire program together. It terrified me, but when it was over and I turned the television off, Mel yawned and said, "That was the stupidest thing I've ever seen, Arek."

"Oh," I said. "Yeah. Me too."

I decided I would look for happier discs if I was ever going to watch television with Mel again in the future, maybe smarter ones too.

I couldn't sleep. My heart pounded, and I didn't understand what it was trying to say to me—if it was struggling to decide whether or not we should go back to the hole or, maybe, wondering what made Mel think it was a good idea to stow away on this ship that was destined to sink.

But mostly I couldn't sleep because I was straining to listen to Mel. The lull of her breathing as she slept was like a song to me. Like Robby—and like Connie, their mother—Amelie Sing Brees seemed to float above everything with an attitude of comfortable wonder. I wished I could be more like that.

And that night, as I lay there listening to Mel's breathing, the wind came.

I had never in my life heard wind blowing in the darkness of night. Think of it—all these new and eternally ancient things outside the hole, without end. It was almost too much, and it was frightening, too. At first the wind made soft whistles as it slashed itself open on the edges of our van. But soon the wind came screaming over us with such force the Mercedes shook and shook.

I got out of bed.

Mel was still asleep.

"Mel?"

She opened her eyes. "What's wrong? Are you okay?"

I kneeled beside her bed and leaned my face over hers. It was so cold inside the van my breath made wisps of smoke, just like it did when I'd stand inside the kitchen's freezer room in the hole. "Listen."

She moved. The sleeping bag rose and fell. I wished I could be that bag, covering her, keeping her warm.

Mel said, "What is it?"

"Whether or not you believe it, you are listening to the actual sound of Iowa wind in its natural environment."

"Oh."

Mel closed her eyes. Her shoulders relaxed.

"Well, I was just checking to see if you were scared or anything," I said.

"Not really. Are you?"

The van shook. The wind howled, without end.

I was scared.

"Of course not."

It was so frustrating.

I stood up and cupped my hands around my eyes and then pressed my face against the window so I could look outside the van. I was half convinced I'd see an army of Bigfoot monsters, preparing to invade.

Outside it was snowing.

I did not think Bigfoots would come out in such a snowfall, so in many ways I felt a sense of relief. And although I'd seen snow falling before, since the only times I was ever technically allowed out of the hole were very brief in duration, in the daytime, and also in the middle of winter, I had never seen such a storm, in the howling wind and in the dead of night.

Snow blew in great gray-white blobs parallel to the ground, smearing across my vision. It made me feel dizzy, as though we were speeding forward uncontrollably, heading for an inevitable cliff.

It was dreadful. I had never before been so convinced I had made a mistake, never before felt so convinced that I was going to die, and very soon, too.

And I thought, *What if I'm wrong?*

My father had told me a story about this question one time, during one of my many lessons on before-the-hole history.

Dad drew comics. I'd seen all of them, I think. Many of them went all the way back to the time when he was my age, even younger, when he was struggling with all these conflicting feelings he had about Shannon—my mother—Robby, his school, church, family, the town he lived in, and how all these things connected to, and tugged relentlessly on, his life.

I loved my father's comics.

When he and Robby went out on their scavenging runs, my father almost always brought back some comic books to keep in the library in our hole.

"Do you know what I learned about these guys in comic books, Lucky?" my dad had asked me.

"No. What?"

We'd been sitting beside each other, our knees touching on the floor of the library, looking at a comic book. I can't remember the exact name of it, but it was about a very powerful man in a very colorful outfit, and he was capable of the most outlandish feats.

Dad said, "It was an incredibly American thing, you know, both inside the stories and in the real world—the idea of the superhero. He was the guy who could destroy anyone and anything, and he was always absolutely convinced—beyond question—that he was right."

"Oh."

"And you know what they never did, Arek? Superheroes never once would ask themselves, *What if I'm wrong?*"

There was so much I could never understand about what it must have been like to be a before-the-hole human being. I sometimes thought my father had made it all up—all the murders and war and cruelty and inhibitions and destruction, without end—as a kind of entertainment. The movies we saw were like that, but Dad, Robby, Wendy, and the others always pointed out specific details for me and Mel and told us, yes, that's really the way things used to be.

And I said, "It must be nice to never consider the possibility you've made a mistake. Like math practice."

My father taught me math. I was awful at it.

"It's worse than that," he told me. "It's a monster. Thinking like that will eat you alive. It ate my mother. And my father, and my brother, whose names are your name."

I watched my father, straddling time as he was, and his eyes changed when he told me that.

What if I'm wrong?

So, as I looked out at the snow, shivering not just from the cold, asking myself that same question, I realized I was not much of a superhero—or American, for that matter.

"It's snowing," I said.

Mel shot up in her bed. "It *is?*"

I never knew so many things. Like, I never knew Mel was excited by snow.

She pressed her face up against the window. I could almost feel something—an energy—radiating from her and into me through the cold glass.

Mel said, "Can we go out?"

Amelie Sing Brees was incredible.

Arek Andrzej Szczerba was horrified at the thought of going out into the dark and wind.

"Why?"

"I want to see what it feels like," Mel answered.

"But there could be . . . *things* . . . out there."

Mel laughed at me. "Are you serious?"

I cleared my throat. "Yes. Yes, I am serious. Um. Mel."

She laughed again. Then she slid her legs out from beneath the covers and put on her shoes. "Well, you can wait for me by the door, then. I'm going out."

I inhaled deeply and stood there, dumbstruck, watching Mel open the door and step out into the whirling rush of the infinite world.

After she shut the door behind her, I whispered, "What if I'm wrong about this?"

Then, frustrated beyond what I had assumed were reasonable limits, I jammed my feet into my unlaced boots, pressed the hunter's cap Dad and Robby had given me snug over my hair and ears, and, dressed in nothing more than a set of red long underwear, followed Amelie out into the snowstorm.

A Ladder from Jupiter

We were new humans, as alien to the world as if we had just climbed down a ladder from Jupiter.

Mel ran through the snow, laughing.

And before I could even catch up to her, I was covered in white flakes that stuck to me everywhere.

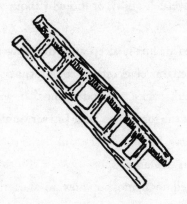

"Isn't it amazing, Arek? Isn't this beautiful?"

It was everything, all in one freezing half minute, without end.

"It's cold, Mel. We should go back inside."

She held out her hand, palm upward, catching flakes that melted instantly when they touched her skin.

I grabbed her hand and pulled. "Come on."

The Exact Opposite of Stuck

In the morning I was overcome by a sickening feeling.

I think it was guilt.

One time I asked my dads about having sex, not that I'd had sex, well, with another person, because I was only fourteen at the time. And Dad told me that feeling guilty happened when you did something good, when all the before-the hole rules told you it was not.

So I had never felt guilty, or thought about what it could be, until then.

I'd managed to finally sleep after dragging Mel back inside the van. We dried ourselves off and took turns brushing the snow from each other's backs with our hands. It was innocent and confusing, all at the same time, and I never wanted it to stop.

"This is crazy," I said.

"This is fun," she argued.

We managed to figure out how to start the motorhome's generator in order to warm the place, and then we went back to our separate beds without saying a word.

I opened my eyes when the windows glowed a dull gray light. I lay there, trying to hear if Mel was also awake, but I couldn't tell. It was the first time in my life I had ever awoken to a light that did not come from some kind of device inside the hole, the first time I had ever opened my eyes outside the hole.

And then I thought about what must be going on back there now—how Wendy, Mom, and Connie would be talking about us, most likely getting everything wrong.

I thought about the wrong things they'd say.

What if I'm wrong?

And I thought, *If this is what's going to happen to my head and my heart after leaving the hole, I don't want any part of it.*

"I hate myself," I said.

Apparently, Mel had been lying there, awake, too.

"Why do you hate yourself?"

I stared up at the ceiling of the Mercedes van. It was white, with a very pale green pattern of geometric shapes.

"Sorry. I didn't mean to say that out loud."

Mel said, "But you did. So, why do you hate yourself?"

"I think Wendy and my mom are probably very upset with me."

"So, based on that, you would let the fear of someone being mad at you keep you in the *hole*—as you call it—for the rest of your life?"

I rubbed my eyes. Damn Amelie Sing Brees's matter-of-fact grasp of everything.

I said, "I don't know."

"Well, if it makes any difference, I left my mom a letter. They'll know where we are. Not *exactly* where we are, I mean, but they'll know I came with you to look for your dad and Robby," Mel said.

"You did?"

I heard Mel shift in her bed. "Like you said, they couldn't have stopped you. And I'm sure they wouldn't have wanted you to go alone. I didn't want you to go alone. That's why I came."

"Mel?"

"What."

"You remember that day when I caught all those fish with my dad?"

"Yeah. Why?"

"That day, we stood on a lake that was frozen. I was afraid the ice was going to break, and we would all fall through. That's what this feels like now."

"We're not on a lake, Arek. We're on a road."

I got out of bed and put on my outside Iowa-boy clothes and hat. I felt awkward, self-conscious, and embarrassed getting dressed in front of Mel in our small space. She watched me and said nothing. I said nothing. Something new was happening to me, and I didn't like it. I worried I was transforming somehow into a before-the-hole human being, afraid that maybe I'd start doing all the terrible things I'd read about in books or seen in movies that human beings used to always do to themselves, without end.

"I brought some food. Are you hungry?"

We ate eggs and biscuits that Louis had stored in the kitchen in the hole.

We were going to run out of food and water. I would need to find gas tanks and siphon fuel for the Mercedes. I'd have to use the .22 to shoot rabbits and birds for our meals. And Mel didn't have proper clothes to be out here. I was done suggesting—or even hinting to her—that we go back. My head swirled and roiled like the sea in Max Beckmann's painting.

It was all so much, without end, this eternal expanse of the world outside the hole.

This is why Dad and Robby kept coming out.

The wind and snow stopped before sunrise.

This was only the second time in my life that I'd been out of the hole at the beginning of a day. Although we could see through the side window above Mel's bed, the windshield was completely covered with snow.

Mel didn't want to take my gloves and coat, but I told her she'd have to, and that we were going to scavenge for some non-hole clothes for her. Then we went outside to clear the snow from the windshield.

"Fuckbucket!" I said.

Mel laughed. "What's wrong now?"

I stretched out my arm and pointed in the direction the van was facing. "The road is gone."

Only a few inches of snow had accumulated from the storm in the night, but it was impossible to tell where the road was and where it was not. Everything was covered beneath a perfectly white blanket. Something else I hadn't thought of: Roads could simply vanish overnight.

Mel said, "That's beautiful."

"We're stuck," I said.

"We've *been stuck* for sixteen years. This is the exact opposite of stuck."

I shaped my hands into shovels and swept lines of snow from the windshield. It was so cold it stung, but all I could think about was how I needed to try to see things more like Mel did.

While I scooped away the snow, Mel walked up the road ahead of the van. I could just make out the shape of her reflection in the windshield.

"We're going to have to wait a bit, to see if it clears up enough to drive," I said.

And Mel answered, "That's okay with me."

"Everything's wrong," I said.

"What do you mean?"

"My dad tried to assemble a model of the world for me, down in the hole. And now we're barely pissing distance away from it, and I can already see that he didn't get anything right."

"I bet he got some things right, Arek."

I finished. My hands felt like I'd been stabbed by a thousand needles. I brushed them off on the front of my overalls.

And Mel said, "Arek, look. Something's over there."

She pointed off to the right side of the road.

At first I didn't see what Mel was talking about. But I quickly cursed myself for allowing us to come outside without bringing a rifle and one of the guns Robby and Dad used against the Unstoppable Soldiers.

If I didn't start being significantly smarter, more careful, Mel and I were not going to make it very far at all.

Then I saw what Mel was pointing at. Across a flat, snow covered field, just at the edge of a picket line of bent black trees, two wolves crept slowly from the edge of the woods. They kept their heads low to the ground as they quietly moved out into the field. Then they began running, directly toward Mel.

I was going to tell her to run back to the van as fast as she could, but she had already decided to do exactly that before the words could get unstuck from my throat.

I slipped in the snow and fell face-first at the front of the van. Something tugged at the suspender straps in back of my overalls, and I thought if this was what being torn apart by sharp teeth felt like, it didn't hurt as much as I thought it would.

But it wasn't sharp teeth pulling at me. It was Amelie Sing Brees, and she was telling me to get up and move.

The wolves seemed to fly across the field without making any sound at all. It was an amazing thing, too, because I'd seen wolves in books and on film, but this real-world thing that had been happening to me since I left the hole was almost too much to take in.

"Get up!" Mel pulled on the Y where my suspenders came together in the back.

I managed to stand, and we made it back into the safety of the van. We watched the wolves through the big side window. They paced around the van, watching, waiting for us to come out. They'd get close and sniff around. One of them pissed in the snow, then took a shit right by the front door.

And I said, "I think we're going to have to make rules about going outside, Mel."

In the Middle of a Disappearing Road

This new world was dangerous and beautiful.

In many ways, it was like the world in *The Sinking of the Titanic*. Mel and I were in our lifeboat, but our lifeboat was completely in the hands of the sea.

When we lived in the hole, the most dangerous thing we would ever have to face was maybe losing electricity, and that had only happened one time—the last day Mel and I were allowed to take our bath together, when I was eleven and Mel was ten. Everything else in the hole was completely sterile, routine, unsurprising. The hole offered us limited diversions: We could bowl, play pool, exercise, watch movies, read books, dance to music; there was even a shooting range where we'd all learned to fire rifles. But the hole lacked the sound of the wind, the bitter sting of wet snow falling, sunrises, and so many other things I couldn't even begin to imagine after just the one day Mel and I had spent away from the place.

We did not watch television that night. I lit a candle—we people of the hole kept candles everywhere—and I told stories to Mel about how I'd constructed the model of the outside world, only based on artifacts in the library or things my father had told me. Of course, like Breakfast, my visible man, I had no way of knowing for certain whether or not my model was an accurate representation, if it was better, or maybe if it was worse than the truth had been.

During the night, the wolves retreated to the edge of the woods. More came. They howled and yapped a song about hunger and loneliness while they stared across the field at the light inside our van.

I thought they sounded like Bigfoot, but I wasn't going to say that to Mel.

We lay in our beds listening to them, listening to all the noise of the world for the first time. And Mel and I talked about all the things we would look for out here, out of the hole, until we fell asleep.

The following day it rained, and by midmorning the vanished road reappeared ahead of us.

One of the things my two fathers had left in the motorhome was a collection of softcover books containing road maps of all the states in the United States of America, none of which existed anymore, as far as we were concerned. The page for Iowa had been marked with a red X where the hole was located. I couldn't help but trace my finger over that mark and feel the grooves of it, wondering whether it had been intentionally left for me by Dad or Robby.

I studied the map in my bed, listening to the music of the rain as it sang against the skin of our lifeboat.

"Mel, do you know we are on Highway 20, in Iowa, which is in the United States of America, which is on the continent of North America, which is in something else and something else, and on and on, without end?"

Mel looked up from her narrow couch-bed and smiled at me. "Doesn't the rain sound like magic?"

So, naturally, before I started the van to drive down the now-visible highway leading toward a place called Waterloo, Mel insisted we go outside one more time to feel what rain was like.

This time I brought the small rifle.

The wolves had given up on us, I think.

I peed in the road behind the van while Mel stood guard with the rifle in the rain. She licked her lips and splashed the bottoms of her shoes in the roadway, where the rain pooled inside circular walls of the melting snow.

We climbed up into the front cab on the van and left the place where we'd gotten stuck—and unstuck—in the middle of a disappearing road.

"Robby knows how to fly," I said.

"He *what*?"

I could sense Mel's confusion as she turned in her seat to face me. I kept my eyes on the road. I was not very good at this driving thing.

"I wasn't supposed to tell anyone. But it doesn't matter now," I said. "Anyway, if anyone bothered to look closely at the books your brother was bringing into the library, it wouldn't have been much of a secret. Robby knows how to fly."

Keeping secrets in the hole was impossible.

Except, maybe, for the one I kept from Mel.

Secrets had their own fondness for chewing their way out of the people in the hole, where, as my father had told me, we lived like hippies, without embarrassment or inhibitions. It was like the time Louis, who is Amelie's father and the official cook for the hole, confessed to us all that he was actually married to someone else besides Connie, who is Robby and Mel's mother. Robby had a different dad.

Louis's wife lived in China. Louis came to America to work and find a place for his family to live. He found Iowa and Connie Brees instead.

Louis confessed this over a dinner of roasted rabbit in wild-onion gravy with apples. He said he couldn't stand holding the secret inside any longer, that it was eating its way through his chest.

Later that night, Dad told me where China was located. Then he explained to me what being married was, which is when he confessed that he was never married to my mother, or to Robby, for that matter; although he told me he and Robby had pretended to get married in a Lutheran church in Cedar Falls when Robby was eighteen and Dad was just seventeen years old—a little more than one year after they came to the hole. I didn't understand it. Pretending to be married looked just like being married to me, but what do I know? It was all very confusing—all this never-being-married and being-married confusion, and China, Cedar Falls, Robby and Dad, and Lutheran churches.

Dad and Robby were strictly opposed to us pretending to do church things in the hole, even though Wendy had forced me to do it after the incident with my penis in the bath. Wendy and Shannon, my mother, made us celebrate Christmas, too. This was one of Wendy's rules for the hole. Christmas. I had no idea what it all meant, how it assembled into a model of my life.

Sometimes, a lot of times, it felt like the hole was crushing me.

What else didn't I know about life as a human before the hole?

When Louis made his confession—and he wept openly, by the way—everyone looked at Connie, to see what her reaction would be. Louis pressed his hands to his eyes and sobbed. A bubble of snot came out of his right nostril, and a little bit of gravy ran down his chin. I looked at Mel. We were scared, I could tell. Displays of emotion like that never really happened in the hole, which, as I said, infected us all with a kind of bland sterility.

But Connie laughed so hard I was afraid she might stop breathing right there during dinner.

The rabbit was good.

She said, "Louis! We've been here for more than ten years! How the hell does that matter now, after all this?"

That happened around the same time I was forbidden to take baths with Mel. It was all this marriage stuff, and inhibitions, and the electricity of being naked with someone that must have done me in, I decided.

But what I'd meant when I told Mel that Robby could fly was that her brother had learned how to fly an airplane. And that Robby had kept his airplane at a small airfield outside this place called Waterloo.

This was what my father and Robby had confessed to me.

Well, among other things, I mean.

Robby kept dozens of aviation manuals and flight-training films in our library in the hole. I had asked him about them, so it was not a secret. And although I'd asked Dad and Robby about flying, Dad said that Wendy and my mother would most likely disapprove if they found out *the boys* would sometimes go up into the sky, and that they had even flown as far away as a place called Kansas at one point.

They did not find any people in Kansas.

Dad told me they'd landed Robby's plane in a place called Junction City, so they weren't expecting to find human beings, anyway.

When I asked them if I could sneak away and go up in Robby's airplane with them, my dad's eyes changed. It was because Mom had said *never*, and slapped my father, on that one day when I was thirteen and *the boys* had taken me with them, away from the hole.

That was not a secret either.

Robby showed me pictures of the type of plane he'd learned

to fly. It was called a PA-46 Malibu. It made me sad and anxious to learn that Robby's airplane could carry six people. I desperately wished that I could see the world from up in the sky, that I could detach myself from the hole and the pull of all this gravity.

Robby's airplane looked like this:

Dad told me that he'd had to get very drunk before agreeing to go up in an airplane with Robby, even though he'd waited on the ground a number of times and watched Robby prove he was capable of operating it. It was hard to get used to, he told me, because although he trusted Robby completely, my father didn't trust the plane, in general.

I would have gone without getting drunk first.

The PA-46 Malibu was actually Robby's third airplane.

Robby's first airplane was something called an ultralight. He said the ultralight was uncomfortable and cold, but it was as easy to use as a lawnmower. Then he had to explain what a lawnmower was, even though he confessed—and this was no secret—that he'd never mowed a lawn in his life.

Robby crashed the second plane, which was also a PA-46 Malibu. It skidded on ice, just like the Ford truck I learned how to drive, and then it went in a ditch and sheared off its left wing and bent the propeller. Dad and Robby laughed about that story.

When they laughed like that with me, I could always see how much they loved each other.

Like I said, the hole was usually very sterile, as far as emotion was concerned.

So Robby got himself a new plane, which was the one they'd taken all the way to Junction City, Kansas, and back. Robby told me they were going to fly farther and farther away from the hole, and that he was sure they would eventually find other people and some place better than the hole. Thinking about such things made my rib cage feel like it might explode. I wanted to fly with Robby and Dad so bad my mouth watered.

And Robby said, "I'm trying to learn how to fly a jet. There's a really sweet Citation sitting in the hangar next to my Malibu."

My father told him, "I will *never* get into a jet airplane with you, Rob. Never."

But my dad did not say "never" the same way my mom did that day when I learned to drive. When my dad said that, he had those *before* eyes, the kind that straddled time and brought him back to when he and Robby were boys my age.

"I would get into a jet airplane with you, Rob," I said.

And Robby put his arm on my shoulders and said, "You're my man, Arek."

So I told Mel all about Robby's airplane, and how we were

going to drive around the outskirts of the place called Waterloo until we found where all the airplanes were kept.

"You're not thinking about trying to fly one, are you?" she asked.

"Mel. I can barely drive this van we're in. And let me apologize now for whatever crashing takes place in our future. But I saw all the books Robby had to study in order to fly an airplane, and I could never do what your brother does."

A Walmart Is a Place of Spirits

My father was wrong about something.

There is no such thing as the end of the world. The world can't end; it can only change, and change, and change, without end.

That's what happened to us. Change. It's what brought us to, and kept us in, the hole.

I had always loved looking at the books about history we kept in the library, particularly ones with photographs. The photographs showed things I had never seen—city streets crowded with automobiles, sidewalks packed full with every color, shape, size, age, and style of human being, all dressed in outside-the-hole outfits.

But there were no people here. There was only empty silence, and square buildings made of stone, some with windows, and many with vacant black rectangles framed with teeth of glass.

It rained all day. It was Mel who figured out that there were mechanical things on the windshield of the van that could be turned on and would swipe away the rain, which was fortunate for us because I couldn't see very well and nearly did crash the van, as I'd warned her I might do.

"Later, let's look around in here and see if we can find an instruction book for the van," I said. "I don't think I'm nearly smart enough to put everything on this machine together."

We did not find Robby's airfield that day, and it was getting late.

"We're going to need to find some gas tomorrow," I said.

I stopped the van in front of a long, flat-fronted building with white letters that spelled out WALMART above the doors, which were for the most part empty frames of aluminum. Some of the doors still had pieces of glass in them. There were a dozen or so cars and trucks scattered around the flat, blacktopped lot in front of the building, and here and there small trees sprang up where the surface had crumbled apart. The cars and trucks all sat low to the ground on tires that had long since gone flat.

I took a deep breath. I was scared.

There could be *things* out there.

I tried to see inside the dark cavern of the Walmart but could not make out any shapes or movement.

And I thought about the time Robby had brought down the two lightning bugs in a jar for me to see. We took them back up the ladder, and I watched from the hatch while Robby let them go into that summer night. The ghosts of Johnny and Ingrid, as Robby called them, obviously did not want to remain inside the jar.

On the other hand, I suppose when you've lived inside a jar for your entire life, getting out of it—as desirable as that may seem from the inside—can be overwhelming and complicated. I'm sure all those people in the lifeboats and in the sea in Max Beckmann's painting would have been very happy to get back inside their little holes in the *Titanic*.

The world, with all its color and sound, was wild and powerful.

I wondered if cicadas, upon emerging to the surface, ever asked themselves, *What if I'm wrong?*

"Let's go inside and see what we can find," I said.

"Is this where the airplanes are?" Mel asked.

"No. I think it's something else."

"What do you think it is?"

"Well." I thought about it for a moment.

I listened to the *tick tick tick* of the rain.

I said, "A Walmart is a place of spirits. A place where people who had lost things in war would come to look for them. That's why they had to be so big. Humans, my dad explained, were the most inhuman creatures on the planet. So the people who had lost things, like their homes or family or people they were in love with, they could all come to the Walmart, and here they would be able to talk to the spirits of those things and the spirits of the people they lost. Because most humans lived in a natural state of loneliness, my father told me, and they missed those things that had been unfairly taken from them. Johnny and Ingrid, and Adam and Eve, too, spent a lot of time here in Walmart, because they had all been very old, and, as a result, had lived through many times of war, and had suffered tremendous losses."

Mel sat facing me, her legs crossed on the passenger seat. I liked the way she always seemed to be so comfortable. And I liked telling stories to her.

Mel always believed me.

She said, "Losing someone you're in love with would be very sad."

"It *is* very sad. But it used to happen all the time. Like I said, that's why Walmart had to be so big. There was a lot of that nonsense in the world before the hole."

And, as always, Mel asked, "Is that true?"

All stories are true the moment they are told.

I bit my lip and looked past her, at the doors of the Walmart. "It is totally true, Mel. At least it will be true until we go inside, I think."

"Oh. Are you scared?"

"Of course not." I had never lied to Mel when we were in the hole.

Outside of the hole, I was becoming a fucking liar.

I added, "But let's bring the guns. You know, just in case."

"Yeah," Mel said. "Just in case."

Leaving Miss Sour Eye, Entering Are Can Sass

"I wonder what happens when we drive ourselves through that big open mouth, Olive. Ha-ha!"

The ambulance had broken down a week before. Breakfast and Olive had spent days trying to find a car that worked. Most cars did not.

So they walked. The houses still standing along the highway had been built far apart, and most of them were swallowed up by the jungle of vines and trees that had overtaken southern Missouri in the last nearly two decades.

And there had been tornados, too.

Breakfast and Olive slept where they could—in an abandoned gas station one night, a collapsing barn the next, then a rotting riverfront cottage, even a rusted locomotive that said MISSOURI & NORTHERN ARKANSAS down its side—until Breakfast finally managed to find a septic-pumping truck that he could get running.

He did not know what STATE LINE SEPTIC SERVICE meant. Breakfast hoped the big bean-shaped tank behind the cab of the truck was filled with gas.

It was not filled with gas, he would later find out.

They had not seen any of the Unstoppable Soldiers since the one Breakfast had spotted having sex with a John Deere tractor's front grille outside a mobile homes sales yard. But they were out there, Breakfast thought. They were always out there.

And it was hot now too.

So Breakfast, being the wild little boy he almost constantly claimed to be, stopped wearing clothes altogether.

The big open mouth Breakfast was about to drive his septic-pumping truck through was actually a concrete arch that spanned the roadway. At the very top of the arch, in all capital letters, was the phrase that Breakfast read aloud to Olive. He was pretty sure that Olive, who could not talk, also could not read.

But how can you be certain when someone doesn't ever talk? Breakfast thought.

The boy said, "Entering Arkansas."

Olive nodded excitedly.

Breakfast had pronounced it *are-can-sass*, having never in his life heard such things as the names of states in spoken language. As a result, Missouri had always been *miss-sour-eye* to Breakfast, who, all things considered, was pretty smart for a just-turned-twelve-year-old, post-public-education, new-human, naked, non-American boy.

"And damn if I'm not hungry, Olive," he said.

Olive bounced approvingly in her seat in the septic-pumping truck next to Breakfast. Olive was hungry too.

"And you know what else I am, Olive?" Breakfast asked.

Of course Olive knew what Breakfast was, but the naked kid at the wheel said it anyway: "Rich and wild, Olive. Rich and wild!"

He pulled the truck into a gravel drive that led down a sloping bank to a creek. The septic truck whined and scraped as it snapped saplings and branches that nearly obscured the track. Breakfast laughed and scratched his balls. They climbed down from the cab of the pumper truck, and Breakfast went for a swim and washed the filth from his skin and hair, while Olive watched from the shore. Olive did not like to swim, but she'd step slowly into the creek and cup her little hands and sip the cool water that pooled in her palms.

Breakfast was good at catching crawdads. He'd learned early on how to tip rocks in the shallows away from him and let the creatures back into his fingers, so he could grab their tails without getting pinched too much. It wasn't a perfect method, and he did get pinched once in a while, but in the long run it was worth it. He loved to eat the things. Cooked or raw, it didn't matter to Breakfast, who was wild, anyway.

His hair, knotted in thick ropey locks, mopped over his shoulders. He would have to cut it all off again soon, he thought.

"Shit! Motherfucker!"

Breakfast flailed his right hand wildly. A big male crawdad had clamped its pincer on the chubby underside of Breakfast's index finger. Olive was entertained by this. She waved and smiled at the boy in the creek.

Breakfast filled a small plastic bucket with crawdads, and two bluegills as well. He was very good at catching fish with his bare hands, but then again, Breakfast was completely wild. Sometimes he would cook their food, but he preferred eating fish raw. Olive gathered dandelion greens from near the highway. They ate until they were full, and Breakfast stretched out on a sunny place in the dirt and fell asleep. Olive lay down next to the boy and put her head on his chest and her hand on his belly.

Olive dreamed about Breakfast, and Breakfast dreamed about money and police cars.

In the new world, sounds like the noise of machinery struck the ears of new humans with the subtlety of an avalanche.

Breakfast opened his eyes and shot up to a sitting position. Olive got to her feet.

An airplane was coming from the north.

Breakfast strained to hear if it was getting closer or receding away from them in the sky. The growl of the engine was getting louder.

"Motherfucker!" Breakfast jumped up.

There was no way the man in the sky would see him and Olive there in all those trees by the creek.

"Come on, Olive! Hurry!"

Breakfast pulled Olive's hand, and the two scrambled up into the cab of the septic-pumping truck. Breakfast smashed and tore the truck back up the narrow gravel drive and out onto the highway, blasting the horn while he drove. He could not hear the plane, but the truck was far too loud, anyway. He slammed the brakes and parked the truck in the middle of the highway; then Breakfast and Olive climbed up onto the roof of the cab.

Breakfast saw the plane. It was only about three hundred feet up, coming directly toward them. The wild naked boy waved his arms and jumped up and down, over and over, on the roof of the truck.

Olive did too.

And Breakfast shouted, "Motherfucker! I have money! Motherfucker! Motherfucker!"

The plane kept coming closer and closer.

The Library for Vegetables and Clothes

As it turned out, Walmart was not a spiritual center.

It was a terrible mess, though, and it was hard for us to see what was inside because the only windows were up front. Mel wanted to go back to the motorhome to get a candle, but I was too scared to let her go alone. So we both went.

"I don't think this is a place of spirits," Mel said.

"Maybe depressed and dirty spirits."

Near the front of the Walmart were rows of walls that almost looked like library shelves, only empty ones. The shelves had little signs on them, with numbers, labeled with the names of fruits and vegetables, most of which I had never seen in my life. Not that I was seeing them now, either.

The floor was covered in a slippery green muck that was dotted with countless thousands of little animal tracks that looked like this:

There were no human tracks, with shoes or otherwise, anywhere.

Behind the library for vegetables were large open areas with signs suspended from the ceiling: WOMEN, MEN, SHOES, and so on. Clothes hung from metal rods or were folded, stacked on more library shelves. Many of them had been torn apart, like the nests in the hole our chickens lived in, and many more had become part of the mulched debris-muck on the floor, but there were still plenty of things that had not been ruined, and even packages of socks and underwear that were sealed inside plastic bags.

"Look at all this!" Mel said.

It was an amazing find.

How many more places like this were out here, out of the hole?

No wonder Dad and Robby kept coming out here. I wished they had taken me; I wished they had been allowed to take me.

I said, "It's time for you to break the rules and get rid of the uniform of the hole."

I wanted to break every rule there ever was with Mel.

And then I felt stupid and embarrassed, because I realized how badly I wanted to watch Mel undress in front of me. It was almost as though I could feel my eyes grow larger, just so they could take in every detail of her shedding her clothes—like some magnificent painting, a before-the-hole Max Beckmann. And I had seen Mel undress hundreds—thousands—of times, but now that we were here, out of the hole, alone with no rules, things were immeasurably different. Now there was a tightness in my chest, and I had to reach down and adjust myself, trying to stop my penis from doing what it wouldn't stop doing when I thought about Mel taking off her clothes.

Mel didn't notice.

I held the candle, and Mel foraged for new clothes.

It ended up being almost like Christmas, but without the rules and the dead tree, and the inevitable anger and disappointment that Wendy's holiday always inflicted on the hole. We did not take too much, and we found all the right things to dress Mel up like a real dynamo Iowa girl, as Robby would have called her.

When it came time for her to get into the new long underwear we found in the men's section, I put the candle down and turned away because I didn't want Mel to feel embarrassed, or anything else a before-the-hole girl might feel when she's naked in a Walmart with a boy.

But I really wanted to watch her.

Maybe Walmart really was a place of spirits, and the spirit of Wendy was making me feel guilty and ashamed, that I needed to segregate my feelings and my body away from Mel's.

"What are you doing?" Mel asked.

I said, "Turning around."

"Why?"

"Um. I don't know. I think a spirit was talking to me."

"Stop being silly, Arek. You're acting weird."

"I know I am acting weird. Ever since I left the hole, I feel like something's happening to me. Don't you feel it?"

"No," Mel said. "Okay. I'm dressed. You don't have to turn your back to me anymore."

I turned around as Mel fastened the final button just below her neck. I gulped. I had never seen anything so beautiful as Amelie Sing Brees in a trashed-out Walmart, standing there in front of me in a set of white size-small men's long underwear. In the dim light thrown out by our candle, she looked like a sculpture. If I were back in the hole, I would have made some excuse so I could get away to somewhere private and be alone. But being out here with Mel, I was never going to get to do that, and realizing this made my stomach hurt.

I wished my dads were here so I could ask them about what was happening to me, and if it was ever going to stop. I did ask them about masturbating—if it was bad, on account of things Wendy had told me—and my dad laughed and said masturbating was the opposite of bad.

"Why are you staring at me like that?" Mel said. "Your eyes look like fish eyes."

"Oh. I don't know. I apologize."

"Weird."

We found Mel a hunter's cap like mine and some boots that left interesting tracks in the slimy mud all over the floor. Then we took sheets and blankets for Mel's little bed, and I found a plastic hand-operated well pump in an area where there were lots of tools and metal things that I had no idea what function they might possibly have served.

I thought the hand pump would be good when we found places with gas.

I'd seen Dad and Robby use one before on a big tanker truck they kept in the field of the three holes, behind my mother's and Wendy's ancient, collapsing house.

I took three movie discs that had colorful pictures on their covers, assuming they would be happy shows to watch. And we picked up some toothbrushes sealed inside tiny plastic coffins, and razors, even though I hadn't started shaving yet, except for the couple of times I played at it with Dad or Robby. Mel took a box of tampons. She told me it felt like she was getting her period. I felt bad for her. It wasn't a secret or anything. Like I said, we grew up like *dang hippies*—naked half the time, uninhibited.

Dad and Wendy told me everything they knew about sex when I was maybe five years old. Dad said he didn't want to be like his father —all hung up and embarrassed about things—so it was no big deal, no secret. What Dad and Wendy didn't tell me about sex, Robby, my other father, did.

But I still felt bad for Mel. I hoped she didn't feel sick.

I imagined getting a period felt like being hit in the balls, which was probably the worst thing that I'd ever experienced. It happened to me one time, when I was fourteen, and I will never forget it. Mel and I were playing a game where we stood at opposite sides of the hole's rec room. The game involved throwing bags that were filled with small pebbles at a target in the middle of the floor. I got too close to the target, and Mel overestimated her throw and hit me in the balls with her little bag full of rocks.

I dropped.

I screamed and cried. My guts convulsed in tightening spasms of agony.

I thought I was going to die.

Mel thought I was going to die.

She ran and got Dad and Wendy, who was a nurse, besides just being the SPEAKER OF THE RULES. Dad laughed about it and said welcome to the club. If I could have spoken, I would have told him I did not want to be in that fucking club, but all I could do was moan and cry. Wendy made me unzip my jumpsuit so she could look at my balls. Everyone in the rec room was standing over me, looking at my balls, including Mel. Like I said, this was not something anyone who'd been born after the hole would think was any big deal at all, but Wendy got angry at Mel for looking at my balls.

At least I was happy Dad was there. I will explain: Ever since I was eleven, Wendy had been talking about having me circumcised because, she said, all boys in her family always got circumcised. I was terrified she might have brought along something sharp while she was in the neighborhood. Dad would not let her circumcise me. He said no after-the-hole boys would ever go through that again.

Still, I couldn't tell if she had a clamp and a knife.

I couldn't see anything, because of all the tears and stuff.

In any event, Wendy told me I would be fine; then she made a rule about Mel never looking at my balls again, and also not playing games that involved getting hit in the balls either.

At that time I was very envious of Mel for not having balls.

I hoped Mel didn't hurt like that. I honestly hoped nobody ever felt anything as bad as getting hit in the balls with a bag of small rocks.

It was a fun game, though, up until that point.

I can't remember who won. Mel did, probably.

Next to the racks where we'd found Mel's boots, far in the back of the dark Walmart building, was a place called INFANTS & TODDLERS. It was full of very small, soft, and colorful things.

I watched as Mel lifted a yellow outfit that looked like an Eden jumpsuit, only miniature, and with built-in foot coverings. And even though I suppose we'd seen each other as infants or toddlers, it was hard for me to imagine that human beings came in such small sizes. I could tell she was thinking the same thing, and it was frightening and lonely.

Mel said, "Do you think there are people out here somewhere?"

"I'm positive there are."

Mel put down the little yellow suit.

I said, "We should go before it gets dark."

We carried our finds through the maze of walls and shelves up toward the broken front doors of the Walmart. I could see the van outside, and it made me feel better, as though we were anchored to something safe and predictable—a little mobile hole without so many rules. To the right of the doors, set back in a little alcove, was a counter with a sign over it that said MCDONALD'S.

I hadn't noticed it when we came inside.

In front of McDonald's was a low counter with a bank of machines resting on top of it. Above the counter, covered in filth, hung a wide sign. Most of the sign was obscured with muck, but on the far left was a picture of something that looked like a kind of giant layered cake with dots on it. The sign said BIG MAC VALUE MEAL next to the cake thing.

"What do you think that is?" Mel asked.

"I have no idea."

I leaned over the counter and looked inside the McDonald's.

There were bones scattered on the floor. I saw two human skulls, which I do not want to draw, sitting among other bones in the soupy muck of the floor. I had seen plenty of pictures of human skulls. I even built a little one that went inside Breakfast, my visible man science assembly project, so there was no doubt what I saw there.

Mel must have noticed that I jerked back in shock. I couldn't help it.

She said, "What is it?"

I shook my head.

"Nothing. It just smells really bad in here."

I was becoming such a liar.

The One-Month Lifespan of an After-the-Hole Cicada

I suppose I'd spent most of sixteen years wondering what exactly happened to the others—Dad, Robby, Connie, Louis, Shannon, and Wendy—after coming to the hole.

I knew it changed them. That was obvious. Maybe the people they were before the hole really did come to an end, and who they became inside the hole were quite possibly no longer recognizable as humans to the people they had been. After all, each of them could straddle time, while Mel and I were stuck on one side of that immeasurable rift. I found myself thinking about this more and more as I spent those first days away from the hole—that maybe the reason Dad and Robby retained any optimism or humor at all was that for all these years they dared to risk themselves by stealing away.

The rest of our little society were all resigned to the permanence of our drudgery, or, worse yet, utterly without hope, and even worse than that: angry.

Maybe the one-month lifespan of an after-the-hole cicada was all it took to shrug off all that.

I really wanted to find my father. I had so many things I now realized I needed to say to him.

And I never wanted to go back to the hole, no matter what happened to Mel and me.

· · ·

The last Christmas inside the hole—the one that came only a few months ago—turned out to be something like an after-the-hole Max Beckmann painting.

One day, I will try to paint it if I can.

Wendy, as usual, transformed into a tornado about one week before the holiday; and my mom, Shannon, was so depressed and sick she spent days in bed, not speaking to anyone. She shut herself away from everyone, inside the quiet dark of her room.

I had never seen a tornado, but one did tear the roof from Shannon and Wendy's house when I was wearing infant-size clothes, and in the spring fourteen years later—the year I got hit in the balls by a bag full of rocks—another tornado thundered past the hole, just over our heads. We could all feel the rumbling of its power and hear the chaos of the tornado's rage. This was how Wendy could be at times, especially, for whatever reasons I will never understand, at Christmastime, when she would consistently enforce her holiday-observance rule.

So, by mid-December, Wendy insisted *the boys* bring a wood-burning stove down into the hole. She said she had lived too long without a fire on Christmas, and there would be no peace in the hole unless Dad and Robby fetched the woodstove from her and Shann's old house and lowered it down into the hole.

My two fathers tried to reason with Wendy, suggesting that nobody wanted to die of carbon monoxide asphyxiation, which I thought was a compelling argument. But Wendy would not listen to them. She told Dad and Robby—*the boys*—to bring down the stove's chimney pipe, as well, so that they could run it up through the hatch in the entry room, just so we could have a real fire on Christmas. She said that was all she wanted; she didn't care if anyone else gave her any gifts, which I knew wasn't entirely correct, on account of the fact that everyone was so scared of Wendy nobody would *dare* not give her a gift.

Christmas was her rule, after all.

In the end, my dads had no choice but to accede to my grandmother's demands.

They were both angry about Wendy's lack of reason. They got even, though, Robby told me. Robby and Dad had smashed through the French doors on Wendy's old house with a tow truck and driven it into the great room, where the wood-burning stove was located. It made sense, Robby said, since the stove weighed three hundred pounds, and they had to use a winch to move it, and then to lower it down the hatch, as well. Robby said the entire west wall of the house collapsed after that, but Wendy, who was never going to leave her empire of the hole, would never know anything about how *the boys* had driven a truck through her living room.

So Wendy got her woodstove. *The boys* put it right in the center of the floor in the round entry chamber to Eden—the hole.

Dad and Robby ran the stove's chimney pipe up to the hatch, which would have to be opened if the stove was in use, but that would not happen until Christmas morning. Then, a few days before Christmas, Dad and Robby went hunting for our holiday meal and also to kill a pine tree and drop it down the hole.

That was the thing about Christmases that always saddened

me—the killing of the trees. It was one thing—a justifiable one—to kill food for our family, but trees were beautiful, and I could see no purpose in their killing as a means to celebrate a holiday that was supposed to reflect generosity, kindness, and love.

I didn't understand any of it.

There was a chapel in the hole. Wendy used to take me there on Sundays after I turned eleven—this started just after the incident with Mel and me in the bath. Wendy told me Bible stories that she remembered, ones about circumcision and God and Jesus and floods and leprosy, and all because I had been observed getting an erection. I think the intent was to make me a better boy, but it only ended up confusing me.

The part about the circumcision actually made me sick with worry.

Wendy told me she thought I should be circumcised before I got too much older.

I had to talk to my father, who told me the best way to deal with Wendy was to smile and nod at her, like you agreed with what she was talking about even if you weren't listening to her at all; and that there was nothing wrong with getting an erection; and, also, that he had decided a long time ago to disregard anyone who suggested cutting off part of your penis was a good thing to do.

I was so relieved.

After Wendy started making me go to church with her, my first waking thought every morning would always be to wonder, *Is this going to be the day when part of my penis gets cut off?*

I loved my dad so much.

So my two fathers brought a dead tree—circumcised at its

trunk—down into the hole. They set it up in the same room with the woodstove. The entry chamber was our new Christmas Hole. They also brought down a wild pig they'd shot. Wendy, who'd asked for a goose or a turkey, was disappointed.

That night, as we lay in our beds, talking like we usually did, Dad sighed and said, "Wendy has been disappointed with me ever since I was about fourteen years old."

"I got hit in the balls with a bag of rocks when I was fourteen," I said. "To me, that was very disappointing."

"These things have a tendency of embedding powerful memories, son."

I asked, "Why did Wendy not like you when you were just a kid?"

"I think she liked Robby better. She wanted Robby to be your mother's boyfriend."

I laughed. "That's the dumbest thing I've ever heard. Well, outside of church, it is."

"I know. What can I say?"

"I bet it's just because you're not circumcised."

My dad laughed too, and I said, "Merry Christmas, Dad."

And Dad said, "Ho-ho-ho, Lucky."

Christmas morning came.

It was time to light a fire in Wendy's woodstove.

Wendy rang a Christmas bell outside Dad's and my door at a ridiculously early hour. We were both very much asleep. Wendy went from room to room, ringing her bell, calling everyone out to the official routine—the ordeal—of Wendy's Christmas.

I did not get dressed. I came out to the kitchen shirtless and in boxer underwear, a protest to the death of the tree and the ringing of the bell. When Wendy told me to get some clothes on, I smiled and nodded, like Dad had told me to do, and then I did not get some clothes on.

We all gathered in the kitchen, just like any other non-Christmas morning.

Mom was silent. Connie and Louis looked placidly content. Robby, in a T-shirt, boxer shorts, and socks, said good morning and sat next to Dad. Wendy never said anything about how Robby dressed or didn't dress, but then again, as I found out, she preferred Robby to Dad. I think Wendy preferred Robby to me, too.

Robby and Dad lit cigarettes.

For some reason I could not understand—and still can't—I kept staring across the kitchen table at Mel, who looked especially beautiful that morning. I thought about devising some way to innocently brush my foot against hers, but there was no innocence to my thoughts at all. Maybe it was just that I was excited about the gift I'd gotten her, about seeing her reaction when she opened the present. It was a silly thing, in all honesty, because she knew what I'd gotten her, and I knew what she'd gotten me, too. We'd made square-knot bracelets for each other. Robby had taught us how to make them after he brought back colorful thread from one of his and Dad's trips outside the hole.

As long as I could remember, Robby and Dad always wore such bracelets they'd made for each other. I thought it was something a *dang hippie* would probably do, like coming out to a family Christmas breakfast in your underwear.

In any event, I did not brush my foot against Mel's that morning, innocently or otherwise, because I did not want to face the prospect of having any discussion with Wendy about an inevitable new rule prohibiting getting an erection under the kitchen table during Christmas breakfast with the family when you are only wearing boxers.

Louis, who had been roasting the pig since before Wendy got out of bed, cooked pancakes and eggs for everyone. And before we could finish our breakfast, Wendy told *the boys* to start the fire, so we could all gather around the dead tree and open our Christmas presents.

Disaster was just moments away. It was as ubiquitous as the smell of the pig roasting in Louis's oven.

Dad worked at getting the kindling inside the stove's belly to catch a flame, and Robby climbed up the ladder to open the hatch, in order to save us all from dying from Christmas-morning carbon monoxide asphyxiation. The rest of us sat on the curved benches around the wall of the entry/Christmas chamber, with Wendy at the twelve o'clock position, nearest the tree. Every year Wendy would distribute the gifts, one at a time, so we could all watch the person opening each gift like it was some kind of show.

The fire caught.

Wendy said, "I finally have a fire after all these years!"

There was no joy in her voice. She was simply narrating the successful outcome of one more of her rules.

But I was almost fooled into thinking this Christmas was going to be nice. The fire was pretty, after all. It smelled good too—wild, the exact opposite of the sterile predictability of everything inside the world of the hole.

Then Robby opened the hatch. It was sleeting outside. Within seconds it was sleeting on all of us.

Robby said, "Holy fuck, it's sleeting!"

But we already knew that.

Connie, who was Mel's mother, said, "Fuckbucket!"

Nobody dared move, however.

It was also windy outside, and the wind that came in through the mouth of our entry hatch made a wet and slushy whirlpool of despair inside our Christmas hole. I looked at Mel. Our eyes laughed a silent chuckle to each other that seemed to say, *Fuck Christmas.*

Robby was drenched, up on the ladder in his underwear. And I was drenched, freezing in my underwear on a bench facing a dead tree, while my dad tried to extinguish the fire so Robby could shut the hatch without killing us all.

I stood up, hugging my arms across my chest. "It's fucking freezing, Grandma."

That was probably the wrong thing to say, considering everything that was happening.

And it turned out that my father was going to have a difficult time putting out the fire in Wendy's stove, because after I said what I'd said about it being fucking freezing and all, Wendy said, "Nobody here knows how to do a single goddamned thing right!"

And then Wendy began picking up presents and stuffing them into the belly of her wood-burning stove, which, fortunately for the rest of us, began giving off a relatively decent amount of heat, despite the fact that it was fucking cold and we were all getting wet and slushy.

So that was Christmas in the hole.

This is what my Max-Beckmann-after-the-hole painting would be called: *Last Christmas in the Hole*. There are two families here, huddled in a hole, where they have been hiding for a very long time. A ladder extends beyond the top of the image, so you can't tell where it leads to—if it is potentially a means of escape, or merely the method by which the people were brought here. In the center of the image is a bleak crematory, its smokestack rising up, off-parallel to the ladder. Inside the doors of the crematory are bright flames and charred skeletons. There is a dead boar stretched out in a pool of blood on the floor in front of the crematory, its black eyes frozen open, tongue lolling from its mouth. Up on the ladder is a man with clear skin; you can see all the organs and musculature inside his body. He has wings and is smoking a cigarette. Beside the crematory, a woman and girl sit together on a curved bench. The woman is dressed all in white, her eyes are closed, and her hands are folded on her lap, while the girl next to her looks across the front of the crematory at a pale young boy. There is a determined look in the girl's eyes, which at times appears to be an expression of love and at others seems to be a challenge, a competition. The boy is standing, barefoot and shirtless, nearly naked, wrapped like Jesus in nothing more than a small rag that ties at his hip. The boy has a frightened expression. He stares down at the gates of the crematory, where the tools of a mohel rest beside the pool of blood: a Mogen clamp, a milah knife. It is the day of his circumcision. There is a spiny black tree that rises behind the smokestack, and four shadowy figures: a woman with a black mask covering her face, a smoking man with his hands and feet tied together, a woman holding a stringed instrument that looks like a mandolin, and a weeping Asian man, seated, with a rabbit on his shoulder.

One day, I will paint that.

An Unfortunate Choice Outside Rebel Land

"They saw us, Olive! Motherfuckers saw us! Yip-yee-hoo!"

Olive knew when Breakfast was excited and happy. She smiled and hugged the boy, patted his back.

The plane passed overhead, slightly to the east of the highway. Then it took a wide turn and looped back around at a lower elevation. But Breakfast was mad that the plane didn't stop. He didn't know anything about flying machines or how they got down from out of the sky, or even if they could. He had seen planes on the ground before, had even tried to drive one, but he couldn't make it work.

But Breakfast was certain that whoever was inside the plane had spotted him and Olive as they waved and jumped up and down on the cab of the septic-pumping truck.

The plane disappeared to the south, and the whirr of its motor faded into the wind.

"Dang!" Breakfast sighed. "Well, at least we know we ain't alone. I always knew that, anyhow, though. Come on, Olive girl, let's see if we can't get down that way and find where those people are heading to. Dang!"

Olive nodded.

Olive would do anything for Breakfast, who was completely wild.

Their State Line Septic Service pumping truck ran out of fuel in northwestern Tennessee the following day. It stopped running in the middle of a once-wide highway that had been narrowed by the overgrown trees on either side of the road to the extent the truck could barely squeeze through in places. The pumper truck coughed to a stop beside an enormous fenced-in park called Rebel Land.

"If there's no gas in that big tank back there, maybe we'll find a state trooper car at Rebel Land, and then load up all my money and our goodies," Breakfast said. "Wild, Olive! Wild!"

Olive wiggled in her seat.

Breakfast climbed down from the cab and went around to the back of the truck. *There must be gas in that big tank,* he thought. *What else would anyone keep inside such a large container?*

At the rear of the big steel tank, just above the truck's bumper, were two valves that clamped shut the mouths of wide steel pipes jutting out from the bottom. Breakfast decided he would open the lower of the two valves.

He wanted to see if it really was fuel inside the big tank.

Breakfast, who was very strong, grunted and strained as his little calloused hands nudged loose the brass closure on the pump truck's valve. Breakfast scratched his balls and picked a wad of wax from his ear and smeared it like butter on the bumper of the truck.

Then Breakfast twisted the valve cap around a half turn, and then just one more.

"I'm wild!" he said. "Hoo-hoo! Wild!"

Olive thought it was funny.

Olive stood above Breakfast at the edge of the pumper truck's bed just when the wild boy opened the lower valve cap on the tank. A great gushing fountain of sixteen-year-old, ash-black shit and septic fluid hosed into the boy's belly, knocking the wind out of him and toppling Breakfast down to the roadway.

The spouting geyser of stewed shit coated Breakfast like a county fair corn dog in a batter of something so magnificently foul Breakfast instantly began vomiting and wishing for death, all at the same time.

But Olive clapped and smiled and jumped on the bed of the truck, joyously entertained by the spectacle of the wild naked boy flopping around in all that greasy sewage. She also began to feel a little bit dizzy from the powerful gaseous stench that rose like a steaming fog around everything.

Breakfast, who almost never got mad about things, was enraged.

"Fuck! Motherfucker! Gah!"

The contents of the tank gushed and gushed, all over the roadway, all over the boy, who could not get to his feet in the slippery goo.

Breakfast flopped and wriggled like an eel on a mudflat, spitting, cursing, and choking.

Olive wanted to help the boy, but she wasn't about to get down from the truck and wade out in the spreading slick of muck.

Roaring incoherently like an animal, which basically is what

Breakfast was anyway, the boy finally managed to stand up. He flailed his arms and shook his wild knots of hair, spitting. He vomited again, and then ran from the roadway, twisting and thrashing through the brush, screaming in rage and agony, over and over and over, running, running, running.

Olive jumped up and down on the truck bed, clapping.

Breakfast always put on such great shows.

Breakfast was very fast. He ran, swearing and gagging, desperately looking for water or mud—anything he could jump into or squirm around in to get all the shit off him.

"Motherfucker!" he screamed. "Who the fuck would drive around in a truck filled with shit and piss?"

It was a reasonable question.

And now Breakfast knew what State Line Septic Service meant. It meant: This truck is filled with shit.

Breakfast was wild with rage, naked, and covered in a thick sludge of fermented human waste that was older than he was. He was also not paying attention to his path. He had no idea where Olive was, or the truck, for that matter. But Breakfast decided he never wanted to see the fucking State Line Septic Service pumper truck again, anyway. He just kept running blindly, dripping shit.

The boy had gotten inside Rebel Land. Breakfast did not even consciously recall scaling the ten-foot-high chain-link fence that surrounded the place.

Breakfast had never seen anything like Rebel Land, which used to be a theme park. In the moment, he cared nothing about the colorful displays of human beings in scenes of battle, or the large wood-and-metal structures that looked like elevated, twisting railroad tracks, because he had spotted a large green lake on the other side of a spiked wrought-iron fence.

A sign over the arched gate said BATTLE OF HAMPTON ROADS THRILL RIDE!

Breakfast vaulted over the fence. He dashed to the edge of the lake and jumped.

Beside the gate stood a painted plywood sign that looked like this:

Breakfast did not stop to measure whether or not he was too tall to live through the Battle of Hampton Roads Thrill Ride! But he did notice, in passing, the way people at Rebel Land spelled "probably." And although the twelve-year-old boy was actually tall enough to die a horrible death if he rode the nonfunctioning Battle of Hampton Roads Thrill Ride!, what at that moment was more likely to kill Breakfast was something else entirely.

First Day in Cicada School

Inside our hole, my father, Austin, had assembled a model of the world for me in pictures and words.

His model was intended to inform and educate me, perhaps to prepare me by serving as some sort of map.

I realized as I drove with Mel around the place called Waterloo, or wherever we were, that my father had always anticipated, straddling time as he did, that I would at one point in my life feel compelled to leave the hole.

But the model—like Breakfast, my visible man—is not the *thing*.

Think about it: My father's model of the world was supposed to *represent* everything that was outside the hole. The only thing that can re-present anything real is the thing itself. No models can ever adequately perform that job.

The model presents—and re-presents—only the model, and nothing more.

And the data—what's really outside the hole—does not call to us, so we must go to it, and then interpret its meaning with our incompetent human minds. The data is mute; we give it an imperfect voice.

And that's exactly why, after he got out of his hole, Max Beckmann painted the way that he did. He understood this, and as a result, his art was more real than all the mute things in the world that it captured.

One of the first things Max Beckmann painted after coming out of his hole was a portrait of Adam and Eve, the first new humans.

· · ·

The next day I used the hand pump and a five-gallon gas container that was fastened to the back of the motorhome to draw fuel from a tanker truck we found at a place called Kum & Go.

I wondered why people in Iowa used to spell like that.

There was so much to learn.

All the windows at Kum & Go were broken.

It was a lot of work, filling up the van. I made a mess, too, and got gasoline all over myself, which smelled bad and made me feel a bit woozy. There were so many things I hadn't considered before leaving the hole—like cleaning my clothes, for example.

Mel and I put together a new world. It was thrilling and frightening, all at the same time.

Mel found the instruction notebook for the motorhome's equipment, and while I filled and spilled, she studied it. I heard her inside, flipping switches, turning motors on. The van, like the world, I suppose, was full of things I had no idea were there. I wondered if not knowing things were out there actually prevented their existence, and if, with each new thing Mel and I stumbled upon, the universe was increasing in size.

"We have hot water here," Mel said. "There are solar panels on top, which provide all the electricity. And if you turn on the water pump, you can take a shower."

I didn't say anything. It made my chest ache, thinking about taking a shower with Mel.

Why couldn't I tell her? In three days, I had transformed into a hung-up, inhibited, before-the-hole sixteen-year-old human being who kept asking himself over and over and over, *What if I'm wrong?*

And our universe kept growing bigger and bigger and bigger.

I stopped the van that afternoon outside a three-story, boxy brick building with top-to-bottom plate-glass windows fronting its entrance and the floors above. The place was called Henry A. Wallace Middle School. It was fascinating to me for two reasons. First, I always wanted to see what an out-of-the-hole school was really like, especially after hearing all the stories Dad and Robby had told me about how deeply school had affected them—and not in particularly pleasant-sounding ways, either. And second, Henry A. Wallace Middle School was one of the very few structures we had driven past whose windows and doors had not been smashed and broken.

Apparently, there was not very much inside a middle school that anyone might have found attractive during the great extinction of before-the-hole Iowans.

Still, I wanted to go inside.

"Why here?" Mel asked.

"We are assembling the world, Mel."

"I thought we were looking for your father and Robby."

"This is part of finding them. Trust me," I said.

I had never asked Mel to trust me before. It had never been necessary inside the hole, but then again, so many things had been unnecessary there.

Mel carried the rifle, and I carried the other gun—the one that could kill the creatures, the Unstoppable Soldiers—and we went along the sidewalk to the front of the school.

The day was cold and clear. Wind blew strands of Mel's black hair from under the flaps of her cap around her face in thin whips.

"What?" she said.

Mel caught me staring at her. I felt my cheeks radiate heat.

"Nothing," I said. "It's just so strange being out here. Seeing us out here together. Are you afraid?"

Mel said, "No."

We walked up the concrete steps to the front doors at Henry A. Wallace Middle School. The bottoms of the doors had been piled up with sixteen years of rotting leaves and windblown garbage. I pulled, and then tried to push, the door's handle.

I could not open the door.

"Okay. Let's leave," Mel said.

I argued, "The fact that it's sealed is a good thing. There won't be anything inside."

"If there's nothing inside, then why go in?"

This was a typical challenge from Amelie Sing Brees, and it's why I liked her so much.

"You know what I mean, Mel. Aren't you even a little bit curious about what things were like for kids before the hole?"

Mel shrugged. "A little bit."

I used a rock to break the window on one of the doors. After that, I could reach my arm inside and push against the bar on the opposite door. It popped open an inch but got stuck in the wedge of all the muck and debris that had built up along its threshold.

From there, I wedged my fingers in the opening and pulled the door outward.

Mel and I went inside.

"This is our first day in cicada school," I said.

The door opened onto a massive hallway. To the right, behind another wall of glass, was a place called Administration. The floor was polished, still glossy after all these empty years. And at the end of the hall, which was lined with at least a dozen windowed doors, some still propped open, a wide stairway rose to the left.

On the wall opposite the Administration place was a long glass case filled with golden trophies and plaques and photographs of boys and girls. They must have been students at the school, I thought. At the back of all the display was a triangular flag that said *Henry A. Wallace Middle School Wolverines*.

I think Mel and I, fascinated as we were by this display, studied it for half an hour, at least.

She said, "What are wolverines?"

"It's a kind of animal," I said. "I have read that they are very mean, and dangerous, too."

"Do you think there are wolverines here?"

I shook my head. "Not enough for them to eat anymore. I'm sure they used to keep the wolverines here as a deterrent to children against breaking the rules."

"They used to feed children to wolverines?" Mel was horrified.

"Did Robby or my dad ever tell you about the things that happened to them in school? It was a terrible place."

Mel grimaced, thinking about wolverines roaming the hall, no doubt.

But it was the photographs of all the kids that made us both feel sad and lonely.

Mel said, "I can't even imagine what it would be like to be around so many other people, around so many kids."

One of the photographs had a caption on it that said *Henry A. Wallace Middle School Boys Basketball—2014 Iowa City Tournament Champions*. There were twelve boys in the picture, posing in two lines of six. The front-row boys were on one knee, and the back-row boys stood. All the boys were smiling, and nine of them had their hands raised with an upward-pointing index finger signifying, I assumed, the number one. And every one of the boys had a thick purple ribbon around his neck with a large gold medallion hanging from it.

A dark-skinned boy in the back row had his medal clamped between his teeth. They were all dressed oddly, too: in big, baggy, white boxer shorts and T-shirts that had their sleeves cut off.

Wendy would not approve of boys being dressed like that.

The boys' shirts all said HAWMS WOLVERINES across their chests, and below this each one had a different number.

One of the boys in front had a big orange ball with narrow lines on it resting on the floor by his foot.

"I wonder what those boys were doing there," Mel said.

I had no idea what any of it meant. But I answered, "Basketball was apparently a form of punishment. The numbers on the boys' shirts list how many times each boy had broken the rules. That one there, in the back with forty-two on his belly, was probably the first one to be handed over to the wolverine."

Mel laughed and shook her head. "I don't think so."

Under the photograph was a caption that listed the boys' names. Number 42—the big breaker of all the rules—was named Julian Powell. Standing next to him, the boy with the medal clamped between his teeth was named Denic Jackson.

Names and faces.

"Clearly they are rule breakers. You can tell by looking at them. Before the hole, boys were simply not allowed to come to school like that, in their underwear. Before the hole, everyone in Iowa was all hung up, exactly like Wendy is right now."

"I think basketball was a kind of game," Mel said. "But it's stupid that it was only for boys. Why couldn't girls play with them?"

Of course I knew she was right about basketball being a game. I only wanted to put the world together without all the instructions, without all the rules.

Then, unable to let go of my past, I answered, "Maybe girls were not allowed to play because the game had something to do with tossing small bags of rocks at your balls."

Mel laughed and put her hand on my chest. "You're never going to forget that, are you?"

"Trust me. It would be impossible to forget it, Mel."

I wanted her to keep her hand there on my chest forever, but she dropped it, and we sidestepped around a few seconds of awkward silence and gulping, and continued studying the display. It turned out there were photographs of girls in the trophy case at Henry A. Wallace Middle School too, but the girls were all shown doing different things than boys did, and they were all segregated too.

Iowa had been filled with Wendys.

We saw pictures of a girls' volleyball team, a dance team, and something called "cheer." To be honest, neither Mel nor I had any idea what the function of the "cheer" team must have been. I theorized that they were responsible for telling jokes and lifting kids' spirits after they got hit in the balls, or possibly after wolverine rampages against rule-breaking middle school boys and girls in the halls.

"This is the dumbest thing ever," Mel said. "Why would they make the boys and girls do different things apart from each other?"

"Maybe they were afraid."

"Of what?"

"I don't know. Maybe bags with rocks in them."

Mel pushed me.

If I were on a basketball team, I would want Mel to be on it too, rocks or not.

The Last Dance of the Year!

With all its unbroken windows, there was plenty of light inside Henry A. Wallace Middle School.

Past the trophy case we saw an enormous hand-painted banner made from blue paper. It had been taped to the wall sixteen years ago, decorated with stars and balls and colorful squiggly lines that advertised what was called the Last Dance of the Year!

The banner, after many years on the wall, had become so desiccated that it was cracking apart and shedding small flaky scales.

It was a lot to take in: The Last Dance of the Year was going to be held on *This Friday!* which was May 9. It was to take place inside the gymnasium, beginning at six p.m., and would be free to all sixth-, seventh-, and eighth-grade students.

Also, the sign said this: *Be sure to turn in parent permission slips to Mr. Dougherty by Thursday!*

In fact, every phrase on the sign had been punctuated with at least one exclamation point. It made me feel like I was being screamed at by a twelve-year-old.

Paradise on the Shore!!!
Last Dance of the Year!
Wear Hawaiian Style Clothes!
Hot Dogs $1!!!

Although I wondered why they did not want the boys and girls of Henry A. Wallace Middle School to wear Iowa-style clothing, which I rather liked, it was the last exclamation that I found most puzzling.

I could not remember ever hearing or reading about "hot dogs." There were no hot dogs in the model of the world assembled by my father.

So I said, "Hot dogs were specially trained miniature wolves that taught kids how to dance at these events. You know, like how Robby taught you and me how to dance in the hole. And although it may seem impractical to have a miniature wolf teaching kids how to dance, the advantage was, in having four feet, that one hot dog could instruct both dance partners at the same time."

"But why were they *hot*?" Mel asked.

"It was symbolic," I said. "The miniature dance-instructor wolves had rings of fire—actual flames—circling their midsections, to discourage boys and girls—or boys and boys, or girls and girls, for that matter—from getting too close to each other on the dance floor. The world before the hole was a vast conspiracy of rule making and inhibitions about sex and the closeness of peoples' bodies."

Mel laughed.

I built this world.

And all stories are true at the moment they are told.

We found the school's gym across from the staircase at the end of the hallway. It was still decorated for the Last Dance of the Year.

Unfortunately, the Last Dance of the Year at Henry A. Wallace Middle School most likely turned out to be the Last Dance for all Eternity, as far as the before-the-hole world was concerned.

It was all very surreal.

The gymnasium was massive, and it echoed with a sad emptiness when our boot soles squeaked on the varnished wood floor, which was painted with narrow lines that made meaningless geometric shapes. They were probably some strange type of regimented dance boundaries, I thought.

The walls of the gym were adorned with construction-paper palm trees, dolphins, women wearing skirts made from leaves, and bare-chested men with wreaths on their heads who appeared to be wrapped in colorful, floral-patterned towels.

"Could you imagine this place, filled with dancing people?" Mel said.

"And the occasional couple engulfed in flames for touching," I added.

Then Mel said, "We should dance, Arek."

Like nearly everything else I'd encountered these past few days outside the hole, Mel's suggestion filled me with wonder and fear. I felt myself choking up, consumed with thoughts of putting my arms around her, twisting my fingers in her hair, collapsing together onto the floor in a ball of fire.

"But." It took a good ten seconds for me to get the rest of the words out. "There isn't any music."

Mel just smiled and gave me a look like she thought I was crazy, which I was. And it was also crazy to be dancing with her to no music here in an empty Iowan middle school gymnasium decorated like a bad imitation Gauguin. But that's exactly what we did.

"We must look really stupid," I said.

"Nobody's watching," Mel answered.

Thinking about nobody watching us—and all that could possibly mean—caused me to start sweating.

"I could sure use a hot dog right now," I said.

"You're sweating."

"These long underwear are definitely not meant for dancing in."

"Dancing in the tropics," Mel added.

"There should be a rule about that," I said.

When we stopped dancing, Mel and I walked around the perimeter of the gym, looking at all the clumsy decorations.

"It must have been nice. I mean, to have been here with maybe two hundred other kids, with music, dancing," I said.

At the back of the gym, on opposite sides of the floor, we found doors that led to what were called locker rooms. One was marked BOYS, and the other said GIRLS.

All those rules, over and over, without end, I thought.

It turned out locker rooms were not prisons for unruly middle schoolers, as Mel and I had theorized. They were, in fact, very much like the big shower room in Eden, the hole, but not nearly as nice. And they were belowground too—beneath the gym at the bottom of a damp and moldy flight of stairs. The showers were rusty spigots poking out like drooping chrysanthemums in evenly spaced rows along two walls of stained tiles. Mel and I went into the locker room for boys, which, even after all these years, smelled like sweat and urine. It was dark, illuminated only by the gray light that squeezed inside through high, narrow windows glazed with swirled glass that you couldn't really see through. There were discarded socks and underwear scattered randomly on the floor, and a bank of urinals and toilets separated by five low sinks and a wall mirror that no longer reflected anything.

Everything in the locker room seemed to be enclosed behind mesh walls, too, so it actually did have a prisonlike atmosphere. And there were lines of metal cubbies with doors in front of long wooden benches. Some of the open cubbies had articles of clothing drooping from them, like the tongues of tired dogs.

I found one of the orange balls, just like in the picture of the boys' basketball team, but it was wrinkled and deflated. And there was a row of metal cabinets that had the white sleeveless shirts we'd seen in the photograph of the basketball team boys with medals too.

"Look!" Mel said. "It's number forty-two."

It was the same shirt I had seen—the one worn by the boy I suspected was the top rule breaker at Henry A. Wallace Middle School, the boy named Julian Powell.

I held it up in front of me, pinned to my shoulders. Julian Powell must have been very tall as a middle school boy; the shirt's tail hung down to the middle of my thighs.

Mel said, "That would look good on you."

"I. Um." I cleared my throat. Why was I being so stupid? "Do you think I should keep it?"

"Have you broken forty-two rules?" Mel asked.

"Maybe I should look for a bigger number."

Mel smiled. "I think you should have it, Arek."

"Well. Just as long as we keep our eyes out for irate wolverines," I said.

I Don't Care About Houses

Henry A. Wallace Middle School gave wordless testimony to the wild nature of the world before the hole.

And Mel and I were the jurors who would ultimately make the final decision as to the details of what had happened. This is how truth works.

We found the library upstairs.

We kept hundreds of books in the library of the hole—but the one here at Henry A. Wallace Middle School must have had thousands. It smelled like everything. There was always something that struck me when reading a book, holding my index finger tucked behind the page I was on while breathing in the smell of all those read and unread words.

It was a magnificent place. I wanted to open every single book there, but I knew it would take days and days, without end. The funny thing was that I'd found a number of books in Henry A. Wallace Middle School's library that we also had in the hole. Up until that precise moment, I had lived my entire life simply assuming that books only existed as single copies. It had never been explained to me, nor was it included within the model my father had assembled, that there were, in fact, many copies of the same book in the world before the hole, and that people all over the planet could be reading exactly the same words at exactly the same time.

I was so excited about this discovery I waved a worn copy of *Slaughterhouse-Five* in front of Mel and told her about it.

"Think of all the people, everywhere, who read this same book that I did."

She was as surprised as I was, but then again, when your entire world has only eight people in it, you just have to stumble onto these truths in your own way, I suppose.

I couldn't even begin to imagine what all those people would have been like, or what this library would look, sound, and smell like with so many books being opened and read by dozens and dozens of other boys and girls, without end. It was almost too much to consider.

In the end, I took a book with photographs in it that was about how to play basketball. As Mel had suspected, basketball had not been a form of punishment, and I decided I would try to learn how to play and then teach Mel, so that we could have a basketball team that didn't just have boys on it.

I also decided that, before we left the school, I'd go back down inside the boys' locker room and get a shirt with the lowest possible number on it for Mel, as well as some of those big shorts, too, just so we would look like we knew what we were doing, even if we had to make up the entire world and all those rules from the beginning, all over again.

Mel was very smart, and I was sure she would no doubt be able to outplay me in basketball. I also thumbed through my book very quickly just to be certain the game had nothing to do with sacks filled with small rocks or throwing anything at my balls.

Mel found a dictionary, resting open like some sort of religious object on a thick wooden pedestal at the front of the library. We had a dictionary in the hole, but this dictionary was massive. I marveled at how the smallest pieces of every idea that had ever been considered, every story ever told, and every line of poetry, without end, were trapped inside the dictionary's pages.

Mel looked up "hot dog."

"It says this: 'A hot dog is a frankfurter sandwich on a split roll, usually topped with mustard, ketchup, pickles, or sauerkraut.'"

Then she had to look up "frankfurter," and those last four nouns as well.

"It makes me hungry, thinking about all the different things people had to eat before the hole," I said. "Let's go back to the van and eat. And tomorrow we should probably look for food somewhere."

So I took an armful of clothes and shoes from the boys' locker room, and I used one of the toilets, which did not flush, and then hid behind a bank of metal boxes so Mel could go too and not be embarrassed—if that was possible for her—about me watching.

I did not think Mel would ever be embarrassed about anything around me. Mel was strictly an after-the-hole human being.

We stayed that night outside Henry A. Wallace Middle School. We ate venison meat and small potatoes and carrots from jars I'd stolen from the kitchen in the hole, and afterward Mel showed me how we had hot water, so we could take showers, and she told me I needed to take off my gasoline-smelling clothes.

It all made me so nervous—the thought of us taking showers, and how Mel had told me to take off my clothes.

"I. Um," I said.

"Stop being so weird, Arek."

Mel opened the door on the little bathroom inside the van. I heard the water splash down from the showerhead.

She said, "There. I turned it on for you. It's warm. Now go."

I didn't know what to do. Mel could see it. I'd never been afraid to undress in front of anyone, but being here in such a confined and private place, alone with Mel, made all things from the world we'd left behind in the hole irrelevant and foreign.

"Go on. You're so dumb. Is this what happens to boys when they start getting boy periods?" she said.

"I don't know."

How could I know? As far as I knew, I was the only boy in the entire world, and Mel the only girl. How could we know about these things, or about ourselves, without making it all up—assembling a model and drawing flawed conclusions from Breakfast Papers and books and paintings?

My face turned red. My hands shook.

I'd never felt like this—not once in my entire life. I thought I could possibly be dying.

I took off my hat and, fumbling, started to unbutton my gas-reeking shirt.

Then Mel left me alone and went up to the front of the van. She sat down in the driver's seat and watched all the quiet nothingness and everythingness of the outside world as the shower water splashed down like rain.

Under the water, warm and alive, I combed my fingers through my hair and scrubbed my skin with thick-lathering soap.

There is a line from a book I'd read in the library of the hole.

When I was confused, when I was trying to construct the truth about so many things, I asked my fathers.

This was just a few days before they'd woken me up in the dark to change me into out-of-the-hole boy clothes and take me fishing—our secret mission.

We were in the library, and I'd asked my dads if it made me a degenerate that my body had been doing things that I couldn't really understand. I told them I'd had dreams—twice in the past week—after which I'd woken up with sticky stuff in my underwear and on my bedsheets. It scared me. I thought something was wrong with me, or broken inside me.

My dad—Austin—smiled and patted my knee. He explained what it was and said, "There's nothing wrong with you, Lucky. It's a totally normal thing that happens to every boy when he gets to be a certain age."

I didn't think being certain had anything at all to do with it.

"I was afraid I'd have to tell Wendy about it, and she'd get mad at me for making a mess."

I figured since Wendy was our nurse, she would know if I was a degenerate, or if I needed some kind of medical treatment to make me stop leaking.

And Dad explained that this was something that boys before the hole were too inhibited to talk about with their fathers, or grandmothers for that matter, so he was proud of me for being a *new human*.

I didn't get it. If you couldn't talk to your dads about the things your body does, how were you supposed to figure out anything at all about being a boy?

Robby puffed a cigarette and said, "It happened to me almost every night, from about the time when I was twelve, all the way until after we moved down here—particularly whenever I dreamed about your dad, which was pretty much all the time."

I looked at Dad. His cheeks reddened, and his eyes turned before-the-hole.

I did not tell them it happened to me because I dreamed about Mel—specifically about touching her. I felt like a liar for not saying that, but I believed they knew without my admitting it. Dads know these things, I think.

"Will it ever stop?" I asked.

Robby sighed. "Sadly, yes."

I shook my head. "It's just—I mean, sometimes I can't stop

thinking about certain things, and the only way I can get those things out of my head . . . well . . . I mean . . . I go find a place to be alone. Is it bad for you—I mean, will masturbating do harm to a boy's body?"

Dad looked at Robby. They both smiled at my question.

And Dad said, "It is the exact opposite of harmful, son. Don't worry about it. Just make sure you clean up after yourself, because, you know—"

"Yeah. Wendy."

My dad lit a cigarette. He looked strangely happy and proud, and I couldn't begin to understand why, but then again, Dad could straddle time.

He said, "I am happy you asked us about this, Lucky. I am happy to know that you'll never be afraid of talking to us about anything."

And Robby said, "We both love you very much."

"That's the other thing I need to know about," I said. "How will I know when I fall in love? And I don't mean like the love I feel for my dads or my mom. I mean the different kind of love they make up poems and paintings and stories about. How will I ever know?"

Robby told me about this book called *John Thomas and Lady Jane*. He told me the book was about everything you could feel about another person, and that when he read the book, it made him feel whole.

The book was written by a man named D. H. Lawrence.

D. H. Lawrence had gone through a hole, much as Max Beckmann had. And like Max Beckmann, many people considered D. H. Lawrence to be a degenerate.

The line I remembered said this:

You are home to me. I don't care about houses.

At the time when I read that passage, at just-turned-thirteen, I don't think I really understood what Lawrence meant. I never knew what home was supposed to be, to feel like, because I never knew what not-home was.

This was home.

The water was good.

The shower made me feel like a new person, but that's exactly what we'd become after coming up from the hole, wasn't it? I came out from the bathroom dressed in my new basketball shirt and shorts, my hair dripping and hanging down into my eyes.

"See? That *does* look good on you," Mel said.

"Oh. Uh. Thank you."

I went up front, distracted, trying not to look back, because I knew Mel was going to get in the shower next. I tried everything I could think of to make myself not imagine being in there under the warm water with her, or becoming the water itself, but it was useless. I wondered if she felt like this was home, and if she didn't care about any other places. And while the water ran and Mel was inside our bathroom, I climbed under the sleeping-bag covers on my bed and opened one of the movie discs I'd taken from Walmart.

The movie was titled *Alfred Hitchcock's The Birds*. I'd chosen it because I liked the cover: It showed a blue sky with veils of thin white clouds and the pitch-black silhouettes of three birds. And there was a pretty gold-haired woman who carried a blue purse and wore a blue dress cinched at the waist by a wide blue belt.

She had a blue jacket on too. It was all blue, blue, blue, except for the birds, and that's why I liked it. It reminded me of Max Beckmann's *The Sinking of the* Titanic painting for some reason.

Other than that, I had no idea what the movie was about. I only hoped that it was about birds, which were nice, as opposed to the terrifying film about Bigfoot that I'd watched on my first night.

I was also happy that I had stopped obsessing about Mel in the shower. At least I'd stopped thinking about her until I heard the water shut off behind the door.

I turned on the television and willed myself not to be staring at the door when she opened it.

"What are you watching?" Mel asked.

You, I wanted to say; *I am watching you.*

You are home to me.

"A movie about birds."

Mel was wearing the white long underwear we'd taken. I wanted to tell her it looked good on her, but I couldn't. I wanted to ask her where home was, but those words would never come.

"Oh. Nice. Can I sit down next to you?"

I wondered if she could see my heart beating. The pulse in my neck was so loud inside my head that I almost couldn't hear her.

"Sure."

I scooted over, and Mel sat down beside me. I gave her a pillow without looking directly at her face. If I looked at her, I was certain Mel would ask me why I was acting so stupid, and I didn't have any answers, only questions and words I was too afraid to make into truth.

I said, "If you're cold, you can get under the sleeping bag."

"Oh. Okay. Thanks."

Mel pulled back the top of the sleeping bag and then slid into bed next to me. When she did, her foot brushed down along the outside of my leg. My pulse got even louder. My penis was so stiff it hurt, but I didn't want to touch it. I felt embarrassed and dumb, like a before-the-hole boy, and I couldn't move. I desperately hoped, from sheer terror, that I would not end up having a wet dream just because Mel had gotten under the covers to watch a fucking movie about birds with me.

Mel said, "This is fun, Arek. And thank you for dancing with me today."

I attempted to swallow the knot in my throat. I tried to think about anything that wasn't about Mel and me in bed together and having a goddamned wet dream.

"Um. Well. We broke the rule about Hawaiian-style clothes."

The movie came on.

The Battle of Hampton Roads

Breakfast did not calm down for a long time.

He was very mad about being covered in sixteen-year-old piss and shit.

It turned out the reason people as tall as Breakfast were not allowed to ride the Battle of Hampton Roads Thrill Ride! was that the attraction included actual cannon balls fired from two metal contraptions—ships on opposite sides of the lake. The riders on the Battle of Hampton Roads Thrill Ride! sat in low boats pulled along an underwater track, while each ship fired cannon balls that sailed directly over the unprotected heads of the fortunately diminutive passengers, missing their Tennessean skulls by mere inches.

There were no guns firing now, no ships under steam, just an algae-clogged, lukewarm, man-made pond filled with catfish, pollywogs, and leeches, along with a thrashing and naked little boy, wriggling and twisting like a hooked alligator, scrubbing and scratching, wringing his hands in the knotted locks of his wild hair, swearing and spitting as he attempted to rid himself of the filth that came from the pumper truck.

And beside the swampy lake stood a small wooden shack with a sign across its porch that said:

BALL'S BLUFF BOILED PEANUTS

"Fuck! Motherfucker!" Breakfast scrubbed and scrubbed. He spat. He swished green soupy water in and out of his mouth and nostrils. He poked the tips of his fingers into his ears and rotated them. Breakfast's hair became matted with thick clumps of algae.

And beside the sagging front porch of the boiled-peanuts stand, a starving and emaciated Unstoppable Soldier pivoted its head and rubbed its folded spiked arms like twin violin bows, aroused by the motion of a human being not thirty yards away in the shallow dirty lake.

Unstoppable Soldiers, although they could sometimes digest other things, could not survive without human meat. Unstoppable Soldiers only want to eat one thing—that is, when they're not eating other Unstoppable Soldiers they're engaged in sexual intercourse with—and that one thing, like a receptive mate, was getting harder and harder to find. But here was one now, writhing and twitching deliciously in the water, and the Unstoppable Soldier perched beside Ball's Bluff Boiled Peanuts, mesmerized by the twelve-year-old boy in the pond, salivating and hissing, nearly dead from starvation.

Breakfast finally calmed down.

When the boy stood up straight, the water in the lake only came up to the middle of his chest.

Breakfast wiped his face in his palms and blew chunks of snot from each nostril.

He spat again.

He screamed, "I hate you, motherfucker shit truck!"

And saying that, Breakfast realized he could not remember where the shit truck was, or what might have happened to Olive. He tried to think if he'd seen any cars when he was running, but it was all a blur that escaped his frazzled memory. Breakfast turned around, at last taking in all the strangeness of Rebel Land.

"Wild!"

When Breakfast wiped the murk away from his eyes, he saw what looked like a fantasy image of twisting, looping train tracks, red sky baskets hanging from overhead cables with stars painted inside blue Xs, and a big building called DOC SAWBONES' FIELD AMPUTATION HOUSE OF HORRORS!

The building was adorned with plastic arms and legs with waxy fake blood at their severed ends.

"Hoo-boy! This place is as wild as me!"

And behind the boy, the hungry giant mantis, drooling and pumping its glistening, jagged mandibular structures in and out, open and shut, crept closer and closer to the shore.

Breakfast poked his index fingers into his mouth and whistled.

When he was especially loud, Breakfast could kill small mammals with the pitch of his whistling.

"Olive! Hey! Olive!"

Breakfast whistled again, louder.

Unstoppable Soldiers are mostly deaf. They have just one tiny ear opening, and their hearing is tuned only to very high frequencies. The Unstoppable Soldier quietly stalking Breakfast at the edge of the pond heard the boy's whistle and froze. It tilted its enormous triangular head, and then dipped its razor-barbed front arms into the water, reaching down to probe for the bottom. Unstoppable Soldiers also hate bodies of water, but this one was moments away from death by starvation and needed to eat Breakfast.

"Olive!"

When the creature jumped into the murky lake, Breakfast, thinking the motion he'd caught at the edge of his field of vision was Olive, spun around to see what was there.

The thing was in the lake, awkwardly wading toward the boy, and it was very, very hungry.

"Motherfucker! Olive!" Breakfast screamed.

The Unstoppable Soldier pushed forward, scrabbling and slipping on the goo-covered concrete bottom of the pond. As it came at Breakfast, it created a wake that rippled away in a V. It gathered a thick belt of green algae skirting its midsection.

"OLIVE!"

Breakfast gulped air and dove beneath the surface of the lake. He kicked off the bottom and swam as fast as he could away from the massive predator just as the Unstoppable Soldier's spike-clawed arms speared down at the spot where the boy had been standing.

The monster came up waving arms draped with ropes of mossy green algae. It thrashed and stabbed into the water again and again, but the boy was gone. The Unstoppable Soldier slashed and raked his spiked arms over and over at the surface of the water, insane with hunger.

Breakfast's chest pounded. Stroking his way along the lake bottom, blinded by the pale foamy green of the Battle of Hampton Roads Thrill Ride's fake river channel, he held his breath until he began to feel weak and dizzy.

Breakfast came to the surface on the other side of a flat-topped metal structure that said MONITOR along its side. He kept his head low, huffing as much air as he could and listening for the thing that was hunting him on the other side of the ship.

Something moved on the shore in front of Breakfast. The boy got ready to go back under again. Breakfast was a good swimmer and fighter, and he was not going to just give up and let a goddamned giant bug eat him.

Then he realized he was looking directly at Olive, who waved her arms and grinned at Breakfast.

"Olive!" Breakfast hissed a whisper. He held up his palm, and then hitched his thumb backward in the direction of the monster in the lake. "Go get him, girl!"

Olive focused on the Unstoppable Soldier, who still hadn't

noticed her in his starving, unrelenting hunt for the boy in the water.

Olive chirped and grunted. She waved her arms overhead so the thing would become aware of her movement. The Unstoppable Soldier stopped its frantic spearfishing for the boy in the lake and stood, upright and shaky, on its back legs. The monster's pinpoint pseudopupils tightened inward and then dilated when its eyes fixed on Olive. It pushed back, trying to get away from her. The giant bug's carapace opened, and sets of useless wings churned through the stew of algae on the surface of the lake.

Weakened by hunger, and weighed down by the water and muck on the surface, the Unstoppable Soldier gave up and tumbled backward into the lake, fizzling and burbling as it went under. Only the two front arms periscoped above the surface, twitching slightly for a few seconds before locking stiff in the grip of death.

Olive jumped up and down on the shore.

Breakfast clapped and splashed in the water beside the *Monitor*.

"You are my gem, Olive! A real gem! Yip-hoo! Welcome to Rebel Land, girl!"

Breakfast kicked forward, dipped below the surface, and swam for shore.

Olive was happy to see him.

Breakfast came up, spouting tepid lake water from his mouth and nose. Strands of fluorescent-green algae braided themselves into the boy's wild dreadlocks.

"I got all that shit off me! Hoo-boy, I *never* want to relive that experience, Olive!"

The boy braced his hands on the sidewalk that edged the lake and launched himself up out of the water. Olive jumped up and down with excitement and hugged Breakfast as soon as he was on his feet.

"Awww, thank you, girl! I love you, too," Breakfast said.

Breakfast was spotted all over with leeches. There were dozens and dozens of them, slick and black, attached to the boy's skin everywhere.

"Well, fuck that!" Breakfast said.

Every leech he plucked left a running trail of Breakfast's blood, comingling with the lake water and algae that clung to him. Olive had to help pull the parasites off Breakfast. The boy couldn't even see the places where half of them were.

And Breakfast, streaked with his own watery blood where the leeches had pierced his skin, just shook his head and said, "Wild!"

Olive ate most of the leeches and algae she plucked from the boy.

It took them nearly half an hour, and when they were finished, Olive dipped handfuls of dried grass into the water of the attraction's fake lake so she could sponge away the blood that had dried to Breakfast's skin.

"Thank you, Olive. I don't know what I'd ever do without you," Breakfast said. "Did you see any police cars or ambulances when you followed me in, Olive?"

Olive shook her head.

Breakfast was very smart. "Well, a place like this would have to have a parking lot somewhere. We just didn't see it, maybe on account of all the trees and stuff. And I don't want to, but we're going to need to go back to the shit truck and get our guns and all my money."

So Olive took Breakfast's hand, and the two of them walked out the entrance to the Battle of Hampton Roads Thrill Ride! and past the sign that told tall riders they might die here.

Breakfast looked back one time at the lake and said, "Come on, girl. Wild!"

"Hey, you! Hey, you boy! Stop! Who are you? Where'd you come from?"

Breakfast and Olive turned around.

"Wait! Don't run off! Wait!"

Someone, waving both arms enthusiastically, had come down the steps that led to Doc Sawbones' Field Amputation House of Horrors! and was running right toward Breakfast and Olive.

Wild.

This Isn't How I Thought It Would Be

I thought, *If this is what birds do, then maybe we should go back in the hole.*

What if I'm wrong about everything?

"Fuck birds," I said. "I never want to see a fucking bird again as long as I live."

It turned out that *Alfred Hitchcock's The Birds* was the most horrifying thing I had ever seen. Mel had fallen asleep beside me, and I was so scared that I didn't have the nerve to turn off the television, partly because I didn't want Mel to wake up and go to her own bed, but mostly because I kept waiting for someone to come on the screen and tell me the story was all made up—it was all a joke, and none of this was true or could ever happen.

But all stories are true the moment they are told.

What if birds got inside our van?

The film, on the other hand, definitely made me stop thinking about my penis, and how Mel and I were in my bed together, completely alone and outside the limits of any rules, at least until it was over and the screen went blank.

So I lay there for a few minutes, telling myself how the movie was all just made up, that it could not be the truth, that people before the hole would never have lasted with all those birds, and Bigfoot, wolverines, Unstoppable Soldiers, and wars and such. It was all too much to think about, how life before the hole must have been as frighteningly insane as being trapped inside one of Max Beckmann's most terrifying compositions.

I had to do something, but what if everything I did turned out to be a mistake?

Mel shifted slightly. Her hair was damp, and she smelled sweet, like the soap we had in the shower. I wanted to kiss her so bad. I decided I would—just a nice kiss, the way my dads would kiss me on the cheek or on the forehead when they'd tell me *I love you* every night before I'd go to sleep.

I could do that. It would be okay.

I leaned my face closer to hers. Mel was so beautiful and smelled so nice.

But I did not kiss her.

Kisses are things that cannot be secret.

Nobody had to tell me that rule.

So, moving as quietly as I could, I lifted the covers and got out of bed, making sure not to wake Mel. I was barefoot and had nothing on under those baggy basketball shorts and the sleeveless shirt with the number 42 on it.

Mel slept so quietly. I could see in her face that she was not worried or afraid of anything. And I thought, if I had anything to do with Mel feeling safe and comfortable, then maybe what I was doing was right.

If I were one of my dads, I suppose at that moment I would have lit a cigarette and gone outside in the quiet. One time, when I was fifteen, I asked my dads if I could have a cigarette with them. We were in the library inside the hole, and both of them had been smoking. My father was reading aloud from an anthology of poems written by a man named Wallace Stevens, his favorite poet.

My question surprised them, I think, because I saw them look at each other with this kind of wordless conversation that considered assent and simultaneously argued the fact that both of them had started smoking—above and before the hole— when they were younger than me. And even though I could have secretly experimented with cigarettes on my own, there was no sneaking in the hole, no secrets or things I hid from anyone, except for maybe my feelings and confusion about what had been happening to my body, and what I thought about Mel.

I think I'd asked them if I could smoke because the smell was something I so strongly associated with my fathers, almost as though the smoke itself became a physical manifestation of their love for me, and for each other, too. So, at that very confusing age of fifteen years, as we sat there in the library and listened to poetry, I asked them, flat out, if they would allow me to have a cigarette with them too.

Dad—Austin—didn't answer. He lay the book faceup on his lap and shook a cigarette out from the pack that was resting on the table between our chairs. I watched as he put a new cigarette into his mouth and then lit it from the coal of the one he'd been smoking.

He handed the cigarette to me.

I knew how to do it. I held my hand up in a gesture of *stop* when he began explaining the method for smoking a cigarette.

I said, "I've seen how to do it for fifteen years, Dad."

And Robby, my other dad, said, "What else have you seen how to do for fifteen years?"

I thought about it. I held the cigarette in front of my nose and stared at the glowing orange eye at its tip, looking at the sea and the boats and the humanity in Max Beckmann's painting.

"I've seen how to make pancakes, how to fish, and how to drive a car, although, admittedly, I'm not very good at it. I've seen how people really love each other, and I've also seen how sometimes people can hold their anger inside and keep it trapped in a sealed jar like insects."

"You should be a poet," Dad—Austin—said.

I put the cigarette in my lips. I sucked a mouthful of smoke in, then inhaled the air of the library—that was how to do it, I knew. The smoke stung and tore at my throat, but I did not cough. When I exhaled, a tear rolled out of the corner of my eye.

"Are you *crying*?" Dad leaned toward me. He laughed.

I felt so dizzy, like I was being tossed on the sea in one of those crowded lifeboats.

I said, "No. But this isn't how I thought it would be."

I gave the cigarette back to my dad.

Naturally, there were cigarettes inside the Mercedes van. My dads would never prepare a vehicle without including such things as they considered to be necessities. The cigarettes were stored inside a drawer in the kitchen area. I looked at them. I did consider taking one out and smoking for only the second time in my life, but I shut the drawer and left them untouched.

I can't say that Mel actually had anything to do with it. I think that maybe I was crazy because of what was happening inside my body; being out here above the hole, alone; and being frightened by the newness of everything, by the volume of that newness. Like that first cigarette, nothing was how I thought it would be. There were so many things I'd never done.

In a cupboard above the stove, in racks that clamped the bottles and jars so they would not topple out when the van was moving, I found a bottle that said KENTUCKY STRAIGHT BOURBON WHISKEY on it. The top of it had been sealed with black wax. I picked it up.

I looked at Mel again as she lay motionless in my bed.

Although it was cold, without putting on warmer clothes, I slipped outside the van, into the dark Iowa night.

Lonely Thing in the Night

I marveled at all those brilliant stars and planets, at the calloused face of the moon.

Growing up in the hole, I felt as though everything real was always segregated away from me, always on the other side of walls and barriers. It was why my father worked so hard to build his flawed model.

But now that I was outside, I looked up at the sky—at the moon—and became finally aware that everything was all inside one room now.

My room.

I felt like it was a simple matter to reach my hands up and touch that cold and lonely satellite.

I walked over to the front steps of Henry A. Wallace Middle School and sat down on the damp and freezing concrete. In the world before the hole, they should never have built schoolrooms inside walls, I thought, because behind walls, all you were left with were models and rules.

There was probably a rule against barefoot kids in Wolverines basketball clothes drinking whiskey at Henry A. Wallace Middle School. And despite the fact I expected that it was bound to not be how I thought it would be, I wanted to try the whiskey anyway, hoping that it might change something inside me, that it would force me to grow up and stop thinking about all the things I could not control.

It was hard to open.

There was a tab in the wax that when I pulled it cut a band around the circumference of the bottle neck. That alone took me several minutes to figure out. I struggled with simply trying to twist off the top to the point where my hand became sore before I discovered that little tab.

I was shivering in the cold, cursing myself for coming outside barefoot, practically naked, when I could have been back inside the van with Mel. But I also felt strangely alive in a way I don't think I had ever experienced before.

The bottle had a cork stopper in it, and when I removed it, the smell of whiskey wafted up, sweet and warm, stinging my nostrils, setting fire to the night. I set the cork down on the step next to me and raised the bottle toward the moon, the way I'd seen my dads raise bottles when they drank together.

"Here's to you, lonely thing in the night." Then I pointed the bottle to the van and said, "Here's to you, Mel. I'm sorry if I've gotten you into something we may not be able to get out of."

And I added, "I love you, Mel. I am so fucking in love with you, I think it might kill me."

Then I took a swallow.

My dads must have had concrete lining inside their throats. The whiskey seemed like a living organism, because it clawed at my insides as though it were fighting against my swallowing it. And then when it hit the bottom, it sprang up like a protesting rabbit in a snare.

I coughed, and the smell of the whiskey seared the insides of my nose.

I no longer felt the cold, though, so that was a good thing.

The whiskey stopped burning by the time I'd taken my third swallow. It had transformed into something sweet, reminding me of the desserts Louis, who was Mel's father, cooked for us down in the hole. But it also made me experience a confused mixture of so many things: I was very relaxed; my body felt so good, like I was sleeping in the most comfortable bed I had ever slept in; and everything—the school, the van, my naked arms and legs, the number 42, wolverines, the cheer team, hot dogs—had somehow become so astoundingly funny.

Maybe the cheer team gave people whiskey.

I wanted to wake Mel up, to explain to her how happy I was about everything. I imagined staying up with her until sunrise and telling her everything that I'd been afraid of, and how I was now willing to release those things and make them into fiction. But there was still that small and possibly sensible part of me that warned against ruining our journey right here and right now, on this cold night.

I took another swallow and corked the bottle.

Then I said:

"*The Birds* is not true.

"Bigfoot does not exist.

"Johnny and Ingrid were the last people from earth to visit the moon.

"Yellow bass are not yellow.

"Those were not human bones I saw.

"I will find my fathers.

"All stories are true the moment they are told."

And I thought, *I should go back inside now. I am not afraid.*

This is hard to explain, but when I stood up, it felt as though the "me"—the ghost or spirit of who I was, the thing that was occupying the awkward and self-willed body of a wet-dream-plagued sixteen-year-old boy—was left behind, separated, still seated on the steps of Henry A. Wallace Middle School.

I had to wait a moment for the contents to get back inside the package.

I laughed. It was funny, after all.

Then the ground tilted slightly beneath my feet, and I took a couple of crooked steps backward to keep the package from tipping over and cracking his goddamned head open, spilling his contents on the concrete steps. That was funny too.

I turned back toward the van.

Something moved down the street, just beyond the fenced-in end of the schoolyard.

It was something big, and it was coming toward me very fast.

It was one of the monsters.

A Number 42 Midnight Special

I had broken my own goddamned rules about going outside.

I had nothing to defend myself with, and the thing was closer to the van than I was. There was no way I could get back inside now. What would happen to Mel?

She would never even know why I was gone.

I ran up the steps and entered the school, trampling through the broken crumbles of glass where I'd shattered the door earlier with Mel. I felt the jagged pieces cut into my feet, but it didn't hurt. And my blood slipped like oil beneath each step I took as I ran down the dark hallway.

The Last Dance of the Year!

At the end of the hall, just at the door to the gym, I glanced toward the front. The Unstoppable Soldier had followed me into the school. I could see its shadowy form and hear its clattering feet as it scrambled down the hall after me.

I was not afraid, which may have had something to do with the whiskey. I was more angry at myself because I'd put us in a position where Mel might end up alone, and the thought of that made me feel desperate and sad. And it wasn't as though I didn't have a plan. I knew exactly what I was going to try to do, even if it may have been completely stupid.

I yelled, "Fuck you, fuckbucket!"

I went inside the gym and ran as fast as I could for the door at the back—the one that opened onto the stairwell down to the boys' locker room—aiming to get myself inside the caged-in area where the basketball team's lockers were.

The place was so dark now; all I could see were bands of gray up above where the ground-level narrow windows allowed just the faintest moonlight inside. I ran right into a bench at full speed, bashing my knees and ending up with my belly on the floor and my face in an ancient Iowan boy's cast-off dirty socks or something.

I was breathing so hard I couldn't hear if the thing had managed to follow me down into the locker room.

My head spun. I got up and felt my way down along the bench to the basketball cage. And I thought, *Iowans before the hole weren't dumb; they built steel cages inside locker rooms to keep their basketball teams from being eaten by enormous bugs, right?*

"That's right!" I said.

I found the door to the cage and slammed it shut behind me. Now I only had to hope that bugs were too stupid to know what doorknobs did, because the one on the cage would not lock, and it was the only thing between my contents and me and the thing that wanted to eat a number 42 midnight special.

I only first started to feel the hurt when I sat down on the concrete floor and hid behind the bank of lockers. My feet were bloody and slashed, and my knees throbbed. I calmed my breathing and tried to listen for any sign of the creature.

Water dripped from one of the rusted showerheads.

And outside, I heard it.

Tick-tick, tick-tick.

The thing was coming downstairs.

Tick-tick, tick-tick.

Everything was suddenly so loud. The creaking of the door hinge as the Unstoppable Soldier pushed its way inside the locker room was as loud as a car crash, and then came the sizzling buzz of the creature's excited wings and the clicking mechanisms of every jointed appendage on the monster as it moved along, hunting for me.

Tick-tick, tick-tick.

Tick-tick, tick-tick.

I pulled my legs in to my chest, trying to make myself as small as possible behind the cold metal wall of lockers.

Tick-tick, tick-tick.

Then, absolute silence that seemed to last an eternity. It was more than silence—it was a smothering vacuum of nothingness. And maybe it was just the whiskey, but I found myself facing the realization that there is nothing more effective at getting a sixteen-year-old boy to stop thinking about his penis than the impending prospect of his being eaten by a freakishly gargantuan bug.

That, and the terrorizing explosion of sound when the Unstoppable Soldier slammed its massive spiked arms into the steel mesh of the cage.

I gasped a little scream.

And the thing kept thrashing, pounding and pounding itself against the cage.

I had to look.

I peered around the edge of the lockers. In the dim gray light, I could make out the shape of the monster on the other side of the cage's meshed steel bars. It flailed and pounded its triangular head against the cage. The front two arms of the thing—the spring-loaded, tooth-lined bear traps the Unstoppable Soldiers used to capture their prey—had gotten caught inside the narrow openings of the steel cage. The thing was trapped and angry, and it bashed and bashed its face and mouth uselessly against the steel.

I curled up behind the metal boxes, shivering.

The bashing and clanging got louder and louder, wildly violent. This must have been the sound of the dying *Titanic*. This is what you hear before you die.

I shook like I was being electrocuted, without end, inhaling chopped hiccups of terror.

The Unstoppable Soldier braced its four hind legs against the cage and kicked.

The noise was so loud it hurt; I could feel the vibrations shudder through every bone in my body.

The thing kicked and thrashed.

The two front arms tore away from the bug's thorax, and the rest of the creature went flying back into the same pile of dirty clothes I'd landed in only moments before. The outside segments of the arms flexed and twitched spastically, still caught in the cage bars like some ghastly trophy, spraying wild, gushing splatters of fluid. Some of the goop landed on my legs and splashed in my hair.

The rest of the now armless monster rolled around, kicking at the air and hissing, spurting pus-like globs of its innards everywhere.

At that point—and, again, maybe this was due to the whiskey—I decided that I would never have another wet dream as long as I lived.

The arms stuck in the basketball cage stopped twitching and relaxed.

Drip-drip.

The thing on the floor also stopped moving, surrounded by a glistening lake of snot gravy. The smell was disgusting. I had to puke. I did it in an open locker.

Maybe it was the whiskey.

So, what do you do when you're barefoot, inside a cage in a moldy, dungeonlike boys' locker room, and there's a presumably dead monster that had just been trying to eat you spewing a fountain of frothing, milky snot all over your only path out?

I waited.

I watched the thing on the floor.

It had to be dead, I thought; it wouldn't be pretending, just to lure me out of the cage. Bugs aren't smart enough for those kinds of things.

Besides, all its contents had pretty much ejaculated out of the holes where its arms used to be.

Cautiously, on stinging feet, I approached the bars of the cage. I wondered if there had ever been any human beings who'd been so close to the spiked death-trap arms of an Unstoppable Soldier and lived to tell about it. I was fascinated and disgusted, all at the same time. This was like living inside *The Night*, that horrible scene captured by Max Beckmann.

I actually touched one of the spikes on the monster's severed arm. It felt like the point of the sharpest, hardest knife I had ever felt.

The arm twitched at my touch.

The hair on the back of my neck prickled.

"Hey!"

I watched the thing on the floor to see if it moved at the sound of my voice.

"You're fucking stupid!"

Motionless. No self-esteem issues.

I wrapped my fingers through the meshed bars on the cage and shook it, rattling and clanging.

The thing was clearly dead, but that didn't make me any less nervous about going outside the cage. I opened the door and stood there for a moment.

The Unstoppable Soldier must have had nearly twenty gallons of goop inside its body. The gut soup smelled like rotting meat, and I could feel heat rising from it. The nearest dry spot on the concrete floor was at least fifteen feet away from the cage. I did not want to walk through the stuff barefoot, so I closed the door and only had to look through a few of the lockers before finding a pair of white Wolverines basketball socks and shoes that fit me.

Maybe they had at one time been worn by the boy named Julian Powell too.

Names and faces.

I stepped outside the cage and into the puddle of guck. When I took a second step, my shoe made a sickening slurping noise and then a sound like I was walking through warm egg yolks. Certain the thing really was dead, I took off running for the door out of the locker room, but my feet slipped in the viscous slop, and I fell down onto my hands and knees, barely saving myself from planting my face in the unstoppable goo.

Feeling it on my hands and legs was worse than I could imagine. The stuff was hot and slimy, wriggling with wormy coils of unnamable horrors, and it smelled so foul I could almost taste it. I slipped again trying to get to my feet and caught myself with my right forearm. When I managed to get up, snotty ropes of the stuff hammocked down from my arms and legs.

My stomach turned, but it had already been emptied once.

Carefully, walking on tiptoes, I made it through the miserable lake.

I felt around blindly in the locker room and found a towel and a discarded T-shirt lying on the floor. Gagging, I used them to wipe myself off, and then I left Henry A. Wallace Middle School.

I abandoned the sloppy shoes I'd found on the front steps next to the bottle of whiskey that was still sitting exactly where I'd left it when I took off running from the Unstoppable Soldier. I had no idea how much time had passed since I'd left the trailer, but I had no intention of staying outside any longer. So I picked up the bottle, and, staggering, I took two more big swallows of the stuff before opening the door on our van.

Inside smelled safe—like Amelie, soundlessly asleep in my bed, with the lingering scents of soap from the shower and the food we'd shared for dinner.

I took a deep breath and thought about what I might tell her, or might not. I put the whiskey back inside the cupboard and took off my shirt. Then I wrapped myself up in the covers on the small bed—the one Mel had been sleeping in—and fell rapidly into a deep and dreamless black void.

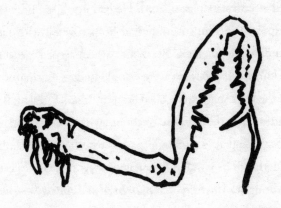

Edsel and Mimi

In all his life, Breakfast had never seen anyone as old as Edsel and his wife, Mimi.

They must have been a hundred years old, Breakfast thought.

Edsel and Mimi lived inside Doc Sawbones' Field Amputation House of Horrors!, and it was Edsel who'd come running out after he spotted Breakfast and Olive walking together beside the fake river-mouth battlefield of the Battle of Hampton Roads Thrill Ride!

"Wait! Don't run off! Wait!" Edsel shouted and ran as fast as he could, which was actually slower than Breakfast's normal walking pace.

"Oh my gosh! Olive! A person! Another real live person!"

Olive jumped up and down and stroked Breakfast's thigh.

Edsel was out of breath by the time he caught up to Breakfast and Olive. He doubled over, panting, like he was staring at his feet, which were gnarled and shoeless. The old man wore greasy work pants that were frayed and threadbare, held tight to his waist with a knotted electrical extension cord. He had no shirt, and every inch of the exposed skin on his body had been covered with tattoos— smudged drawings, as far as Breakfast was concerned, since the boy did not know what tattoos were. Breakfast was fascinated by the image of the rattlesnake that coiled around Edsel's forearm. Breakfast had no idea what the purpose of the drawings was, especially ones like the car with flames coming out of its wheels and the skull with a knife underneath its jaw and fiery flames spewing from its eyes.

He thought, *Maybe the old man lived at a time when everything in the world had been engulfed in flames.*

"Where did you come from?" Edsel, who still had not raised his face to look at the two, asked.

"Over yonder." Breakfast pointed.

That was when Edsel, who was actually not a hundred, but more approximately sixty-five years old, looked up and, for the first time, clearly took in the image of Breakfast and Olive.

"You're naked," Edsel, who had lived the majority of his life before the hole when people were inhibited about such things as nudity, pointed out.

"I'm wild. Rich and wild," Breakfast said. "And me and Olive don't like to wear nothing. What's the point?"

"But you're a person, and she's a chimpanzee," Edsel said.

Breakfast picked his nose and scratched his balls. "A *what*?"

Breakfast didn't know what chimpanzees were.

And Olive, who actually was a chimpanzee and never argued anyway, didn't argue about it.

"A chimpanzee," Edsel said.

"She's just a girl with a bunch of hair on her," Breakfast said. "You're not making fun of her, are you?"

Breakfast was ready to fight the guy, even if he was a hundred years old and apparently frail. But Edsel, having developed such a pronounced degree of patience after spending so many endless days and weeks holed up inside Doc Sawbones' Field Amputation House of Horrors!, especially during the first few years, when the infestation of the creatures was particularly bad, continued attempting to explain to the twelve-year-old naked wild boy the fundamental differences between human beings and chimpanzees.

Breakfast wasn't buying any of it.

He took Olive's hand. "Come on, Olive. We're leaving. Let's go get our stuff from the shit truck and find another vehicle, so we can get the fuck out of here. I don't like that old man with the pictures on his skin."

Breakfast and Olive turned back in the direction they'd been heading when Edsel came running for them.

"Wait! Please! You can't leave," Edsel said.

"Sure we can. Who needs you?"

"No. I mean you *can't* leave." Edsel's voice was flat and cold.

When Breakfast turned around, the old man was pointing a pistol directly at the boy's belly.

And Edsel said, "I'd just as soon shoot you both here and now, and then gut you out and have Mimi stew you up with some dumplings, as let you walk out of here."

Breakfast didn't know what to do. He'd never in his life been in or even witnessed a situation where a human was threatening to kill another human.

It didn't make sense to Breakfast, who was wild.

Part Two

All Stories Are True

PART TWO

Number 42 Breaks Every Rule

"I was beginning to think you were going to sleep all day. I even checked to see if you were still breathing."

It was like being dead, and then coming back to life.

I could tell by the color of the sunlight in the windows that it was afternoon. And then I thought, *How did Mel check my breathing? Did she lay her hand on my bare chest? Did she put her face close to mine?*

"Oh. Uh." I sat up in Mel's little bed.

I was starving. She had been cooking food while I slept. The smell of it must have been what called me back down to earth.

"Is something wrong with you?" Mel asked.

It would take me at least an hour to answer that one honestly, I thought.

"No. I'm okay."

"I watched that movie about birds this morning while you

slept. I don't think things like that ever really happened, or else people used to be incredibly dumb, right?"

"Uh. That's what I think too."

And Mel said, "Sorry I fell asleep last night and missed watching it with you."

"It's okay."

"Well, why did you go to sleep over there?"

Because if I fell asleep next to you, I would have ended up embarrassing myself, I wanted to say.

But what I did say was, "Um. I don't know."

"Well, I apologize for taking over your bed. I made some food, though, if you're hungry."

Mel didn't know anything about how I left last night, how I was nearly killed. It all seemed like a strange dream, like a bad movie from before the hole about how stupid people used to be.

And I was exceptionally stupid.

"I'm starving," I said. "And I need to pee. I'm going outside."

"You can't go alone."

"It will be okay. Trust me. I'll stay right by the van."

But when I stood up, I was reminded about the broken glass I'd stepped through and the wooden bench I'd slammed my knees into. I groaned and grabbed on to the counter beside the sink to keep myself from falling down.

"Oh my gosh, Arek! What happened to you?"

Mel bent down to look at the purple marks on my knotty knees and the dried blood on my borrowed socks.

She gently touched her fingertips to my legs. It felt so cool and healing.

And then I remembered I had absolutely nothing on except for some very loose, very thin basketball shorts, and that Mel was bent down in front of me, touching my naked legs with her perfect hands. I clutched myself and said, "I really need to pee. I'll tell you the story when I get back."

I limped for the door.

And Mel said, "But you have to leave the door open, and I'm standing right here with the guns."

I tried not to groan when I stepped down to the pavement below the van but was not successful in the attempt.

Mel stood in the doorway, and I went to the front of the van. It was a beautiful day—clear and warm. I felt bad that Mel had had to stay inside all day while I slept. It must have made her feel trapped and bored.

"Are you watching me?" I said.

Behind me, Mel said, "Yes. Stop being weird, Arek."

"I can't stop being weird, Mel."

I hobbled back to the door with an apologetic look on my face. We went inside, and Mel sat me down on the little bed. She said, "Now, let me see. And tell me how this happened."

"I must be a sleepwalker," I said.

"Bullshit."

"All stories are true the moment they are told," I said.

"That moment ended immediately," Mel pointed out.

So I told her everything: about how I drank whiskey and had to shut myself inside the boys' locker room cage in order to avoid being eaten by a monster.

Mel kept asking *why*.

Why did I drink whiskey—I didn't know.

Why did I go outside, unarmed, alone at night—I didn't know.

Why did I think it was okay for me to risk leaving her entirely alone—I did not know.

I had completely devolved into a hung-up, before-the-hole teenage boy. I couldn't understand it.

I felt terrible. And to make things worse, while we talked, Mel gently took off my ruined socks and cleaned the cuts on my feet with warm soapy water. It stung.

In the end, I could do little more than apologize to her and promise I would never be so stupid again. It was probably a lie, I thought; I was bound to be just as stupid as ever.

Mel served us the last of our eggs and jarred potatoes from the night before.

She said, "We are going to run out of food today."

I nodded. I'd been thinking about that too.

So I asked her, "Do you want to go back?"

Mel shook her head. "I miss my mom and dad, but I don't want to go back, Arek. I had no idea that all this was out here. Now I want to see more of it. And we need to look for Austin and Robby, besides."

"There are others out here too. Dad's found signs and stuff from someone who calls himself Breakfast."

Mel said, "Breakfast? Like the model you built?"

"Yeah. It's why I named him that," I said.

"Does it scare you at all, the thought of finding people?" she asked.

I thought about it. "It kind of does, Mel."

"Me too."

"It's going to get warm," I said. "The Unstoppable Soldiers are going to be out now. Like last night."

"I know."

"Well. I guess that one wasn't so unstoppable, right? He pretty much got his ass handed to him by a boys' locker room basketball cage."

"And a drunk barefoot kid."

"Number forty-two breaks every rule," I said.

Looking for my fathers was only an excuse that got us out of the hole to begin with. The moment we found what was out here, the instant Mel stood, laughing, in that first snowfall, I believe we both recognized that the excuse, despite all the risks, had become a pretense we both laid claim to, perhaps as a means of disguising what it was Mel and I were truly looking for.

And maybe I was fooling myself with that, too.

What if I'm wrong?

This was, without end, the barrier I'd built between myself and Mel: Neither of us had the freedom to choose the other. There was no one else. We were, as Dad liked to call us, Adam and Eve. What if Mel felt nothing special toward me? What if, given a choice, given the opportunities that before-the-hole human beings had, I would become repulsive to her?

And what if I was wrong about that?

I shut up and ate.

Two Notes and One Picture

We came to the airfield the next day outside a place called Independence.

It was Mel who'd first spotted the lone airplane, tilted half on its side with a broken wing, nearly obscured by the brush that grew up alongside the runway. I was too busy concentrating on avoiding debris in the roadway. It was everywhere—windblown branches, entire sections of roofs, the charred remnants of tire fires, abandoned cars and motorbikes. And when I pulled the van around through a chain-link gate that had been battered down, we both saw the car that Robby and Dad had been driving the last time they left the hole.

It made me excited, anxious, and sick, all at the same time.

Mel knew it too.

I'd been driving around without any real idea of direction or distance. It was almost as though an unseen hand had guided us to Independence.

Our plan for the day had been to go inside abandoned houses. Dad and Robby had always told me there were plenty of houses in Iowa that had belonged to people who called themselves *survivalists*, which I thought was funny since they clearly did not succeed in becoming what they claimed to be. Dad told me to look for their holes, because *survivalists* religiously kept stores of food and water that could last a lifetime.

That part—the part about lasting a lifetime—was very accurate, I thought. Possibly an overestimation, in fact.

The car was a white BMW four-wheel-drive vehicle. We both

knew it was Dad and Robby's without looking inside. But we looked inside it anyway. It made me more than a little bit sad, and worried, too, because this was the first time I'd considered the possibility that my two fathers may have had some kind of accident, that something terrible had happened to them.

Inside, we found cigarettes and bundles of extra clothes in the backseat. There were a few jars of food, too.

"I don't think Dad or Robby would mind if we borrowed some of this stuff," I said.

"I'm sure it's okay."

So I took all the food and some new T-shirts and socks and boxer shorts because I didn't really have any spare underclothes.

But the most important thing in the vehicle was a note, written by Robby. He'd left it facing up on the dashboard.

My name is Robert Brees Jr. I am flying a Piper Malibu. Departed on February 23 from IIB, Independence, Iowa, with my husband, Austin Szczerba. We are looking for more people. We spotted two groups of survivors last winter near what we believe was the city of Winnipeg, Manitoba, but were unable to put the plane down due to ice and snow. We are going south today, heading for Nashville, TN, or perhaps Atlanta, GA, depending on conditions and fuel. Looking for a person named Breakfast and his companion, who has indicated he observed us flying overhead, and is also heading south. There is a group of us—eight in number, the

*youngest, my sister, is almost sixteen years in age—
living in an underground shelter outside the town
of Ealing. Directions to our shelter, called Eden,
are below. We will come back again, depending on
conditions and fuel. We can make a return flight
from Nashville without refueling. If we go as far as
Atlanta, that will have to be determined.*

*I'm sorry if this sounds like some kind of police
blotter report. We don't really talk like this. Good
luck, stay alive, and we hope to see you soon.*

Austin says you can have a cigarette if you'd like.

—Robby Brees and Austin Szczerba

I read the note aloud to Mel.

I said, "He's right. My dads don't really talk like that."

"That sounds like something Wendy would have written."

I nodded. "If I read this, I would not follow the directions to the hole."

Mel said, "Not a very good sales pitch."

We considered our choices. The fact that my fathers had been gone for more than a month ruled out a round-trip with no refueling. It could have meant something terrible, but neither of us wanted to say that out loud. Waiting at the airfield didn't make much sense to us, given the time that had already gone by, and since the motorhome was stocked with every imaginable road map, we decided to head south and try, if it was at all possible, to get to those two places—Nashville, which was in Tennessee, and Atlanta, which was in Georgia, both of which were in North America, which was floating between the Atlantic and Pacific Oceans, and on and on, without end.

And despite all the potential dangers, I had a sense Mel was as excited as I was about going farther and farther away. I thought about those two lightning bugs Robby had brought down for me when I was thirteen, which was a very sad year in my life—how happy they must have been when Robby took that jar back up to the surface and opened it, freeing them.

I had no idea.

"It is a very dangerous thing we are doing," I said.

"I know."

"Are you scared?"

"No."

"Neither am I," I lied. My chest felt like I'd been inflated with a frenzied swarm of tiny fluttering birds, like the ones in the movie, which also terrified me. But I would do anything to stay with Mel, who was much braver, and far more sensible, than I was.

Before we packed up the van to leave, I wrote a reply to my fathers and left it on the dashboard beside their official, rule-constrained-sounding note.

Dear Dads,

No thanks on the cigarette. I tried that once, and Mel does not smoke either. So your

cigarettes will be waiting for you when you
come back, unless someone other than me or
Mel comes by first.

If you have not guessed by the salutation, it is me,
your son, Arek Andrzej Szczerba, and Robby's
half sister, Amelie Sing Brees. I just thought of
something: Is there anything wrong with me
and Mel being together? Because we aren't really
related, right? I mean, not that we're "together,"
because we are not—trust me. Anyway, I don't
know why I am even thinking of that. Well,
actually, I do know why I am thinking of that,
because, as you know, I still can't stop thinking
about Mel and me. And no, Dads, I have not said
anything to her. So you know what that means for
me at night (ha-ha).

Also, if you have not guessed by virtue of the fact
that Mel and I are here at Independence Airfield,
we have left the hole. I hope this does not make
you mad. Which reminds me, I have never seen
either of you mad at me. So don't be now. I
had to leave. I was not only sick of living in the
hole—and I think this was mostly your fault for
taking me fishing that time, which, until now,
was probably the greatest day of my life—but I
felt useless if I did not come looking for you, and

useless as far as the others in the hole (except Mel)
were concerned.

I told Mel I was leaving the day before I did it.
I did not know that she had hidden inside the
vehicle until late the first night I was gone. But
then it was too late. At least she told Connie she
was coming with me. So at least everyone knows
what we are doing. And no matter what anyone
"thinks" I am doing—I am not.

I really wish I could just talk to you, like we used
to talk about things. But not in the library. Not
in the hole. I don't think I ever want to go back. Is
that bad?

What if I am wrong?

I took some clothes and food from your car. I
hope you don't mind. I am driving that big black
Mercedes van. I have not crashed it yet (ha-
ha). We decided to go to Nashville, and then to
Atlanta, to look for you, or to look for whoever is
out here.

You never told me it would be like this, Dad.

I love you both. Mel loves you too.

I know we will see each other again.

Arek
PS I drew a picture for you.

The Church of the Screaming Stag

The hole we found was located beneath the floor of a garage in a house that had been burned down, outside a town called Rome.

The entire town of Rome was about the same size as the hole I'd lived in my entire life, but at least it was aboveground and had a view of the sky.

We'd been looking through houses for two days. Mostly, the work was disappointing, and even though neither of us admitted it, we were hungry. Starving. We found some clothes and interesting objects that neither of us could identify, but the most troubling things were all the photographs—pictures of children, of family gatherings, weddings, and old people.

There had been so many people, without end, and now they were all gone.

A few of the houses had the heads of dead animals and preserved fish hanging on the walls. I did not understand the purpose of such things.

"Maybe it was a kind of religion, one that was different from the Christmas religion Wendy made rules about," I theorized.

"What kind of religion would put dead things on the wall?" Mel asked.

On that day we were inside a two-story house somewhere south of Cedar Rapids.

I thought about it. I said, "All religions put dead things on walls."

Hanging above the fireplace, which had probably been used to incinerate hundreds of Christmas gifts, was the head of an enormous deer—a stag, with sharp racks of antlers rising like frozen flames from its skull. The stag's neck was turned, and his mouth was open, as though he were screaming something. Whatever it was the stag was screaming, it must have sounded horrifying.

"I wonder why his mouth is open like that."

I could see the stag's teeth.

"Maybe he was screaming in pain because he was being circumcised," I said.

"What's that?"

"Well, when Wendy started making me go to church with her, she told me about it. It was one of the first stories she shared with me. According to Wendy, and her Bible, God expected people to cut off parts of boys' penises, to show that they were good, and they believed in God."

"Did people actually do that?" Mel asked.

I nodded. "Wendy said they did it to all the boys in her family. I asked my dads about it, and they showed me things about circumcision in a book."

"Why would anyone ever cut off part of a boy's penis?"

"Before the hole, the world was dangerous and insane, Mel."

Mel said, "Were you afraid?"

"Terrified. I did not want Wendy to get anywhere near my penis with something sharp. I think Wendy was trying to frighten me about my penis, because I was growing up, and, well, this happened right after she made us stop taking baths together."

Mel smiled and looked down. She couldn't possibly be embarrassed, right? Mel would never be embarrassed with me.

She said, "That time when we lost the lights?"

I felt my cheeks getting hot. I looked up at the screaming stag and nodded.

"Did Wendy cut off part of your penis?"

"Dad wouldn't let her."

"Thank God."

"Thank Dad," I said.

"That would hurt."

"Worse than a bag of rocks hitting your balls," I said. "I'll be honest. I cried about it for days, until I talked to my dad, and he told me not to worry, that nobody was allowed to circumcise my penis."

"That's terrifying."

"Maybe in this church, the Church of the Screaming Stag, maybe they never circumcised boys just to show they were good. Maybe they let girls play basketball on the same teams as boys.

Maybe the stag is screaming like that because he took all the unfairness away from people and bore it himself."

Mel did not ask if that story was true.

We both knew that people before the hole were far too stupid to follow such sensible dogmas as that of the Church of the Screaming Stag.

The Rome hole we found was very small. In fact, it was smaller than the refrigerator room in the hole Mel and I were born—and conceived—in. It was mere chance that I discovered it too, because the heavy metal disc that covered its entryway was plastered in filth and ash and blended in almost perfectly with the rest of the garage's floor.

We had a gas lantern with us, so we could see down the little opening and the ladder, which was very much like the ladder down into our hole, only miniaturized.

"Hello!" I called down into the hole.

I definitely did not want to surprise any inhabitants, even though I could tell by the staleness of the air rising up from the portal that there was nothing living down there.

After waiting a sufficient amount of time to rule out the existence of residents, I climbed down with the lantern, and Mel followed.

"This place is really creepy," Mel said.

"You know what I think? When you build a hole, you never expect you'll have to use it," I said. "When you do have to use it, chances are it's already too late."

The thing had been built inside a large, ribbed metal pipe of some kind. I imagined the childish stories I'd heard about people who lived inside the bellies of whales after having been swallowed by them. The hole was barely big enough for me to stand up inside; the confinement of it made me feel as though I had to hunch down.

Along one side of the pipe-hole were two sets of narrow bunk beds, perfectly made as though someone were expecting important guests. Opposite the beds were shelves with a desk and television. The place was wired for electricity, but there was none. At the end of the cramped room were a toilet and a sink basin with a hand pump, and that was it.

It would have been the most terribly oppressive experience, trying to live your life in such a place.

On the shelves were a small gas stove, utensils, and a framed photograph of what I assumed was the family that had lived in the burned-down house above. There were four people in the photograph: the mother and father in the middle, and on each side of them, teenage boys who looked to be about thirteen and fourteen years old, near replicas of each other, with very short-cropped hair, big ears, and comfortable smiles. The family was standing on the front steps of a house, most probably the one that had burned.

I said, "It's sad, isn't it?"

Mel said, "Yeah."

"I mean, I can tell I really would have liked to talk to these boys, to ask them what their lives were like, and maybe if they knew how to play basketball."

"Yeah."

"Maybe, given a world such as this, you could have fallen in love with one of them."

"I doubt it," Mel said.

I was only testing her, and Mel was too smart to fall for it.

There were colorful boxes of games on the shelves too, but no books at all except for one—a Bible.

"Clearly, these people did not attend the Church of the Screaming Stag."

"Poor boys." Mel shook her head. "It's a wonder they could manage to smile, considering what they may have had to endure just to show they were trustworthy to God."

I laughed.

Some of the games we'd had in our old hole—I found playing cards, chess, and checkers—but most of them I'd never heard of before. One of the boxes said this: YAHTZEE—THE CLASSIC SHAKE, SCORE & SHOUT DICE GAME! AGES 8 TO ADULT.

So many rules, without end.

"I don't know if shaking and shouting sounds like a game," I said.

Mel shrugged. "I'd like to play it."

I placed the game box down on the edge of the desk. Then I moved our lantern and saw that we'd both been standing on a large rectangular trapdoor that had been cut right into the wood floor of the hole. And when we opened the door, we found six large blue plastic barrels below the floor, and all of them were sealed shut and dustless.

"This is exactly what we've been looking for, Mel."

"Praise the Screaming Stag."

Fuckers from Space

The only light inside Doc Sawbones' Field Amputation House of Horrors! was a dancing yellow ghost that flickered out from the mouth of the open door on a potbelly stove.

Houses of horrors never have windows.

This was one of the reasons Edsel and Mimi had survived. Before the hole, they had been seasonal carnival workers who traveled the country mostly by hitchhiking, and now they were, in effect, king and queen of the abandoned Rebel Land.

Edsel, who tried to explain things to Breakfast a little too much, insisted that he and Olive were not prisoners—Edsel just didn't want to let them leave, which made as much sense to Breakfast as it did to Olive, who pretty much understood everything she heard, anyway.

"You can't leave without visiting me and Mimi for a while. It would be rude," he said.

"How long is a *while*?" Breakfast asked.

"I don't know. We'll see. Maybe a few months. Maybe you'll like it here. Maybe we'll find you a nice rebel uniform with a cap, so you don't have to run around naked like that. Would you want that?" Edsel said.

Breakfast had no intention of remaining captive to the old man for a few months.

"I don't want no uniform and cap," Breakfast said.

"Suit yourself. Or, un-suit yourself! Ha-ha-ha!"

Edsel and Mimi used to be addicted to heroin and methamphetamine.

Holding the pistol aimed between the boy's shoulder blades, Edsel escorted Breakfast and Olive up a ramp, and then he unlatched the thick metal door marked ENTRANCE to Doc Sawbones' Field Amputation House of Horrors!

"Just follow the path into the hospital," Edsel said. "That's where we live."

The "path" was a very narrow trail through the first room, which was called Sharpsburg. The path snaked through a canyon of garbage that was taller than Breakfast. The floor was slick with a fermented goo that had percolated down through the years and years of waste deposited in Sharpsburg by Edsel and Mimi.

At the very bottom of the muck and rotting slime were the occasional outstretched arms and a couple of bloodied faces from the plastic-prop dead soldiers who were essential decorative components to Doc Sawbones' Field Amputation House of Horrors!

It smelled like death, and there were rats wriggling through the mountains of shit, unfazed by the presence of the three marchers, setting up what looked like potential lines of attack along the ridges.

"This is our rat farm," Edsel said. "You ever eat rats?"

"Lots of times," Breakfast said.

"Mimi! Mimi! I got 'em! Only, one of 'em's a chimpanzee, and the other one's a naked boy!"

"I'm wild," Breakfast muttered.

Once inside the hospital room, Edsel told Breakfast and Olive to sit down at a table next to the stove. Overhead, hanging like a vast constellation from hell, were bloodied limbs—arms, legs, feet, hands—the ambiance of the former fun house. The walls were lined from top to bottom with mirrors that were bent and curved to stretch and distort every image they captured.

"Well, my, my, my. I just can't believe it. We're sitting here with another person—a little boy, no less!" Mimi said. "How long has it been since there were any people here, Edsel?"

"Oh, say!" Edsel's pistol lay on the pitted steel dinner table, pointed at Breakfast's chest. "It must be fifteen years now. Maybe fourteen since that last feller come through."

The table had a mesh-screened drain in the center of it, and at each of its four corners were leather restraints with thick brass buckles on them. Olive fidgeted in her chair. She had her hand on Breakfast's knee beneath the table. Olive stroked Breakfast's thigh. She could tell Breakfast did not like the old couple, and she wanted to make him feel safe.

Mimi, who had no lower teeth, scratched her head. She was mostly bald and had big brown spots all over her skin, but no pictures on her, like Edsel did, at least not as far as Breakfast could see. Mimi wore a long-sleeved nightgown with a white collar that tied in a bow at her neck.

She said, "Yes. Maybe fourteen years back. Do you remember how that man—he looked like he might have come from Ohio, the way he was dressed so fancy—climbed and scrambled all the way to the top of the General Lee's Wild Revenge Coaster, trying to get away from them two big bugs? Ha-ha! What a dummy!"

Edsel nodded and smiled, the fire making little dancing tornados in his dark eyes. "That was the dumbest thing I ever saw anyone try to do in my life."

Then he held his hand over the tabletop and slapped it down. Breakfast and Olive both jumped.

"Spee-lat!" Edsel said, then laughed and coughed a drumbeat of wheezing, phlegmy barks.

Mimi reached across the table and put her hand on Breakfast's.

"How old are you, little boy?"

Breakfast pulled his hand back, repulsed, and said, "Twelve." He picked at his earwax and scratched his balls.

Mimi looked up into the dark, concentrating, counting on her fingertips.

"Twelve? That's a miracle. You don't have no clue, no clue at all about the things that happened, do you?"

"Maybe a bit," Breakfast said.

"It was a invasion. Fuckers from space," Edsel said.

Breakfast had no idea what the crazy old heroin addict was talking about.

"Maybe you might tell us all about what you did—how you come here, and how you managed to live like this on your own," Mimi said.

"It wasn't on my own," Breakfast said. "I have Olive. She keeps me safe."

"We can be like family now!" Mimi said. "Edsel and I never had no babies of our own!"

"Are you hungry, boy?" Edsel said. "We should have a special dinner for our newest little rebel, don't you think, Mimi? A special dinner. Not rats tonight."

Edsel's narrow eyes were fixed on Olive. He licked his lips and swallowed an obvious mouthful of warm saliva.

Breakfast balled his hands into fists. He had never encountered such cruelty and nastiness in his life, and if this was what other people were like, he thought, he'd just as soon go on with no one but Olive.

"No," Breakfast said.

Edsel put his hand back on the gun, just resting there.

"Dumb little fucker," he said. "If it gots hair on it, you eat it. Good thing for you you ain't got a lick of hair except for that mop-head jungle up top. You wouldn't be the first person we eat. Maybe the littlest, though, huh, Mimi?"

Mimi and Edsel laughed. Drool ran down the old woman's chin.

"I can catch you some catfish," Breakfast offered. "There's lots of them in that pond out there."

"You can catch fish?" Edsel asked.

"With my bare hands. And I can swim fast," Breakfast said. "Because I'm wild."

Edsel was excited. He leaned so close to the boy, Breakfast could feel the sweaty steam rising from the old man's bare chest. Breakfast lowered his eyes, fixed them on the smeary image of two crossed rifles just below Edsel's hairless left nipple.

"Hoo-wee! A boy what can catch fish barehanded! And can swim, too! Mimi, we might want to keep this one around forever!"

Mimi nodded and wiped her chin with the snot-varnished sleeve of her nightgown. "Forever!"

Survival Gear

The supplies from the Rome hole ended up being more than we needed and were also more than we could figure out.

Three of the barrels were filled with drinking water, and the other three contained smaller buckets of rice, beans, spices, and dehydrated food that was sealed inside vacuum pouches, along with other nonedible survival supplies. Among those items we found flashlights and a solar battery charger, a .45-caliber handgun and ammunition, a first aid kit, a handheld fire starter, packages of medicine, a carton of fifty colorful butane lighters, and a plastic-wrapped purple box of something neither one of us had ever heard of before.

The box said this on it:

durex® extra sensitive™ ultra-thin condoms with extra lube for heightened sensitivity

"Any idea what 'ultra-thin condoms' are?" I said.

Mel shook her head. "Maybe it's something to eat. The box is an appetizing color. They're probably sweets. You know, to make you feel good, if you're sensitive about living in a hole throughout the duration of a mass-extinction event."

"I don't get the 'lube' and 'sensitivity' thing. Maybe they're used in a motor or something."

"Yeah, maybe they are," Mel said.

"Or maybe condoms were invented for people who were very sensitive about frightening movies with things like Bigfoot and murderous birds. Condoms are a kind of medicine, which sensitive people would put in their ears and eyes, so they could enjoy terrifying things in the presence of other people who did not have heightened levels of sensitivity to such things," I offered.

"Judging from what I know of the world before the hole, as you say, I think condoms were a definite necessity in that case," Mel said.

All stories are true.

"No doubt, Mel. I'm going to open the box and see what they are used for."

Mel sat down on one of the little bunk beds next to me. She wanted to see what was inside the box too.

It was almost like Christmas, but without the bitterness and arson.

The box contained thirty-six little packets, as well as a glossy pamphlet with very small print and black-line illustrations that gave instructions on how to use ultra-thin condoms with extra lube.

I said, "Oh."

Mel leaned against my shoulder, looking at the diagrams on the instruction sheet.

"They're for your penis," she pointed out.

"Apparently."

She took the page from my hands and read aloud. "'Once the penis is erect, open the condom package. Squeeze the tip of the condom with your fingers, and unroll the condom over the head of the penis until the entire penis is completely covered. Leave a half-inch space at the tip of the condom to collect the semen.'"

I cleared my throat. The temperature inside that little hole had risen significantly.

Mel said, "This is really interesting."

"Um."

"Are you turning red? What's wrong with you?"

"Nuh—nothing," I said.

Sweat dripped from my armpits, tickling my ribs. Despite the fact that I was wearing Julian Powell's rule-breaker Wolverines basketball jersey, it was entirely too hot down here. I was also getting an erection and did not want to stand up.

Well, I wasn't actually *getting* one; I *had* one.

Stupid penis.

And Mel continued, "'After ejaculation, while the penis is still hard, clamp the condom at the base of your penis and then slip it off, being careful not to spill any semen onto your partner.' I guess these condoms were to help boys not get their semen on stuff, or on other people. Have you ever had that problem, Arek?"

"I. Uh. Well."

What was happening to me?

I said, "Yes, I guess I have. At nights, sometimes it just happens in my sleep. I didn't understand it at first, and it makes a mess. So after the first couple times, I talked to my dads about it, and they told me it was a normal thing that happens to all boys."

"Like girls getting periods," Mel said.

"I guess."

"Maybe you should put a condom on your penis at night when you go to sleep. That's probably what these were for. The family who lived here probably needed them for their two boys."

"Um. Uh."

"You're sweating."

"I know."

"Does this make you feel uncomfortable?" Mel asked.

"No." I was such a fucking liar.

"Open one. I want to see what they look like."

"I liked the story about the scary movies better."

"Stop being weird."

"I can't."

"Give me that."

Mel took the box from my quaking hands and pulled out one of the shiny purple packets. She squeezed it between her thumb and fingers. "There's definitely something slippery inside it." Then she held the packet out to me and said, "Here. Feel it."

What was she doing? She was making me crazy. Couldn't she see I was in the process of melting into useless goo?

I did what she said. I squeezed the condom packet.

"It feels weird," I said.

"You're shaking."

"This is kind of awkward, Mel."

"Why is it awkward, Arek? I don't understand you at all," she said.

Mel was right. Too much had changed in me since I left the hole. And none of this would have ever happened if she hadn't stowed away inside my lifeboat. But I couldn't imagine being out here, this far away from the hole, tossed on these seas without her.

I never would have lasted.

And my penis felt like it was about to snap into pieces. Why did this have to happen to me? I willed myself to not look down at my lap. I would have passed out if Mel had said anything about what was so obviously going on inside number 42's basketball shorts.

Mel tore open the packet and pulled out the oily little dome-shaped object.

It looked like a creature from a nightmare.

"It smells weird," Mel said.

She stuck the thing under my nose.

"Um. Yeah. Weird."

"You are so red, Arek."

"Sorry. I can't help it."

Hopefully, Mel had no idea about all the things at that moment I couldn't help from happening in my body.

"I think it's cute when you get embarrassed."

"Um. I'm not."

Mel laughed. Loud.

She said, "So. You put this on the top of your penis, and then you roll it down. Like this."

Mel began unrolling the condom over her thumb.

It was wrinkly and slick with oil.

Mel said, "You should feel this."

She fluttered the little greasy tube in front of me.

"No thanks."

She kept unrolling it.

And then she said, "Are penises really this big?"

I sighed. "Can we put this away now?"

Mel shrugged. "Whatever. But I still think you should put one on if you have trouble with your semen making a mess when you sleep."

"Mel. Please."

"I'm just trying to help, Arek."

"Let's look through the rest of the stuff, then. I think we've discovered enough information about extra-sensitive ultra-thin condoms," I said.

"You are very sensitive, Arek."

"Uh."

Mel got up from the bed and reached down into the nonfood barrel. I was so relieved.

"Look. They have tampons, too."

"Please. Please, don't open them, Mel."

"I don't need to. You already know what they're for."

Fortunately, Mel spent about twenty minutes going through the survival gear, so my blood pressure dropped to normal, which was still messed up, considering I was a sixteen-year-old boy with an uncontrollable penis.

I said, "It's getting late. We should start moving this stuff into the van, and we can finally cook some dinner."

"Oh. So you can stand up now?" Mel asked.

"What's that supposed to mean?" I felt my cheeks getting hot again.

Mel said, "Nothing."

There Are Bound to Be Snakes

Max Beckmann also painted *Adam and Eve*.

It was one of the first works the painter produced after

coming out of the hole of World War I. He painted *Adam and Eve* in 1917.

Maybe it was because of the paintings in our library or the book we had about his work, or maybe it was something else, but I have always felt my life connected with Max Beckmann's—that the models he had constructed had something to do with the models I constructed.

Max Beckmann's *Adam and Eve*, like many of his after-the-hole paintings, is claustrophobic and dark. It seems as though Max Beckmann used only one ashy color to capture the image. In it, the distorted figures of Adam and Eve stand at the trunk of a tree. The tree seems dead and cold, and Adam's eyes are completely black, as though they have been cut from the cloth of a starless night. He is emaciated, starving; and Eve, opposite him, has her eyes lowered, lifting one of her round breasts toward Adam, her mouth slightly open as though she is saying something. Eve appears to be pregnant in the painting. The couple were Max Beckmann's cautionary idea of the world's new humans after the Great War. Around the trunk of the tree coils the body of a serpent, its head poised just above Eve's. But the serpent has a doglike snout. It snarls, baring teeth. Maybe the serpent is whispering to Eve. And one of the only primary colors in the work is the ring of the serpent's eye—a blazing red. The only other, yellow, is on the bloom of a lily that sprouts up from the dead ground behind Adam's feet. Both Adam and Eve, naturally, are completely naked. In many ways, Max Beckmann's *Adam and Eve* shows the first two humans who came up to the surface of earth, after the hole.

"What do you think of that?" my dad—Austin—had asked me.

I was fourteen at the time. He, Robby, and I were talking about the Beckmann book in the library.

My two fathers, who loved each other very much, smoked cigarettes.

The others in the hole had come to accept that *the boys'* general routine after dinner was to retreat into the library, as though it were some kind of private place of discussion for the three of us. Mom and Wendy clearly resented it but did nothing to interfere with the private time I shared with my fathers.

Robby sat between us, on the library's small leather couch.

Dad put his arm around Robby's shoulders so that his hand touched me.

"Is it a model meant to *represent* the story of Adam and Eve, or is this the actual story itself?" I asked.

"We have a very philosophical son," Robby said.

"I think it's Max Beckmann's actual story. Right here. On this page," Dad said.

"It's a good story, but not a happy one," I said.

My fathers kissed each other, and Robby put his hand in Dad's hair.

I continued. "You always say how we're like Adam and Eve—Mel and me. But I hope we aren't like the people in Max Beckmann's painting."

"Well, I mean that you and Mel are like the first humans on earth. You are the new people, without the baggage everyone carried with them, without end, from before. Beckmann's Adam and Eve still carried those burdens," Dad, who could straddle time, said.

"Before the hole and after the hole," I said.

"Yes. Max Beckmann's Adam and Eve are before-the-hole people. There's a hint of a promise they will not make the same mistakes, but only a small hint."

"But then there's the snake, too. So, no chance," I said.

"You won't make those mistakes, Arek," Robby said.

"I hope not."

Then I asked, "Dad, how old were you the first time you had sex?"

Dad got his before-the-hole eyes. He looked at Robby, then at me, and said, "You mean with someone else?"

"Duh. Yes," I said.

"Why?" Dad looked concerned. He asked, "Did you have sex, Arek?"

I admit his question frustrated me a little. "You mean with *someone else*? There is no one else, Dad."

"Oh."

And Robby said, "He was fifteen. I was sixteen. It was the first time for both of us. Your dad stayed the night at my house, because my mom was away. It was such a perfect night. I was so in love with your dad. And know this, Arek, we both wanted to have sex. We talked about it, and both of us said yes, which is the way it should always happen."

"Who asked first?" I said.

"Austin did," Robby said.

Dad, almost simultaneously, answered, "Robby."

Robby shook his head. He bit the inside of his lower lip. "But after it, the next day, your father avoided me and wouldn't speak about it."

Dad didn't smile or look away from me.

He said, "I was confused and scared afterward, because I felt so guilty about everything."

I did not know what guilt felt like. Dad could see I didn't understand the word.

So he said, "Guilt was something from all the rules before we came here. Guilt was because you did something good that the rules said was bad, or because you did something bad that you knew was good."

I said, "Oh."

I cooked beans and rice for Mel, and we stayed that night parked in front of the burned-down condom house in Rome.

The food was good. It was what we needed after not eating for more than a day.

Cooking dinner for Mel made me happy. It made me happier than I'd ever been since that day my two fathers took me fishing through a hole in the ice at Clear Lake.

I never wanted to go back to the hole, and I was determined not to make the same mistakes that Max Beckmann's Adam and Eve made. The world was a new place, full of yellow lilies, everywhere, without end.

Mel and I didn't talk about her falling asleep next to me in my bed that night we watched the movie about birds, the night I snuck away with a bottle of whiskey and nearly died. It wasn't that either of us felt guilty, or at least that's what I believed. But after that, Mel stayed in her bed, and I stayed in mine.

The mature and responsible part of me, which admittedly was not much—the part that planned things out about getting food and fuel, the part that considered which direction we were going—that part of me knew this was the right thing to do. But every particle of the rest of me wanted to feel Mel's body next to mine, to be tangled up with her in the sheets of a bed I'd just as soon never leave.

After dinner, I took a shower and got ready for bed. I was exhausted and full. When I came out of the shower, I was dressed in new green-and-yellow boxer shorts with John Deere tractors on them and a T-shirt I'd taken from my dads' BMW. I was determined to put an end to feeling embarrassed or inhibited around Mel. I was committed to replacing the after-the-hole Arek with the Arek who'd grown up openly sharing everything in his life with Mel.

Mel sat at the little eating area beside the sink. She was wearing the basketball clothes we'd taken for her from Henry A. Wallace Middle School.

"You look good in basketball clothes. We would have a good basketball team, Mel," I said.

Then I felt the heat rising into my face.

"Thank you, Arek. You look good in . . . um . . . your boxers."

Mel stared at me. I watched how her eyes went all the way down the length of my body. I half expected her to say something about if I had an erection, or if I thought I should put on a condom before I got inside my bed, just in case.

What she said was, "I read the rules about how to play Yahtzee."

"Does it sound dangerous?"

Mel laughed a little. I loved hearing that as much as I loved any sound ever.

She said, "It looks like fun. Do you want to play?"

"Does it involve throwing bags of rocks at anyone's balls?"

She smiled and shook her head. "No. There's a cup with these little cubes with dots on them, though."

"How many cubes? How much do they weigh?"

"Stop it."

"It sounds like it has the potential to inflict pain."

"Don't be dumb. Sit down."

I sat beside Mel, resisting the urge to fake an accidental touch, and then immediately damning myself for being so uptight and inhibited.

We played the game for hours until we were so tired we could no longer do the simple addition required by the rules.

Then Mel crawled into her little bed, and I went to mine.

"Good night, Mel. Thank you for teaching me how to play that game. I think it was probably—oh, I don't know. Good night."

"You're welcome, Arek. Good night."

I had almost drifted off to sleep.

"Arek?"

"What?"

"Do you think I tease you too much?"

"Probably not enough, considering all the rules I break."

"Okay."

"Okay, Mel."

It turned out that Yahtzee was probably the greatest thing we had discovered that had been invented by before-the-hole humans.

Who knew it could be like this?

Who knew what else could possibly be out here?

Snakes, I thought.

There are bound to be snakes.

A Roof over Your Heads, and a Bucket

One of the deepest rooms inside the maze of sets in Doc Sawbones' Field Amputation House of Horrors! was called Camp Sumter.

The real Camp Sumter was also known as Andersonville Prison, a notorious place where thirteen thousand captive soldiers died horrible deaths in the American Civil War.

The first night they were there, the room called Camp Sumter became Breakfast and Olive's prison cell inside the lightless and awful former amusement park attraction.

Breakfast, who was clever for a boy who'd never heard or read about nonhuman primates, cooperated with Mimi and Edsel. Breakfast, always alert, and a quick learner when it came to such things as the contents of septic service pumper trucks, was waiting for an opportunity when Edsel and Mimi lowered their guard. They escorted him and Olive at gunpoint out to the pond at the

Battle of Hampton Roads Thrill Ride!, where, during the time that Edsel and Mimi were employees of Rebel Land, no fewer than three rule-breaking and overly tall Tennessee fun seekers had been decapitated by cannonballs.

Breakfast dove into the shallow, murky water, and within seconds broke the algae-carpeted surface with a wriggling black catfish in his wild little hands.

"Look at that!" Mimi hollered. "That boy *is* a wild critter!"

Breakfast tossed the fish onto the sidewalk, and Edsel used the butt of his pistol to club it senseless.

"I am wild," Breakfast said.

He took a breath and went under again and again, until he'd thrown four fat fish out to his captors. Olive jumped up and down and waved at Breakfast every time the boy came back up.

And he was covered with leeches for the second time since he came to this place. Breakfast picked and cursed and blew snot from his nostrils, while Olive examined him and gently plucked— and ate—her share of leeches from the boy's back and legs.

Edsel and Mimi made Breakfast carry the fish back to their house, but they cautiously decided not to risk handing him a knife, so Mimi gutted and prepared them herself. Then she threw the guts, skin, heads, and fins out into the Sharpsburg room for the rats, who would eat anything.

Mimi was pleased with herself, but Breakfast thought she was a terrible cook.

The four of them ate the charred crumbles of catfish with their hands, directly off the tarnished surface of the old operating table beside the stove. And Edsel's pistol lay constantly at the ready, pointed at Breakfast's little chin. It sat just beside the picture of an eagle's head inked on the back of the old man's right hand.

"Tell us what you know," Mimi said. Bits of catfish dotted her chin and hung like small ornaments from her hair.

"I know a lot," Breakfast said. "I'm wild, and I am rich. How much money do you want to let us go?"

Edsel nearly choked. He coughed up a snotty wad of fish meat, then scooped it up with his calloused fingers and put it back in his mouth. "Money? Who the hell needs money?"

Breakfast shrugged. "Everyone needs money. Just like everyone should know how to swim and climb things and fish with their bare hands and be wild like me."

Breakfast held up his hands like he was holding invisible grapefruit-size balls in each one and said, "Everyone."

Then he picked his nose and scratched his balls.

"That's some skills, little boy," Edsel said. "What else can you do?"

Breakfast thought. "I can whistle so loud, I can kill birds and squirrels and rabbits with it."

"Get out," the old man said.

Breakfast shifted in his chair and farted. He needed to pee, too, so he just started urinating on the floor beneath the table. He was, after all, wild, and that meant Breakfast would pretty much pee on anything he wanted to pee on.

He put his index fingers in the sides of his mouth and let rip a shrill whistle that nearly drove both the insane old carnies to the brink of death.

"Quit that! Quit that now, you little fucker!" Edsel yelled. "Ow! Motherfucker!"

Olive bounced in her chair and stroked Breakfast's arm.

Breakfast stopped whistling.

"Good goddamn, you little fuckwad! That hurt!" Edsel rubbed his hairy ears.

Outside, in the Sharpsburg room next door, a dozen rats fell dead and plopped down into the stagnant pool of festering shit on the floor.

And Mimi said, "Looks like we've got ourselves quite a little hunter." Mimi waved her hand across the table, flinging bits of fish. "Well, what's she good at?"

"Who? Olive?"

"Who in God's name do you think I was talking about?" Mimi, who'd been in a state of heroin withdrawal for more than fifteen years, said. "The invisible saloon gal behind your chair?"

Breakfast didn't get it. He turned around.

"Olive's good at finding roots and plants. And the monsters are afraid of her. They'll kill themselves cold dead rather than let her get anywhere near them."

"You say." Edsel didn't believe pretty much anything Breakfast said, and Breakfast was getting tired of the old man.

"I *do* say," Breakfast told him.

"You done eating, then?" Edsel asked.

"I wasn't hungry to begin with," Breakfast said.

Olive had already had her fill of leeches and some of the algae she'd pulled off Breakfast.

"Then come on. I'll show you where you two can sleep."

Edsel waved the pistol at Breakfast and Olive as a kind of invisible hand to brush his guests away from the table. "It's that way down yonder."

There was barely any light at all that managed to ooze through the doorway of the Camp Sumter room. What light there was revealed walls made from pole-straight trees and a variety of ancient metal restraints and shackles that the former amusement park guests could lock themselves into for the purpose of snapping photographs or perhaps babysitting children while adults stole away to the nearby moonshine stands.

There were also human bones littered around the base of the camp's walls. Breakfast did not ask the crazy old couple if the bones were real.

In one corner of the room was a box constructed of wood planks and steel strap bars. Above the door on the box was a crudely painted sign that looked like this:

Mimi pushed open the door.

Edsel said, "Go on. Get in there. It ain't much, but at least it's a roof over your heads, and they's some rags on the floor to sleep on. Ha-ha!"

"I need to make shit," Breakfast said.

Edsel pushed Breakfast through the doorway. "That's what the bucket's for. Ha-ha-ha!"

The door slammed shut.

Breakfast and Olive were locked inside the Hole.

The Prisoners of Camp Sumter

"Don't worry, Olive. They ain't smarter than us. They ain't stronger, and you know what? They ain't wilder, neither. We'll figure out something, girl."

When Mimi and Edsel left the room called Camp Sumter, they shut the door behind them, and Breakfast and Olive found themselves smothered in complete darkness. They could see nothing at all.

Breakfast sat against the steel slat bars of the cage with his arm around Olive, who trembled and pressed her face into the side of the boy's neck.

"It might take a while, but if we try hard and do what they want every day, then I figure they'll start to like us more, and eventually they'll forget to pay attention when they should be paying attention. That's when we'll go. You just have to wait and be nice, and be ready for when I tell you."

Olive whimpered a little.

"I promise they ain't going to eat you, girl, or me, neither. I can get them plenty of other stuff to eat, and you can help too. But, damn, I've never seen people so wicked and cruel as this. And here we've come all this time thinking the biggest monsters was those big fucking bugs, and now look at this mess we got into—and all because our truck was filled with shit. Think about that."

Olive put her hand in Breakfast's dreadlocks and twirled them gently.

"I don't really need to make shit, if that's what you're thinking. I was just saying that to see what they'd do. I did pee under the table when they were eating, though. Serves them right."

Breakfast picked his nose.

"You know what, Olive? I'm wild, that's what. Wild and rich. So fuck those two old motherfucker poor people. I never been in a cage in my life, and I'm not planning on staying put in this one a second longer than we have to. We can do this, Olive. We can do it. I never let you down, and you never let me down, and you know why?"

Olive knew why, but, being a chimpanzee, Olive didn't say it.

"Because we're wild, girl. Rich and wild. Nobody wants to mess with someone as wild as us."

Breakfast, being the wild boy he was, knew he would not easily go to sleep in the cage that night. He stood up and felt his way around each side, measuring, counting each metal slat that held them in.

He was particularly attentive to the door. He traced along its edge slowly with his index finger, which was as good as an eye to the boy when he was doing things like hunting for fish in a deep lake. Breakfast studied the hinges, which were recklessly turned inside. The Hole was never meant to be an actual prison, and with the right implements, Breakfast would be able to break out of it in under a minute.

"Come here, Olive," Breakfast said. "Let's see if you can't get your finger up inside this and push up on the pin."

Breakfast guided Olive's hand to the underside of the lower hinge, but he could feel right away that her fingers were chubbier than his and could not move the hinge pin up. They needed something stiff and narrow to do the job.

"We need to find something like a stick, Olive. Something smaller than our fingers. If we could just push it up a bit, I could pry it the rest of the way with my hands. You know why? I bet you do. Because I'm strong. Wild and strong."

Breakfast and Olive swept every inch of the floor with their palms, trying to find anything that could serve as a tool to force up the pins on the door hinges. They found the rags that were supposed to be their bedding, and the bucket toilet, which was empty and had no handle.

Olive began to bounce excitedly when her hand brushed into a small scattering of rat bones. One of them had to be just the thing Breakfast was looking for.

"What is it, girl?"

Olive gathered up some of the bones and grabbed Breakfast's hand. She turned his palm up and opened the boy's fingers, then placed the bones into Breakfast's hand.

"Hoo-wee! Olive, you are magic! I could kiss you!"

Breakfast hugged Olive, and she kissed him with curled and slobber-slick lips, squarely over his nose and mouth.

"You're a good girl, Olive! A lifesaver!"

Olive jumped up and down. She grabbed the bars on the top of the cage and swung, dangling her legs joyfully.

Breakfast took his rat-bone toolkit to the door and began working on the hinges. The pins gave way easily, and within moments the little wild boy had the door disassembled. Olive clapped and rubbed Breakfast's back.

"We have to think about this, girl," Breakfast said. "We don't really know how to get out without going back the way we came, right into those crazy old people. Now we know we can do it, so let's wait and see what we can learn tomorrow. We have to be safe. I don't want either one of us getting shot by that man with the pictures on his skin. But, hoo-wee, we know we can do it. Let's put the door back on and go lay down and try to rest, and talk about tomorrow."

So Breakfast put the door back on its frame, and then peed out through the slatted bars on his cage.

He said, "Fuck this place. I never want to come to Rebel Land ever again. Who would ever?"

Breakfast picked his nose and scratched his balls.

Then he lay down beside Olive, atop the rags on the dusty floor, and thought about his future.

The Clockwork, Mechanized Routine of a Haircut

When I lived in the hole, every three weeks Connie Brees, who was Robby and Mel's mother, gave me haircuts in the barbershop there.

Although Connie stopped giving me baths when I was eleven, the haircuts, which were events I always looked forward to, continued regularly. I thought about those haircuts frequently after I left the hole. For one thing, my hair was getting longer, and I preferred to keep it short on the sides and back. And I also thought about them because I kept coming back to what my father—Austin—had told me about feeling guilty, which was something I didn't truly understand.

There was so much more out here that confused me now.

I do know this: I would never have allowed Wendy to cut my hair. The thought of being alone in that small and surgical space, nearly bound to my chair beneath a clean white sheet while Wendy displayed an array of sharp and gleaming cutting implements was the stuff of my deepest adolescent nightmares.

The last time Connie cut my hair was just after my sixteenth birthday. My fathers were gone, and I'd been acting like the personification of an after-the-hole Max Beckmann painting. I was sick of everything, haunted by ghosts that weren't there, and miserable. I don't even know why Connie asked me if I'd like to have my hair cut—I was so unpleasant.

But I think it had something to do with the fact that of all our family of survivors who'd endured more than sixteen years in the hole, Connie Brees was the only one who'd had experience with raising a teenage boy. Maybe that gave her some extra capacity for tolerance, or perhaps a natural immunity against the torment a teenage boy's body inflicts on his brain.

Maybe Connie could look at me and see my Breakfast— my visible man science assembly project—as me, with my brain outside my skull, and my body, like a Max Beckmann figure, distorted and in disarray.

So I walked with Connie to the barbershop of the hole, which was next door to our laundry facility. Mel was folding clothes she piled on a stainless-steel counter beside one of the dryers. I saw a pink bra and some pale blue panties there, and my eyes stuck on them for a good few seconds. I took a deep breath, hoping I could smell her fresh-laundry smell, wondering what it would be like to help her fold her things.

Connie ducked her head in the laundromat's doorway.

"Hey, babe. I'm giving Arek a haircut next door. Stop by when you're done."

Mel's eyes paused on mine, but only for a moment.

It was a moment, though.

"Okay, Mom. See you in a bit," Mel said.

And Connie said, "Love you."

The shop had three steel-and-red-vinyl barber chairs that faced a wall-length mirror, and behind them, against the opposite wall, sat another row of chairs with domes that went down over your head to dry your hair. At the back of the shop were three low sinks with U-shaped lips on them so you could sit back and rest your head while someone else washed your hair.

That was where haircuts always started.

I unzipped the top of my stupid Eden Project jumpsuit and pulled it down past my shoulders, while Connie folded a towel that would be a pillow on the lip of the sink. Then I leaned back, and she turned on the cool water and showered it through my hair.

I watched her. I tried to imagine all the things she knew, everything Connie Brees had gone through in her life before the hole, and I wondered if Amelie would grow up to be as beautiful as her mother. Connie combed her fingers through my hair. Her breasts swayed, full and heavy, just above me.

That's how it always happened.

Connie Brees could have been a Siren, an iceberg, and I was helpless on this sea.

She turned off the water and grabbed a bottle of shampoo. The shampoo, which was older than I was, was supposed to smell like kiwi fruit. I had no idea what kiwi fruit was, but the shampoo did smell good.

Then Connie said, "You have such nice hair, Arek."

She always said that.

I said, "Thank you."

I always said that, too.

She scrubbed and rinsed, then smeared conditioner in my hair. The conditioner looked like semen. It made me feel strange when Connie put it in my hair, because I always wondered if she thought it looked like semen too. She probably did, I thought.

So it was always this kind of clockwork, mechanized routine: the same lines recited, me watching Connie's breasts while she washed my hair, the conditioner making me think about semen. But that last time we did this, when she was rinsing the semen-conditioner out of my hair, Connie looked straight into my eyes and said, "It hurts when your dads go away, doesn't it?"

And, as usual, thinking about Connie Brees's fingers and watching her breasts move, I'd been getting an erection until exactly that moment.

I swallowed. "I— Yes. It does."

I closed my eyes. I could feel goddamned tears forming in

the corners of them. I could feel Connie's thumbs wipe them. She kissed my forehead.

"I know, baby. I know exactly how it hurts for you. Robby's dad went away too, when he was just a boy."

"All dads go away," I said.

"What is it with you boys? You just can't stay put, can you?"

I didn't know if that was a rhetorical question or not. I kept my eyes shut. Connie put a towel over my head and massaged my hair with it.

I said, "Louis seems happy here."

"Maybe Louis went away enough in his life." She pulled the towel away from my hair and softly wiped my face with it. It felt so nice. And Connie put her hand on my bare chest and said, "Come on. To the chair, Arek."

She always said that, too.

I sat down, and Connie pinned a sheet around my neck. She always knew how to do it with the perfect amount of tightness so it felt safe, like a hug. Her face was right next to my ear; I could hear and feel her breathing.

She said, "You should start shaving soon."

"Really?"

"All boys start shaving in Iowa by the time they're your age."

"We're not really *in* Iowa," I pointed out. "I don't even know what Iowa is."

Connie opened a cabinet under the counter below the mirror. She did not usually do that. When she stood up, she had a big folding straight razor in her hand. Even though it was Connie, I was still a little bit frightened by the thing.

She said, "I'm going to give you a shave, Arek. For your birthday."

"As long as you promise not to circumcise me," I said.

"Where did you ever get that idea?"

"Wendy wanted to do it. When I was eleven. I was so scared."

Connie said, "Oh. Well. Wendy's kind of . . . um. Fucking insane."

I was so relieved, and not just because Connie would never do something like circumcise me, but because she thought Wendy was fucking crazy, which was something nobody else in the hole ever said out loud. I took a deep breath. I said, "Wendy is already talking about what we're going to do next Christmas."

"Fuckbucket. Somebody's going to end up dead."

Connie made a soapy foam in a porcelain cup and used a soft brush, like a painter, to lather the foam on my face. It felt like I was being licked. Then she swiped the razor down from the top of my ear and traced along the curve of my jaw toward my chin. It was exhilarating. It felt electrical, like being naked in the bath with Amelie.

I imagined with each swipe of the razor that my skin was peeling away to expose the Arek who was underneath the exterior I'd been hiding behind for sixteen years.

Connie followed the same track on the other side.

Then Connie said, "You want to go away too, don't you?"

I didn't know what to say. Was it that obvious? I almost felt as though I had been unmasked in a lie, which was something I never did in the hole, where there was no reason to ever lie about anything. I waited until Connie paused to wipe the razor clean.

I didn't want her to cut my face off if I moved my mouth to talk.

I said, "I hate it here. I went out one time, and if I can ever go out again, I would not come back."

"You know what's funny?" Connie said.

"What?"

"Hold still."

I didn't think holding still was funny, but I didn't think anything was funny at that moment in my life. Connie grabbed the top of my head and tilted it to the side so she could shave my neck.

She said, "What's funny is I totally get that. I can see you hate it here. Just be careful, and know that we will miss you, and we all love you."

The thread was cut.

"Even Wendy?"

Connie finished shaving me, not that there was anything missing on my face afterward. Still, it felt very nice.

She said, "Yes. Even Wendy."

"Okay."

"Okay, then."

Connie picked up the scissors and began clipping the hair at the front of my head.

She always started there.

"Connie?"

"Yep, kiddo?"

"Why did some people turn dark down here, and then others—you, Louis, my dads—why did they hold on to the good parts of who they were from before the hole?"

Connie stopped snipping and sighed. "You ask tough questions, kiddo. I don't know if I have the answer for you."

Maybe it was just a rhetorical question. Maybe Connie did not need to articulate an answer for me, because even at sixteen I knew enough to realize the answer was about love, and about rules, too.

The Three Sisters

"Today is Mel's sixteenth birthday," Connie said.

Connie Brees quietly considered the length of the lifetime her daughter had spent belowground. It didn't feel like sixteen years had passed to Connie.

Shannon Collins, who spun the thread of my life, and Wendy McKeon, the measurer of all things, thought about time too, but they calculated it on darker calendars than Connie did. Shannon and her mother couldn't remember what things were like before the hole, where they had spent an eternity that felt immensely longer than sixteen years.

The hole sank into a fog of semiconsciousness after all the departures.

Occasionally Wendy would check. Most days she'd simply tell Shannon to climb the ladder and take a look, to peek outside and see if there was any sign the missing had come back home to Eden.

Near the hatch, the ladder and the circular walls of the entry chamber were stained with soot from Christmas.

Shannon, who wordlessly resented her mother's manipulations, made her way down from the ladder and said, "It's not like they'd just wait out there for someone to open up and tell them to come inside."

In the library, our Max Beckmann book sat open to a full-plate glossy image of a painting called *The Three Sisters*. I was the one who left the book like that before I went away. The painting always reminded me of Wendy, Connie, and my mother.

To me, the painting straddles time before and after a hole, between the wars that tore Beckmann's Germany apart. In some ways, *The Three Sisters* was like the smoke-stained hatch leading in and out, straddling before and after; but I believe it is simultaneously Max Beckmann's depiction of the Fates.

Like so many of Beckmann's paintings, the perspective of *The Three Sisters* feels cramped and twisted. We see the women in the scene through a half-open window, like we're playing the part of Beckmann's intruders, only offscreen this time. The three women are sitting on a terrace, and the only one of them who seems amused, or even slightly happy, is the woman I imagine to be Connie, who cuts my hair, the one who cut my thread and told me it was okay for me to go away. When I hold the painting in the right spot, it looks as though Connie sees me standing inside the window watching her, and she is smiling at me. Maybe she's smiling because she is ignoring the other two women in the painting. Connie was always good at ignoring Wendy and Shannon. But maybe she's smiling because she's holding something that looks like a giant fish.

Max Beckmann liked fish.

I often get sad when I think of fish.

And when I look at the painting, it's almost as though I can hear things—lonely music being played by a busker, sounds from the street below—even though I have never actually heard such things in my life. Or the women might be Beckmann's Sirens, luring the mortals drifting in the city below their terrace toward the inevitable misfortune of the hole.

The painting conjures the smell of cigarettes.

I imagine my mother, Shannon, who spun the thread of me, is the woman in white. She occupies the entire right half of the painting, and we see her partially through the rippled glass of the open window. She holds a mirror in her right hand but is not looking into it. The mirror seems to be pointing toward the face of the woman in yellow, the rule maker, Wendy, the measurer of all things, who sits predictably at the apex of the painting, between Connie, who is wearing a green dress, and my mother, the one in white.

The maker of the rules, Wendy, the measurer of all things, dominates the painting. Of course she would. And she's preoccupied with herself too, as she fluffs her hair while looking into the mirror held by my mother. She's wearing an enormous lopsided hat covered with green and yellow feathers. But what is so disturbing about the image is that if you look closely, there is a second face behind Wendy, difficult to see at first, like the face most of us in the hole chose to ignore. The face is dark, frightening, and its teeth are sunk into Wendy's left shoulder.

But her hat and hair are perfect.

· · ·

"They wouldn't wait out there," Shannon said. "Nobody would do that."

"We *will* keep looking every day until they *do* come back. It's the least we can do," Wendy said, issuing another rule, the tireless Siren of the hole.

"Actually, we *could* do less than that," Connie pointed out, smiling.

And Wendy, already thinking about the loneliness of church and the next Christmas in the hole with half the population absent, looked directly at Shannon and said, "Don't you even care that they're gone? It's your son. You have to know what they're doing out there." Although she asked the question to Shannon, it was clear she was talking to Connie, whose son was also gone.

"Are you talking about Arek and Mel, or Robby and Austin?" Connie asked.

"They're all so useless. Goddamned boys," Wendy said. "You're lucky she had a daughter, Shann, otherwise Arek would probably have grown up exactly like his disgusting father. Anyway, you *have* to know what they're doing out there—Austin and Arek."

Shannon pondered the unknowable.

She said, "Do I have to know? Will it make anything different for you?"

As though the hole would digest them all if we resisted the call to return.

Connie could smell the bread Louis was baking, far off in the kitchen.

The Machine in the Forest

It was Mel's sixteenth birthday.

After four weeks, the weather turned very warm. Trees exploded with leaves and color. And the only Unstoppable Soldiers we'd seen were dead, empty husks.

Something was wrong. Or maybe something had been wrong for the sixteen years Mel and I had spent in the hole.

Our journey had not become boring, nor was it reduced in any way to a chore. And every day, Mel and I pieced together a larger and larger universe that included such things as baseball stadiums, lightning, Kentucky Fried Chicken establishments, empty school buses, stop signs, hailstones, buildings so tall they were terrifying to look at, billboard advertisements for pregnancy counseling, and a giant water tower painted to look like a pumpkin with a face on it.

We constructed meaning from the data that was available to us, and we were comfortable in accepting our certain incompetence.

On a day when I was not sure about anything, I thought Mel and I may have been in southern Kentucky. It was late morning, and I'd pulled the van onto a gravel driveway that cut through thick dark woods past a sign that said:

SHAWNEE

NATIONAL FOREST

I said, "Why settle for a forest, when you can have a *national* forest?"

Mel sat beside me in the passenger seat. The map books lay beneath her feet, largely ignored on the floor. We'd given up using them days before, because so many of the roads we tried to take had become impassable. As a tool for determining our path, they were useless. The only good they served was in helping us determine where we were.

We had to turn around four times due to collapsed bridges.

So I drove in what I thought was a general direction that would take us closer to Nashville, always in the belief that my fathers were still out here, and they were waiting for me.

"What do you think a *national* forest was supposed to be?" Mel asked.

"Well, clearly, before the hole, national forests were places where all the trees formed separate nations and then went to war with one another, conducted elaborate espionage schemes, and conquered parts of the forest's territory where maybe the water was better, or there were more abundant nutrients. Nations of trees invaded other nations of trees, enslaving them, murdering them, forcing them to adopt new languages, customs, and religions that required circumcision of all boys, because that's what nations have always done. Now, after the hole, there's no entertainment value in waging war of any kind, since there is not a large enough human audience left to enjoy the spectacle. This explains why this particular national forest appears to be so calm and tranquil," I said.

All stories are true.

"In that case, we mustn't do anything to let the trees know we're watching them."

I said, "Definitely. Nobody wants to be held accountable for the renaissance of global warfare."

Mel agreed. "Definitely."

"Let's go see what's out there."

"Okay."

The day was humid and still, and the air in the forest smelled alive, swirling with insects and birds, but not the kind that peck you to death. I carried the paintball gun and a small backpack that held the .45, a knife, and one of our flashlights. I was hoping to find a nice place with water, so I was only wearing boxer shorts and basketball shoes with no socks, and my number 42 rule-breaker tank top.

We learned that sleeveless T-shirts were called tank tops when we found a package of them that were made just for women in a demolished clothing store before we crossed the river into Illinois. In some ways the find was disappointing. The boys' basketball team tank top I had taken for Mel had very large openings around the arms, so I could see the softness of her breasts when she wore it. The women's tank tops didn't do that.

I supposed the before-the-hole gender segregation in terms of clothing design may have served some practical functions, like the fly openings on boxer shorts, for example. And the women's model tank tops looked good on Mel, besides. She also wore girls' sneakers and shorts that were very tight on her, which made her look small and light, like she could float away from me if she only raised up her arms to the sky and willed it to happen.

At the end of the parking area was an arch-shaped tunnel that led us back a few hundred yards into the opening of the forest. As soon as we came out of the tunnel, both of us were struck by an overwhelming and silent awe of the scale and beauty of the place.

It was magnificent.

"Oh my gosh, Arek."

"Yeah."

For all the weeks we'd been driving around on paved roadways that passed through walls of wooded lands, this was the first time that Mel and I had actually ventured some distance out into the trees. I had no idea it would be like this.

At the back of the tunnel was a post that had a carved wooden sign with yellow arrows pointing to different trail openings with names of destinations and distances. We chose the arrow that promised a waterfall in 1.2 miles and started down the trail.

The path we took was overgrown with brush and young trees. In many places, Mel or I would take turns bending back branches to open a doorway for whichever of us was in the back, leapfrogging like this until we got to more open ground. But the trail was easy to follow. We were up on a high bluff, walking along the edge of a stone cliff that dropped directly down to a line of trees and a shallow river that was the most welcoming shade of blue green.

"I want to put my feet in that water," I said.

"So do I."

I swallowed. I thought about being eleven years old again.

When the slope of the bluff we were following began to descend into the tree line, we heard a faint and constant rumble that almost sounded like an idling engine. We stopped and listened, without saying anything.

"Do you think there's someone out there?" Mel asked.

Whirrrrr . . .

It was strange, but for the first time after traveling so far from the hole in search of someone—anyone—the thought of encountering other human beings was suddenly frightening.

I shook my head. I whispered, "I don't know. If we keep quiet, we might be able to see them without being noticed."

We crept farther down the slope.

Whirrrrr . . .

As we moved forward, the sound grew louder, until it became a near roar, some kind of massive machine that must have been as big as a mountain. The closer we got, the more the thing began to sound like an angry fire.

"Maybe we should turn around," I said.

Mel grabbed my hand and tugged me onward. I would have gladly thrown myself into the flames for that confident touch of her hand. She said, "Let's just see what it is."

We rounded a bend in the trail, keeping close to the edge of the woods in order to remain hidden, and when we peeked out from the cover, we found the machine in the forest that had been making all that noise.

Here the river broadened out into a deep circular pool that butted up against the sheer face of a twenty-foot granite cliff. The rim of the cliff sloped down from both sides into a gentle dip, and over the edge spilled a frothy cascade of water.

I had seen waterfalls before, in paintings and photographs from before the hole, but being here in the presence of one so massive felt almost holy.

We could smell the droplets of water floating in the air, feel the marked rise in humidity as the path took us around the pool and closer to the base of the falls, and the sound became more and more intense, rising up in hypnotic vibrations through the soles of our feet.

"Add one waterfall to the universe," I said.

"This is the most perfect thing I've ever seen," Mel said.

And I thought, *One of the most perfect things.*

In seconds I'd kicked off my shoes, dropped the rifle and backpack, and slipped out of my shirt. "I'm going in."

"Be careful."

The rocks at the edge of the pool were slippery and uneven. I stumbled and had to catch myself with my hands. The water was so cold it made my chest and belly tighten. But the bottom fell away quickly, and soon I was wading out to where the water was past my shoulders and up to my chin. It was incredible.

But I didn't know how to swim.

There was never any reason or place for swimming in the hole, but I thought I could do it if I needed to. I was not afraid to try.

I looked back at Mel, who had her eyes fixed on me, waiting on the shore.

"You should come in, Mel. This is fantastic."

"Okay. Just be careful."

Mel slipped her feet out of her shoes and then tiptoed to the edge of the pool.

She said, "It's freezing!"

"It's really nice when you get in. Trust me."

Mel crossed her arms at her waist and peeled her tank top up over her head. She tossed it back to where she'd left her shoes.

I couldn't believe I was watching Mel undress right there in the sunlight, at the most beautiful place I had ever seen in my life. I felt nervous, like I should turn away from her or something, but I knew she would only tell me I was acting dumb and I needed to stop doing that. She stepped out of her shorts and stood, completely naked in front of me, at the water's edge.

Amelie Sing Brees was perfect.

I felt as though I were painting an image in my mind—for the first time in my life—with Arek Andrzej Szczerba's after-the-hole eyes, and I never wanted to look at things any other way. And I felt stupid and embarrassed for myself that I had some goddamned John Deere boxers with pictures of tractors on them, but I couldn't strip out of them now and risk making this day into something forced and unnatural. So I just put up with the fact that of the two of us, Mel was braver and far less polluted by before-the-hole rules and hang-ups.

Why did I have to be like that?

Mel looked directly at me. I wanted to turn away but forced myself not to.

I wiped my hands across my face and said, "Come on. It's really nice. You'll see."

Swimming and Not Drowning

We spent an hour playing in the pool beneath the falls.

And we managed, struggling and awkward, to swim out to where the water was too deep to feel the bottom, just so we could be right beneath the place where the cascading falls tumbled down over the edge of the granite cliff.

At one point Mel tried to steady herself by grabbing my shoulder but only managed to push my head below the surface, and then our legs tangled, and I ended up against her body, and her breasts met my chest. My hands traced down the curve of her spine and over her butt. It was all completely innocent and fun. I marveled at the fact that I was not thinking at all about having sex with Mel, and that I didn't have an erection for maybe the first time in what seemed like a month. So I wondered if there maybe was something wrong with me, but I shrugged it off and allowed myself to simply be here in this moment, after the fucking hole, and share this simple experience that before-the-hole human beings had undoubtedly undervalued for century upon century; to just have fun with the person who was the closest, most dependable friend in my life.

We sat on the rocks and dried in the sun.

Mel put on my basketball tank top and wore it like a dress.

I said, "I'm hungry, but all I brought was a bottle of water."

I opened the pack and drank, then handed the bottle to Mel.

"If I had brought a fishing pole, I would fish," I said. "Do you know I know how to catch fish?"

Mel didn't answer. She just looked at me and smiled.

I said, "And, you know what else? I didn't forget. Happy birthday, Mel."

"Is it my birthday? I hadn't even been paying attention."

I nodded. "I've been keeping track since the night I left. It is, in fact, your birthday."

"Well, thank you."

"Wait. I have something for you. For your birthday." I reached down inside the pack. "You have to close your eyes and open your hand."

"Can I guess?"

"Sure."

"Is it a hot dog?"

"No."

"A condom?"

"Shut up," I said. "Here."

And then I dropped the thing into Mel's hand. It was a knotted bracelet, made from threads in two shades of blue with bands of charcoal gray between them. It was like what we were supposed to have given each other last Christmas, when all the gifts ended up being thrown into Wendy's crematorium of happiness. I'd been working on the thing for nearly a week, quietly at night while Mel slept in her little bed.

Mel said, "Oh, Arek!"

And then she looked at me, and it was very confusing. Her eyes looked so sad and wet, and at the same time she seemed as though she'd been filled up with something lighter than air, like she was about to float away from me.

"How did you do this?" she said.

If keeping secrets in the hole was difficult, secrets in our van were impossible.

I shrugged. "Some nights I don't sleep. Here. Let me tie it on. Robby said that's how it's supposed to work. The person who gives it to you has to make the knot."

Mel held out her wrist. My fingers shook when I touched her. She said, "You're shaking, Arek."

"I know."

I managed to get the thing tied properly, but it was no easy task.

Mel said, "It's beautiful. I love it, and I'm never going to take it off. Thank you, Arek."

"You're welcome. And thank you for going swimming, and not drowning, with me. Happy birthday, Mel."

Amelie held her hand up to my face so I could see the colors of the threads against her skin. Then she touched me just below my ear and said, "Can I kiss you?"

I inhaled.

"Yes."

Then Amelie Sing Brees leaned her face close to me. She pulled me toward her with her palm open on my cheek, and then she kissed the opposite side of my face.

I nearly coughed. It was definitely not what I had expected her to do. I think the only person in the hole who up until this point in my life had never kissed me on the cheek was maybe Louis, but I could even be wrong about that.

Nobody remembers kisses on the cheek.

Maybe Mel sensed that too.

I hoped she did; I hoped it wasn't what she had expected either—that maybe she just didn't aim very well, like I did the first day my fathers took me out to drive a car. Crashing a car into a road sign is the same thing as being kissed on the cheek by someone you're insanely in love with.

But when Mel pulled her face back, she paused there. Our

noses were maybe a quarter inch apart. I could hear every single blood cell thrumming through the strained vessels in my neck.

And the waterfall went:

Whirrrrr . . .

Whirrrrr . . .

Whirrrrr . . .

Then Amelie Sing Brees pressed her lips into mine.

I couldn't move. I was paralyzed. I was more than willing to die here and let this be my eternity and my final memory of the world after the hole. Mel put her hands behind my neck, and then softly and fumbling, our tongues met.

Add one real kiss between a boy and a girl to the universe.

It may have lasted five seconds; it may have only been half of one heartbeat.

Then we separated, and there was nothing but the sound of the waterfall.

Whirrrrr . . .

Whirrrrr . . .

Whirrrrr . . .

Mel looked away from me. I licked my lips to taste her again. I swallowed.

She got up and slipped her feet into her shoes, hair dripping, wearing the dress of my basketball shirt, looking perfect. Mel picked up her discarded clothes from the ground, wadded them up, and stuffed them inside the backpack.

Then she said, "Come on. Let's see what else we can find out here."

She held a hand out to help pull me to my feet.

My knees shook.

"Okay."

Father Jude, the Sister Ladies, Joe, and the Attic in the Church

Breakfast was wild, and he knew it.

But over the years he'd spent traveling with his companion Olive, he'd held on to what he could by talking to her. And Breakfast talked almost incessantly. Despite any limitations he may have had, the one thing Breakfast was certain to be true was that if he did not keep talking, he would forget how to, and after that, the wildness would overtake him.

Breakfast believed there was no fun to be had in being wild, unless you *knew* you were wild and could articulate it.

So Breakfast was wild, and he knew it.

"You know what I am, Olive?" he said. "I bet you know it, girl. I'm wild. That's what I am. Wild."

They'd been locked inside the Hole in the lightless Camp Sumter for nearly two days with neither sign nor sound from the insane Edsel and Mimi.

Olive was scared. She stayed the entire time, always touching, making contact with Breakfast. And throughout the ordeal of darkness, Breakfast talked to her, recalling every detail from his life before and after meeting Olive that he could remember.

He'd never known his parents. Breakfast's earliest memories established themselves as narrative stories in his mind beginning when he was about four years old. At that time he lived with a group of three adults and one teenage boy named Joe Mahan in the attic of a Catholic church. Joe Mahan had been altar boy in the church when the plague of monsters rained down on Missouri. The adults—one man and two women—always wore black, Breakfast explained to Olive, because it had something to do with their being in the church.

"They prayed over me and Joe every night, because they wanted to keep us safe, and they wanted me to not be so wild," Breakfast told Olive. "Praying is when you put your hands together and fiddle with necklaces and ask for something you can never have. They asked for me to wear clothes, mostly, which, every time they'd try to put something on me, it felt likely to make my skin blister and burn, so I always tore it off. Right away. I'm wild, and I don't want to wear clothes unless it's freezing, and even then I don't, but I especially don't want to wear clothes just because a bunch of old people get jittery looking at someone without shoes and pants and such nonsense. And they also prayed for me to stop peeing on the big round colored window at the front of the attic, but it didn't work, on account of me being wild. Did I ever tell you that?"

Olive loved listening to Breakfast's stories.

All of Breakfast's stories were true.

"But it was Joe who took the time to teach me how to read and write. He was my best friend ever, up until I met you. Well, actually, up until Joe got eaten by one of the monsters, I guess, which didn't happen until a couple years after Joe and me moved to the farm with the others. Joe was a full-grown man by that time.

"You know what else was in the attic with us? Bees. Bees was in the attic. And they had such big drapes of honeycombs, just dripping with honey. And you know what else? I was the only one of us who could ever get that honey and not get half stung to death. I bet you already know why, though. Wild.

"Mmmm . . . honey. Doesn't that just make your mouth water, thinking about us going out and finding some honey, Olive? Remind me that's what we're gonna do once we leave this shithole—get us some honey."

Olive held on to Breakfast's hand and bounced up and down. She wanted some honey too.

"Living in that attic was miserable for those other people. Me? I didn't know nothing different. I might as well have been living in this cage for all I knew. I don't have any idea how I came to be there in that church either. But let me tell you, there was nothing to do. That's why Joe taught me how to read. He was clever. Sometimes he would sneak out and go find cigarettes or magazines to help with reading and writing. Joe always kept one or two of the magazines he'd get rolled up beneath the pieces of carpeting we slept on. Those magazines had pictures of naked people in them. I didn't see anything wrong with that, but Joe said we had to keep it secret from the old man and the ladies. Sometimes Joe would bring back bottles of vodka, and the man— his name was Father Jude—would get mad at Joe for bringing back the vodka, but he'd always forgive Joe after he'd had a few swallows from it.

"Then Father Jude would make Joe pray because he felt bad. They always felt bad about something, which is another thing I didn't get. That, and wearing all those dumb clothes. People in Joe's magazines didn't wear clothes. Why should I? The sister ladies drank too, though, but only after the rest of us went to sleep, so nobody would know. But when you're wild like me, you're real good at pretending to be asleep and then watching people sneak off and do things they don't think you know they're doing.

"At the other end of the attic there was a painting on the wall. Sometimes the sister ladies and Father Jude would pray in front of the painting, which showed some naked babies with wings in the sky over a lady who had a dead guy with a beard on her lap. So many naked people everywhere, and still the people in black wanted to pray over *me* to start wearing clothes.

"And back by that painting of the naked flying babies and the dead guy, they had a blanket hanging up, and there was a bucket on the other side of the blanket, just like this bucket here, except the bucket in the church attic had a smooth seat on it so people would be comfortable hiding behind the blanket when they needed to pee or make shit. Is that the dumbest thing you ever heard? Sometimes Joe would go back there with his magazine, too, especially when Father Jude or the sister ladies were out in the town looking for food for us. Joe was wild, but he usually wore clothes.

"On each side of the colored window where I used to pee and sometimes take shits that I didn't hide to do there were small round windows that had crosses in them. They were clear, so you could look out onto the street below. I had to climb up the wall like a lizard to see out those little windows, but I was always good at climbing, and you know why, right?"

Olive bounced.

"That's right. I could climb up that wall like a lizard because I was wild. Hang on, girl. I need to poo now. I'll tell you the rest of the story in a bit."

Breakfast got up from the rags on the floor and went to the bucket.

Olive held his hand and followed.

And Breakfast said, "I don't like people to hold my hand when I poo, Olive. Don't be scared. I'm just right here."

Olive let go of Breakfast's hand, and the boy grunted and farted, because he was wild.

Breakfast went back to their rag bed and sat beside Olive.

"Now. Where was I? So, one time I'd scrabbled up that wall to look out the window with the cross in it. Father Jude and the sister ladies were out in the town looking for things, and Joe had been drinking vodka and was hiding behind the blanket with his naked-people magazine. When I looked out at the town, I remember it had just finished raining because the street below was all shiny. Winter was over, and it was beginning to warm up. And you know what I saw? I saw monsters out there—big bugs, right? They would have shit themselves if only I had you then, but I only had Joe. But I saw not just a few of them, Olive. I saw more of those giant peckerheads than I ever saw before or since—a hundred of them, at least, and every one of 'em was as big as a tree.

"So I said, 'Joe! Joe! Come here and look at this. The monsters are everywhere!' And Joe eventually come out from behind the blanket, buttoning up his britches, and he climbed up next to me, even though Joe could not climb like a lizard on account of him not being completely wild, and wearing clothes and stuff most of the time, and acting like the world was going to turn itself around and go back in time to when we didn't have to live inside this old attic and hide from monsters with three old people in black. And Joe said, 'This is not good, Breakfast boy. This is not good at all. We better stay as quiet as we can and wait here, and maybe we should pray for Father Jude and the sister ladies, so they can be safe.' And I told him right out that it was the dumbest thing I ever heard, on account of I never seen one thing get got that anyone had ever prayed for. And Joe said, 'Yeah. I suppose you have a point there, Breakfast boy.'

"So it was just like this, Olive. Joe and me waited in that old attic for three days with nothing to do except practice reading and writing, and Joe let me look at the pictures of naked people with him. But then we ran out of water, and we ran out of anything to eat, and so on the third night, Joe said to me, 'We can't stay here, Breakfast boy. If we do, we're going to die. Are you brave enough to head out with me?'

"And I said, 'Let's go outside, Joe.' Wild."

There was a creak and a clanging of metal.

Finally, the door to Camp Sumter was opening, and Breakfast could see the silhouettes of the insane old carnies moving through the maze of skeletons toward the Hole.

Hunting for Food in the Dixieland Bayous

Breakfast whistled as loud as he could.

"Ahhhh! Motherfucker! Quit it!" Edsel screamed.

"Shoot 'em both if the little fucker does that again!" Mimi said.

"I'm sorry. I thought you forgot about us," Breakfast said. "We sure are thirsty, and I'd be happy to go out and catch you some food if you let us stretch our legs."

"That's why we come. We're hungry, and we need you to go do some work, so you can earn your keep," Edsel said.

Breakfast did not understand what he meant by "earn your keep."

Mimi unlocked the useless cage door, and Edsel held the pistol pointed at Breakfast's belly. Then Edsel and Mimi escorted their captives back out through the fun house.

"How good are you at gettin' ducks?" Edsel asked.

Breakfast nodded. "I'm wild. I can take down a whole flock of 'em with one whistle. But you two are going to have to plug your ears on account of I don't want you to be inspired to shoot me."

"You just get the ducks and shut up about it," Edsel told him.

The day was so bright it nearly blinded Breakfast and Olive, after having spent two days in absolute darkness.

Edsel and Mimi took their prisoners to an entertainment pavilion that had been built on an immense marsh. The pavilion was called Dixieland Bayous and featured a large stage constructed atop a floating platform.

Breakfast saw there were at least sixty ducks paddling around in the cattail-choked swamp, which was ringed with tall trees that wept massive curls of pale Spanish moss.

Breakfast held up his hand and whispered, "We have to stay real quiet now, on account of I need to get up as close to the water as I can before giving them a blast."

Edsel nodded. "Do what you have to do, boy."

And Breakfast put a hushing finger to his lips and whispered, "You might want to hold your ears once you see my fingers go up to my mouth."

The three humans and one nonhuman primate crept closer to the water's edge. Unlike the foul, sometimes decapitating, artificial-cesspool setting for the battle between the *Monitor* and the *Merrimack*, the swamps encircling Dixieland Bayous were natural and clean. Ducks paddled and flapped over the tiny windswept chop of the waterways, painting an image of the most peaceful and unspoiled scene imaginable.

In life, it had been Breakfast's experience, peaceful and unspoiled scenes frequently preceded those of brutality and death, and this was no exception.

They stood behind a blind of breeze-tickled cattails.

Breakfast whispered, "Okay. Here we go."

Mimi grabbed the bottom of her stained nightgown and wadded it into her ears.

Breakfast noticed her legs were so white they were nearly purple, and the skin on the old woman's thighs draped down in arches that covered her kneecaps.

Edsel jammed the stub of an index finger in one ear and tilted his head to cover the opposite one with a shoulder so he could maintain the grasp on his pistol. There was a tattoo of a spider clutching a nude woman in its fangs on Edsel's belly.

Olive bounced up and down excitedly.

Breakfast was her hero.

The wild little boy inserted his fingers into the corners of his mouth and stretched his lips tight.

And behind the small group, limping and staggering through the wreckage of a broken-down food stand called Granny Gert's Gator 'n' Grits came an old and starving Unstoppable Soldier, a male who had not eaten in two summers, and one of the few of its species remaining in the state of Tennessee. He was zeroed in on a lifesaving meal of human meat.

The Unstoppable Soldier had rotting disease spots on its exoskeleton and open sores that oozed burbling pus around the segments on its abdomen, but it was so very hungry. Glycerine strands of anticipatory saliva dropped in gooey strings from its mandibles.

Clicking softly, the monster stalked his way closer.

Nobody heard a thing.

Breakfast let rip a deadly, shrill blast that lasted a solid ten seconds.

Edsel screamed, "Goddammit! Ouch! My ears are bleeding, you little shit!"

In the long run, it did not matter that Edsel's ears were bleeding.

It did not matter because in one leap, the Unstoppable Soldier could close the distance between itself and the adult humans. It didn't even notice Breakfast and Olive, who were crouching inside the jungle of cattails at the water's edge.

Ducks flapped wildly. A few of them took to the air, managing to only gain a foot or so in altitude before crumpling back down into the swamp. Some of them fluttered in spasms of death, casting off feathers in the wake of their final movements.

Breakfast wiped the spit from his fingers on his belly. "That should do it."

The boy pushed his way through the reeds and waded out into the deep, cool water.

"I'll be right back," he said to no one who would care, except possibly Olive.

Breakfast swam out toward the flotsam of death.

And the Unstoppable Soldier sprang forward, firing its tooth-studded forearms wildly into Edsel and Mimi, who hadn't heard a thing.

Aware of a commotion behind her, Olive turned around in the cattails just in time to see the Unstoppable Soldier snatch both the old carnies in the spiked traps of its forearms. And Olive tried to save them. Olive would have tried to help anyone, but it was already too late.

Edsel and Mimi put up no struggle.

The only sound Edsel and Mimi made was a kind of crunching sound, like Breakfast made when he chewed on raw crawdad tails.

But Olive clapped her hands and jumped up through the scrim of reeds, flailing her arms as she ran toward the distracted predator. When the giant insect-monster saw Olive, it immediately dropped one of Edsel's tattooed legs and tripped over its own feet, slipping backward in a pool of blood and innards that had spilled onto the ground below.

Olive was mad. She did not like seeing people being eaten, even ones who were cruel old heroin addicts like Edsel and Mimi. She bared her teeth and scrunched her face into the scariest expression she could manage, then swiped her inordinately long arms in the air toward the Unstoppable Soldier, who had been so frightened by Olive that it choked and gagged on a portion of femur that had not been properly chewed.

The thing turned and ran with increasingly struggling, slowing strides, dripping gore, wheezing and gagging on the bone lodged in its gullet, until it could go no farther and collapsed in a sighing and hissing heap, satisfied, but mortally stricken.

Olive jumped up and down, careful to not tread in what had formerly been the contents of Edsel and Mimi.

I Only Want to Be a Human

I remember this about my mother, Shann Collins.

Until she lost all of what she had been before the hole, and, like her mother, Wendy, transformed into just my *mother in the hole*, there were moments of softness between us, and between my mother and my two fathers, too.

I remember this.

The anger she carried usually began to grip her during the winters, when my fathers would go away together, ostensibly to bring supplies and trinkets back to the hole for the rest of us, but in reality to also do that which I felt each of them, and myself, were driven to do—to go away. By the time I was twelve years old, my mother's anger had taken hold and did not abate, increasing in pressure to the point at which she actually struck my father, and cursed him, that time we'd gone fishing when I was thirteen.

There was a lounge in the hole. It was a place where we would listen to music. It was where Robby taught me and Mel how to dance, too.

The winter of my eighth birthday, when my fathers were gone again, I sat in the lounge alone with my mother, and we listened to some old music on a tape machine we had there. My mother told me this was my fathers' favorite music. It was music that got inside my bones, I think, and made me want to move, to go away, like all boys, I suppose, but I could not articulate it at the time.

"What was it like?" I said. "What was it like on the outside, to walk down a street and see a hundred faces on people you never knew? Or to be inside a schoolroom with so many other little boys and girls?"

My mother said, "It was just like here, except more crowded."

I could not, even at that time, believe our *Eden* was an accurate model of the world before the hole.

"Will there ever be more boys and girls like me and Mel?"

My mother smiled. She rubbed my leg.

The couch we sat on was orange.

She said, "No, Arek."

I didn't know what to think about that. On the one hand, it saddened me to imagine that I would never have the opportunity to encounter unthreatening strangers—passersby—and let them go on doing their own private things while they let me go on doing mine. All these intersections of privacy and paths without end that would never re-cross. It was impossible to consider. But there was nothing to compare life inside the hole to. Life inside the hole gave me the opportunity to explore nothing of a private existence. I may as well have been sad to know that I would never sprout wings and fly.

This was all there was.

"That's sad," I said.

"Your father always said that sadness was a dominant trait in the genetic constitution of Polish boys."

I knew I was Polish. Dad—Austin—had been teaching me the language from discs he'd scavenged from up above, outside, where there were places with names—like Poland—inside of other places with names, and on and on, without end.

It was impossible to imagine the scale of things.

"But what if I need to fall in love with somebody?" I asked.

My mother didn't say anything. She kept her hand on my leg, and the music played.

"What if I need to fall in love with someone else? What if there is nobody else, anywhere? What if I need to fall in love with a boy?"

And my mother said, "Well, that would be in your genes too, I suppose."

I did not understand what she meant, but then again, I was only eight years old at the time.

"What are my 'genes'?"

My mother thought about it. Then she said, "They kind of

make rules for you before you're born—about what color your eyes will be, and if you will be a boy or not, if your hair will be straight, how tall you will be."

"And my heart, too?" I said.

"Yes, that too."

I started to cry.

Why did there have to be all these rules—more and more of them, invisible ones, all piling up without end?

Max Beckmann thought tears were a sign of slavery, but I couldn't stop them.

The music played and played.

My mother pulled me to her chest. She kissed the top of my head.

Despite my genetic constitution, which tilted toward sadness, it made me feel loved.

She told me not to cry about things, that most things could not be controlled.

The music played.

I said, "I only want to be outside the hole. I only want to be a human."

Names on a Wall

When we walked around the pool where we'd gone swimming, the trail that went along the water's edge led Mel and me into the shade beneath the falls.

Here we found the opening to a cave—a hole as big as a house.

The entry looked like an openmouthed frown, wide, low, and curved downward into sharp points. There was a sense the chamber behind the opening was massive, but from where we stood below the overhang of a granite face, all we could see of it was black.

Mel said, "Let me have that flashlight."

I opened the pack and felt around inside. My hands lingered on the soft things Mel had been wearing before she took them off to come swimming with me. Her clothes were still warm from her skin, or at least I imagined they were.

"You're not planning on going inside, are you?"

To get into the cave, we would have to crawl on our hands and knees.

She said, "I almost feel like we *have to*, Arek."

We had a puzzle of this world to construct, after all; we both knew it.

I took the flashlight from our backpack and switched it on.

Crouching at the cave's mouth, Mel shone the light inside. From behind her, I could see how big the room was, and where the light hit the granite walls, it revealed figures and writing from another time, possibly from before the hole, I thought.

"There's a fire ring right up near the entrance," she said. "Probably to keep things from attempting to come inside."

Holding the light in one hand, Mel got down on her knees and crawled into the opening.

She said, "I'll let you know if it's okay. In fact, I'm pretty certain I'll let you know if it's not okay too."

And I said, "I'm not sure about this, Mel."

"Nonsense. I've got my lucky bracelet on."

Mel disappeared inside the doorway tunnel.

After a minute she called back, "I think you should come in here, Arek."

This was crazy, I thought. I crawled in behind her.

On a day of incredible stacking upon incredible, when I could not be certain where we were, but had finally come to accept that it didn't matter, the things we saw inside the cave behind the falls added new pieces to our model. Those pieces changed everything.

All around the floor outside the black-charred rocks that encircled how many fires we could never guess, we saw the impressions of footprints—human footprints, left behind in the cave's soft, sandy floor. I did not need to make up a story of explanation as to who'd left the footprints there; this became obvious to us quickly, because the people who'd been here—storytellers as we all are—let us know.

And this story was true.

People had been living inside this cave.

Maybe it was out of reverence for the place, and maybe it was from fear, but Mel and I didn't say anything for several minutes while we both studied the signs revealed by Mel's light, taking it in, taking all of it in.

The main room was about twenty feet deep. There was a natural chimney overhead; we could feel the air being sucked inside—inhaled by the doorway we'd crawled through. Against one wall we found what were apparently beds that had been made from tree boughs that were blanketed with old canvas fraying so badly it fell apart in our hands when we touched it.

One of the beds had an actual foam mattress on it. It was wide enough for two or maybe three people to share, and like the canvas beds, it too was crumbling where the cloth seams had separated, spitting out what looked like dry yellow curds of stuffing.

When I slipped off one of my shoes, I saw that at least one of the people who'd lived here was probably as tall as I was. The other footprints—we could not say how many different sets were here—were smaller. There was at least one young child, too.

Mel whispered, "Where do you think they went?"

I looked at her and shrugged.

We'd both seen what had been left behind on the wall above the beds—a sort of tally-mark calendar with names and ages of the people who'd lived here. The singular date that had been written on the wall was only three years before Mel and I wandered in here.

"There are people," I said.

And saying it made truth of something that I had always wanted to believe but had never been allowed to: There were other people out here, somewhere. There had to be others.

On the wall above the beds was a picket line of slashes that ended on the bottom with a date, and beside this record had been written:

Henry Martin, 39 yrs
Joanna Martin, 36 yrs
Davis Martin, 14 yrs
Sara Martin, 5 yrs

"It's a family. And if you figure by the date, Sara is younger than we are. She was born after. After the hole," I said.

Mel counted up the tally marks beside the names.

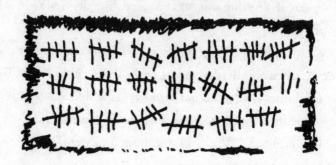

"They stayed here for more than three months," she said.

I nodded. "I think the date must have been when they decided to leave, since it's at the bottom of the scratch marks and the names of the people."

The date was in April, almost exactly three years before Mel and I found this place.

"What do you think happened to them?" Mel asked.

"I think they got tired of living in a hole."

I went back to the fire ring to look for a piece of charcoal. I said, "We need to put our names up here too, and today's date, so if anybody else finds this place they will know we were here."

Mel swung the light around to help me see.

And on the wall across from the ring of stones where the family had tended their fire, we saw the reason they'd come into the hole:

There were some small bones in the ashes of the fire—mostly what appeared to come from rabbits and squirrels—and I found some good-size pieces of burnt wood, too. My hands and shoes turned black from raking through the old fire ring, but I found a piece I thought would work.

We were here. April 10, 20XX

Amelie Brees, 16 yrs

Arek Szczerba, 16 yrs

"Why did you put my name first?" Mel asked.

"I would never have come in this hole unless you told me to, Mel."

When I finished writing, my fingers and wrist were stained charcoal black.

I said, "I'm going to need to jump back in the water."

I looked at Mel. I imagined us kissing again. I dreamed about taking off all our clothes and going back in the water with her, naked.

Then we heard a buzzing sound that came echoing through the entryway of the cave. It was not the waterfall this time.

This was unmistakably the whirring mechanical drone of an engine.

Mel and I scrambled back out through the narrow entrance to the cave.

As we crawled, the sound of the motor became clearer, rising in pitch with each small distance we managed to cover.

When we stood outside, there was no doubt that somewhere out here an internal combustion engine was running. Although the sound was muted by the steady rush of the waterfall, there was nothing else it could possibly be.

"Where's it coming from?" Mel asked.

"I can't tell."

I tilted my head, trying to angle my ears so as to catch the sound better.

Neither one of us breathed.

Just minutes before, we were amazed to find evidence that someone else had been out here—now we were practically face to face with that reality. We went back along the trail, Mel in the lead, with me carrying our pack and rifle.

She stopped at the top of the pool.

"Oh my God, Arek, look!"

She pointed up above the rim of the bluff we had followed down earlier, and then we both saw it—just a glimpse. Up in the air, at a distance that was impossible for me to gauge, we saw a plane heading southeast.

"Hey!" I screamed as loud as I could.

It was stupid, but I couldn't control myself. "Hey! Dad! Robby! Hey! HEY!!!"

It was the same plane Robby had shown me in his pilot books.

We saw it for no more than three seconds, and then it disappeared behind the tops of the trees.

I kept screaming, waving my hands frantically and uselessly at nothing, calling for my dads. I only stopped when Mel put her hands on my shoulders and told me it was okay, and that I shouldn't cry. I didn't realize I was crying until she told me that, and when she did, I finally attempted to suck in a breath.

I felt so stupid and weak, enslaved to something bigger than I could comprehend.

"It's okay, Arek. We both saw them. It really was them. It's okay."

I was suddenly so tired. I was sick of the hole and what it did to us all. I was sick of the world before the hole and the things my father attempted to bring inside for me, and the hidden before-the-hole things the others carried like pathogens inside themselves. I believe at that precise moment, when I saw the airplane vanish behind the treetops, I finally understood how it was possible to straddle time.

I sat down near the edge of the water and pulled my knees in to my face.

Mel didn't say anything.

I was dimly aware that her arm was around my shoulders.

We must have sat there like that, saying nothing, for an hour or more.

Self-Portrait with Champagne

One time, my father, Austin, told me this: "Every great poem, and every great novel, is a self-portrait."

My father taught me how to read. Sometimes we would share a book together and take turns reading it aloud to each other in the library.

That was one of my favorite things to do. The books did not bring anything into the hole from the outside world; they pulled things out from our hearts and allowed us to examine them.

This is me.

It took us two months to read *Moby-Dick* this way.

. . . that in her retracing search after her missing children, only found another orphan.

I read the last pages of the novel to my father. I said, "It's one of the saddest stories I've ever read."

And it was after I read that final line and closed the book that we sat there for a moment in silence, thinking about what had been pulled out and shown to us, when my father told me his conclusion about books being self-portraits.

"Do you mean it's a self-portrait of Melville?" I said.

"All self-portraits examine the identity of the painter, as well as that of the viewer."

I looked at the swirling blue painting of the sinking ship, the people in the icy water, and the lifeboats.

And my father, watching me, said, "'In landlessness alone resides the highest truth, shoreless, indefinite as God.'"

"Are we shoreless here in the hole?" I asked.

My father smoked a cigarette and nodded.

"Some of us are," he said.

This is me.

Max Beckmann wrote this: *The self is the great veiled mystery of the world.*

Max Beckmann was probably obsessed with exploring his identity, with stripping away the function of model and replacing it with the substance of pure data. He painted more than eighty self-portraits in what must have been an exhausting effort to veer away from re-presentation and, in doing so, come face to face, artist to canvas, with an immutable and wordless truth.

This is me.

I am a story.

All stories are true.

Among Beckmann's self-portraits were works in which he depicted himself as a nurse, as a clown, wearing suits with ties, in a tuxedo, as a sculptor, drinking champagne, with white hats and black hats, in a red scarf, holding a crystal ball, carrying horns and saxophones, on a staircase, with his wife—and most of them included the inevitable smoldering cigarette, too.

The thing I find most compelling about Max Beckmann's self-portraits is they all seem to be a little off balance, as though staring at one for too long a time would make the viewer feel dizzy, or that the painting had been hung in such a way that it was crooked. And there's almost always something pushing Beckmann away from center, as though his intent was to make the viewer look beyond Beckmann's sometimes menacing expression and away from his eyes, which seem like insatiable black holes—sucking in all that had ever passed before them—and focus on just a sliver of something that doesn't quite seem to belong in the picture, even if it's an object as mundane as a bit of purple drapery or a potted plant.

My favorite—if such a word could appropriately be used for Beckmann's work—was painted in 1919, when the artist was struggling to recover from his wartime experiences, from going through Max Beckmann's shoreless hole. It is called *Self-Portrait with Champagne*.

The painting shows Beckmann in what is likely an upper-class nightclub, seated alone at a table with a bottle of champagne in an ice bucket, a filled glass in his left hand, and a cigarette in his right. The image is all out of skew, distorted, and claustrophobic to the point where it makes me feel like I can't catch my breath. Beckmann is wearing a suit, with a wing-tip collared shirt and tie, and he is turned, looking over his right shoulder as though either something in the room has caught his attention, or he's trying to ignore what we see in the background. I believe he's trying to ignore what's behind him, even though, or more likely *because*, it is very unsettling. In back of Beckmann we see a kind of demon standing behind a doorway. Although the demonic figure is nicely dressed, he has a pointed ear and a deranged expression, openmouthed like a crocodile, baring teeth, an enormous white eye magnified in the lens of his spectacles. And Beckmann is smiling. It is a very tired smile from someone who has already seen all the horrors in the world before the hole and is therefore resigned to temper his reaction to the immediate present.

This is an image of someone who can straddle time.

Nothing is a surprise.

This is me.

A Familiar Reaction

"I suppose we should get up and go," I said.

I had no idea how long Mel and I had been sitting at the water's edge after seeing the plane in the sky. The shadows stretched across the pool; I could feel the cooling of the shade as it extended its canopy over us.

"You know what I think?" Mel said. "I think maybe your dads went back to Independence and saw the note and the picture you left for them. And now they're coming back to where they said they'd go. Maybe they even flew over the van and saw it."

"Maybe."

Of the two of us, Mel was the braver. And along with her bravery, she was an unwavering optimist, too.

I think optimism requires the highest degree of bravery.

I nodded. "I'm sorry if I ruined your birthday."

Mel put her hand on my arm. It felt cool and loving.

She said, "This has been the best birthday of my entire life. And now, I'm hungry. We should go back and have dinner. A birthday dinner. Maybe we could watch a movie."

"I'll let you pick it out. I'm no good at doing that."

"It's a deal, then. Let's go."

So we followed the trail back to where it rose upward along the forested bluff that would lead us again to the tunnel we'd walked through that morning, when we discovered this part of our expanding universe.

"Hang on," I said.

Something was wrong with the tunnel. I could not see through to the other side where we'd left the van.

Mel noticed it too. "Did it collapse?"

"There's something inside the tunnel, and it's big."

We heard the *scritch-scritch* of what sounded like clawed feet moving across the concrete floor of the passageway, coming toward us.

I dropped the backpack and found the .45 pistol.

"It might be a bear," I said.

Scritch-scritch-scritch.

"I don't think that's a bear," Mel said.

Then we saw the twin tooth-spiked forearms of an Unstoppable Soldier emerge into the light from the mouth of the tunnel. The arms jabbed into the ground to anchor and pull the rest of the creature out onto the trail in front of us.

I put the pistol down on the ground and swung Robby's paintball gun around on its shoulder strap. I knew how to use it—everyone in the hole had to learn how to do it—but I had no idea whether or not this particular one would even function.

Mel and I had gone a long time without testing it, without ever needing to.

Mel said, "Holy shit, Arek."

This was the first time she'd ever seen one of the things.

When the monster emerged from the tunnel and stood upright, its twitching arms spread wide, the beads of its massive compound eyes pinned directly on me and Mel, it was at least ten feet tall. It sizzled and burbled saliva.

I was so scared, I honestly thought I was going to piss myself.

The barrel of the paintball rifle twitched up and down with each surging rush of my pulse.

The Unstoppable Soldier came forward.

Scritch-scritch-scritch.

But there was something wrong with it. It appeared to be limping, as though injured or sick, and there were large brown bruises splotching its abdomen. But it was very hungry, too. There was no doubt about that.

Scritch-scritch-scritch.

It came closer.

I shook, fumbling with the gun's safety catch.

The Unstoppable Soldier was so close to me, when it fully extended one of its forearms, the hairlike sensor at the very tip of the spiked claw got to within a few inches of my feet. Then the thing jerked back, straightened up, and cocked its arms, ready to leap at me.

I pulled the trigger.

Fwack!

A paintball, loaded with the only toxin in the world that could kill one of the monsters—my other father's blood—burst against the creature's left eye. The Unstoppable Soldier froze, confused. It combed one arm across the eyeball, which promptly dissolved, exposing the interior of the monster's skull like a soft-boiled egg.

Fwack!

I shot it again, this time in the pulsing center of its pillowy abdomen.

The second paintball did not burst on contact; it penetrated the creature's body directly through one of the mushy bruise spots. The Unstoppable Soldier took a step around, as though contemplating a retreat through the tunnel. And when it turned away from me, a geyser of acrid yellow goo began erupting, like spouting diarrhea, from the creature's anus.

At this point in my life I was no stranger to the incomprehensible wretchedness that was inside an Unstoppable Soldier, but this was all new to Mel—the smell, the steamy fog of heat.

Some of the torrent of goop skittered along the ground and splashed over my shoes and up my legs, onto my tractor boxers. The heat of it stung my skin.

Mel said, "That's fucking disgusting!"

Her claim left no room for argument.

The Unstoppable Soldier took a final half step, then collapsed in a heap at the entrance to the passage out of the forest, sizzling and squirting like an ignored stove-top espresso maker on a red-hot burner.

"Fuckbucket!" I said.

Mel went pale.

Her mouth turned sharply downward, like the opening to the cave we had found. She looked at me, then at the dead thing slumped in front of us, then back at me, and so on, for a good few minutes.

Then she turned toward the bushes that lined the trail and vomited.

I was also very familiar with that reaction.

A Smoker's Best Friend

"So. Let's see. Where was I? Well, me and Joe left the attic in the church that third night after Father Jude and the sister ladies didn't come back."

Breakfast and Olive had been walking for four days since they'd left Rebel Land. Every vehicle they came across on the way was utterly useless, so they walked.

After coming back from his duck hunt and seeing what had become of Edsel and Mimi, Breakfast took Olive back to their old septic-pumper truck to gather up the things that the wild boy simply would not leave behind: a canvas bag stuffed with money, his rifle, and a few other assorted tools and trinkets.

Then they walked.

"But I'll tell you, I've never been happier in my life as I am right now. Car or no car, Olive. I never want to go back to Rebel Land. I can't tolerate being covered in shit at the start of a day, and then kept in a cage at the end. And you know why, don't you?"

Olive rocked her chin against Breakfast's chest. It was her way of laughing, and answering, too.

Breakfast said, "That's right, girl. Because I'm wild."

On their fourth night walking, they settled into an ancient tobacco barn. Breakfast liked the building because from the outside it looked like a flying saucer from one of his favorite comic books, due to the wide skirt of sloped tin roof that extended outward on all four sides, midway up the structure's walls. On one of those outer walls, in paint so faded Breakfast could barely read it, the barn said:

TENNESSEE CLUB PIPE TOBACCO

A SMOKER'S BEST FRIEND

The interior of the barn reminded Breakfast of the old church attic he used to live in with a boy named Joe Mahan and three sour old people in black who had something to do with the church, which was why he wanted to continue telling his story to Olive.

Olive loved Breakfast. Olive didn't care that she'd heard the story at least a hundred times, but then again, Olive didn't care about anything much at all.

Since there was no window with colored glass, Breakfast peed on a rickety old sawhorse in a dusty corner of the old barn.

They made a bed on a pile of giant tobacco leaves.

Breakfast knew what tobacco was, but he wanted to taste a bit of it. Olive did too. They both decided that seventeen-year-old tobacco leaves were not suitable for eating.

"When we left that night, it was a little bit cold, and it was raining as hard as I ever seen it rain. That was probably a good thing, though, since you know how much those bugmen hate water. Still, Joe tried talking me into wearing clothes, and I told him no. I mean, just look at him—all sogged down in britches and a shirt that drank enough water to double that boy's weight in no time. Besides, like I told him, I was wild. That's how I lived this long, right, Olive?"

Breakfast picked his nose and wiped a stringy amber clot of dried mucus on one of the tobacco leaves beside his head.

"I can't remember the name of the city the church was in. Centerville or Midvale or something dumb like that. It was empty. Every house and building sat quiet like gravestones. I think Joe and me were the last two people for miles and miles.

"We got into a store, and Joe took a bottle of vodka, a pack of cigarette lighters, and a small box of cigars that were supposed to taste like cherries. The only naked-people magazine the store had, Joe already memorized it, frontways and back, so he said he didn't feel like carrying it along too. I'll tell you the truth—I never cared for cigars or vodka, neither one of them. Joe said the vodka made him feel good. I told him thank you, I felt fine as I was.

"Joe and me walked all night in the rain, trying to get away from that town, on account of all the monsters we'd seen when we climbed up and looked out that little round window with the cross in it a few days before. Joe smoked cigars. I tried one too. Let me tell you, Olive, I have eaten cherries plenty of times, and if they ever tasted as shit-stank as that cigar, I'd rather starve to death. And you know what Joe said? He said he was glad to be out of the church, and that he'd wanted to leave for a long time, but the only reason he'd stayed there with Father Jude and the sister ladies was because of me. He said they were all from before the time, and since I was from the after-time, all wild and new, I deserved not to be prayed over and told to wear clothes—but was I sure I wasn't cold? Ha-ha—that's what Joe told me. Wild."

Olive rustled around in the bed of tobacco leaves and sighed. She lay her hand flat on Breakfast's tummy.

"Well. Once the sky started getting light, the rain came even harder. But by that time me and Joe were away from the city, walking through a countryside that was mostly trees and houses spaced far apart, with big fenced-in fields where Joe told me people used to keep horses and hogs and cattle. Can you imagine what that must have looked like? Horses and hogs and cows all kept inside fences, as opposed to running wild. What a time! What a time for the cage makers of the world, right, Olive? Wild.

"But since it was getting light, and we were both tired, and Joe told me he wanted to get drunk, we decided to find a hiding spot and lay low for a bit and see what was going on around here. One of the big fenced-in places we came to had a little brick house sitting out in the middle of a field. Oh, that house wasn't even a quarter the size of this barn, and there was no windows on it neither. Joe said it was a shed or something, probably for tools and such. But since it was brick, with a stout metal roof on it, Joe thought it would make a decent place for us to sleep. It had a stovepipe chimney, too, so Joe said we could maybe get a fire going inside. So I told him, fine, but I'm not cold, but let's see what it's like in there. And then I asked Joe if he was cold, sloshing as he was in those soggy dumb damn clothes. Ha-ha. Wild."

Breakfast stretched and yawned, and Olive, who frequently mimicked the boy, did the same.

"You know what? Let's tomorrow get some fish or some crawdads to eat. I'm getting hungry just thinking about it."

Olive nodded her head and patted Breakfast's stomach.

"So me and Joe jumped over the fence and then tramped our way through this field where the ground was so wet, my feet sank in halfway up to my knees. Joe's did too, and both his shoes come off. And I laughed at him and said, 'See? Dumb clothes. Nature herself wants to take 'em off you, Joe.' But Joe said shut up, wild boy, and let's get inside. Well, there was a heavy wood door on the little brick shed, with an old iron latch on it that Joe had to jimmy up in order to get us inside the little brick house. Despite his being odd about so many things, Joe was a real good guy at figuring things out, and he was smart enough to teach me how to read and write, so that's saying something. But now he was barefoot, and his britches were carrying at least ten pounds of mud on 'em and were pulled halfway down his legs from it, but he got that door opened. Then Joe lit one of his cigarette lighters, so we could see inside.

"So, you know what was inside that shed, Olive?"

Of course Olive knew. She'd memorized Breakfast's story dozens of tellings ago.

"Well, first off, everything inside was bricks. The floor was bricks too. And in the middle of the floor there was yet a circle of bricks, stacked up about knee high, that was made for keeping a fire in, with an old chimney hood over that. But what scared me about it right away was there were steel bars high across the room, and there were two whole pigs hanging upside down by their back legs. They were dead, though. They didn't have no guts, and their skin looked like shiny leather. And there were other big, round pieces of meat too, all hung up from sharp steel hooks, just hanging there over my head. Joe was tall as a doorway, though, and about as skinny straight up and down as a stop-sign post. But I'll tell you, Olive, I'd never seen such a thing as those upside-down hanging pigs and those big chunks of meat. And Joe told me we found a smokehouse, and it was a miracle, and that we were going to eat a ham before we went to sleep.

"I had never heard of such a thing, but Joe promised me it would be better than anything. So we went out again to find things Joe could get a fire going with, and then we lit that fire inside the ring of bricks. Joe drank almost half his bottle of vodka and began acting silly, but I didn't mind. He sang a song he learned from Father Jude, and Joe took off his dumb clothes and hung 'em on the steel bars to dry out, and then he pulled down a big hunk of meat, which he said was called ham, and we tore it apart with our bare hands and ate till we couldn't stand up, neither one of us, but in Joe's case, it was probably more due to the vodka. That Joe was a real good singer, though.

"That ham. My word, Olive, I think that was the best thing I ever tasted in my entire life.

"Oh, what I would give for us to find a smokehouse like that, Olive. I'm practically drowning in saliva just thinking about that ham. You know what? I'd pay one thousand dollars for a ham, I would.

"And you know what I said to Joe? I said, 'Joe, look at you there on the floor with me, with not one stitch of clothes on, muddy, and eating like this with our bare hands. You know what we are, Joe? I bet you do. Wild. That's what we are, Joe. Wild.'

"And Joe laughed and laughed, and then he sang another song. Wild."

In This Version of Adam and Eve

As it turned out, the Unstoppable Soldier I killed at the end of the tunnel was not the only danger we encountered before we got back to our van.

Mel's sixteenth birthday ended up being a universe-expanding day for surprises.

We stepped around the lake of steaming goo that spilled out of the dead monster. Mel wadded the neckline of my basketball shirt up over her nose and mouth.

"Do they all smell like this?" she said.

"Well, I've only seen three of them in my entire life, and they all smelled really bad."

Also, something I hadn't noticed before, but this one's innards seemed to be alive with writhing white worms that were as big and thick as my fingers. The worms wriggled so much, they made a sound like the monster's guts were boiling.

I said, "But I never saw this before. This one was all full with worms. He looked like there was something wrong with him, don't you think? These worm things must have been eating him alive from the inside."

Mel shook her head, keeping the shirt over her nose and her eyes level with the opening at the opposite end of the pathway out. "I am *not* looking, Arek."

By the time we came out the other side and could see our van parked in the gravel lot, Mel had recovered and was able to breathe again. But when we got to within ten feet of the van's side door, a sudden and loud buzzing startled us. It seemed to come from beneath the motorhome's doorstep. The buzzing sounded like something was burning, like an electrical short inside the van, and I immediately thought about how terrible it would be if the van caught fire right here, leaving us stranded in the middle of a forest.

I put up my hand to stop Mel from getting closer when I saw what was making the noise. It was a fat, black-banded rattlesnake with a copper-colored stripe running the length of its spine.

The snake raised its head as we stood there and watched. It hissed and huffed, inflating its body like a balloon to appear more threatening.

To be honest, the snake did not need to appear more threatening. It was the second time in less than an hour when I seriously thought I might pee myself.

We both knew what rattlesnakes were, but books and photographs and old cowboy movies just could not convey how scary they are when you actually see and hear one, face to face, for the first time in your life.

The universe adds a snake.

And the thick, menacing rattlesnake was coiled just below the step up into our home, facing us with a predicament about how—or if—we should go about getting back inside to the relative safety of the van.

"I think he plans on stealing our house," I said.

Mel said, "He can have it."

"No. I need to take a shower and get all this shit off me. Here, take this."

I handed the paintball gun to Mel and took out the .45 we'd found in the hole in Rome.

The gun was heavy, and my hands hadn't stopped shaking since the encounter with the Unstoppable Soldier at the tunnel. When I squeezed off a shot, we both jumped. Actually, all three of us—the rattlesnake included—did.

The shot went right into the rattlesnake's head, splitting it open, and breaking its lower jaw so its mouth hung crookedly agape. But the snake continued to writhe and buzz its rattle for half a minute before turning over and lying there, dead still.

"In this version of Adam and Eve, our heroes kill the serpent, then drive away in their motorhome, start their own basketball team, and live happily ever after, through many more birthdays," I said.

I clicked the safety back on the pistol and put it away. "You know, we could cook this and eat it."

Mel frowned and shook her head. "No. Absolutely not."

"Yeah. I didn't think so."

Camouflage Does Not Make You Invisible

I thought it would probably be smart if we moved the van at least ten miles from the forest where we'd encountered the monster and the snake, just in case there were any more things trying to sneak up and kill Mel and me.

So I pulled out of the lot and onto the unmarked road we'd driven in on.

Mel was in the back, changing out of my basketball jersey–dress and into some regular after-the-hole human being clothes.

In some ways, I was relieved there had been so many distractions that day, but now that we were back inside the safety and isolation of the van, all I could do was think about the kiss we had shared at the edge of the pool. I knew it was going to be something we'd talk about, because it was just like Mel to nonchalantly bring it up in conversation.

I imagined we'd be eating dinner—maybe something dehydrated from a silver pouch out of the survivalists' kit in Rome—and Mel would say something like, *This dinner is great, don't you think?* And I'd nod, and then she'd say, *And why haven't you said anything about that kiss? Did it scare you? Did you even like it?*

And here I was, driving our van and having this made-up conversation in my head, and I could feel myself turning red and feeling uncomfortable and aroused, all at the same time.

It filled me with a kind of nervous dread, too, because Mel was destined to be so matter-of-fact, uninhibited, and unfazed by what we'd done, while here I was, a polluted after-the-hole teenage boy who was capable of feeling a dozen or more simultaneously contradicting emotions and impulses.

I didn't have any idea where we were, and this was not only in reference to our van and geography.

Geographically speaking, the compass in the Mercedes's dashboard said we were going south and east. I figured the next morning we'd eventually run into a town, or a marked highway of some kind, and then we'd be able to use the map books to get some idea of our location.

Emotionally, there were no compasses available whose needles didn't spin wildly without ever settling on one definite point.

The sun was nearly down when, following a welcome sign and another one that said ENTER HERE, I parked the van at a place called Davy Crockett Campground. There were two other billboards that said RVS WELCOME and FISHING! BOATING! SWIMMING! HIKING!

So with all the fun and gracious hospitality promised by the signs, I figured this had to be a friendly and safe, monster- and snake-free place for us to spend the night.

And maybe tomorrow I could show Mel how to fish in nonfrozen waters, I thought.

I parked the van just as Mel came up to sit in the passenger seat. She was dressed in a set of thin plaid pajamas we'd taken from the boys who were supposed to have been surviving inside that very small hole in Rome.

I wanted to touch her so bad my hand shook.

She said, "Where are we?"

"Davy Crockett Campground, which sounds like a very fun place," I answered.

Mel's hair was wet. She'd taken a shower, which only served to remind me that the lower half of my body had been painted with bug guts.

I looked at her, consumed with wondering if we would ever kiss like that again. It made my throat knot up a little.

Mel said, "What?"

"Nothing. I'm just tired."

"You're weird, Arek."

"I know. And I need to take a shower too. I must smell like that awful . . . stuff."

"Okay. I left pajamas on your bed for you. I'll find us something to eat and a movie," Mel said. "And leave your boxers on the floor back there so I can wash them."

I felt my face getting hot.

Mel rolled her eyes and said, "Just go."

Everything I had predicted was coming true. It made me very nervous.

I came out of the shower, wrapped in a towel. It was night, and Mel had the small lights turned on above the little dining table. I'd forgotten to bring the pajamas Mel had left for me into the tiny bathroom and realized I was now in an inhibited, before-the-hole Iowa-boy predicament.

Mel was cooking something called macaroni and cheese from a dehydrated foods package. It smelled good. I was starving. The boxers I'd had on that day were gone, and I could hear the rumbling growl of our motorhome's washer-dryer.

I pretended not to notice anything, but in my nervousness, absolutely everything around me—the sights, sounds, smells—assaulted every sense I had.

"Do you feel better?" Mel said.

"Um. Yeah."

I tried to will myself to be the after-the-hole Arek who'd grown up with Mel, the one to whom nothing ever mattered.

This is me.

What if I'm wrong?

The pajamas Mel had left on my bed were made of soft T-shirt material. They had a green camouflage pattern on them. I thought it was funny, because what would you need to hide from when you're in bed—and then I thought, maybe that's a good idea after all.

I took a deep breath and dropped my towel. Shakily I pulled the bottoms up over my naked legs, trying desperately not to glance up and see if Mel had been watching me.

Of course she was watching me.

I swallowed the knot in my throat.

And Mel, without blinking, said, "Those look good on you."

"How can you tell? I'm camouflaged. You're not supposed to see me."

"Believe me. I saw you, Arek."

"Oh. Uh."

"Are you hungry?"

"Starving."

"Well, it's time to eat."

"Good."

"You're being weird."

"I know. Sorry."

I picked up the towel at my feet and hung it in the bathroom, then sat down next to Mel at the little table where we shared dinner.

The Black Car with the Shiny Treasure Chest

Breakfast found a car the next morning in a small town called Hopeful.

"Ha-ha!" Breakfast laughed. "I was hopeful we'd find a car that worked! Do you get it, Olive? Hopeful? Hopeful and wild!"

Olive did not really get it, and the car was not really a car. What Breakfast had found was a hearse that had been parked behind a place called Shaun Hutchinson and Brothers Funeral Home. And although the wild boy knew what funerals were, he did not know why funerals had homes, or what the long black vehicle with the shiny treasure chest in the back had ever been used for.

"I'll tell you what, though, girl—after what happened to me with that truck full of shit, I am *never* going to open that fancy box back there."

That was probably one of the luckiest random decisions Breakfast ever made.

He said, "In fact, come on and help me, Olive, 'cause I plan on getting that big box the hell out of here before it pops open and turns out to be full of someone else's shit, or hornets and snakes."

Olive was afraid of snakes.

Breakfast wasn't really afraid of anything, except surprises like trucks filled with shit, and he was determined not to be fooled again.

He left the hearse idling and opened the wide and tall back door.

Breakfast grabbed on to one of the silver handles on the big box and grunted. He had to brace his little feet on the car's bumper and strain to get the thing to move. He farted and laughed.

Olive liked it when Breakfast farted.

Finally, the big long box nudged past the tailgate of the hearse.

"This fucker's heavy," Breakfast said. "And I honestly do not care if it's filled to the brim with money, or even ham, but I am *not* going to open this motherfucker *no matter what*."

Olive pulled on the other side of the coffin, and soon the heavy thing slid and tipped, crashing down onto the crumbling asphalt behind the funeral home.

Fortunately, it did not pop open.

"It sure is pretty in back of this car, with all them little fancy curtains and clean sheets and pillows. I bet this car was made for people who got tired when they drove places, so they could just lay down and rest themselves in this big back," Breakfast said. "Looks like we not only got ourselves a car, Olive, but we got ourselves a place to sleep, too."

Olive jumped up and down to show her approval.

Breakfast scratched his balls, sniffed his fingers, and said, "Come on, Olive. Let's drive! Wild!"

As he spun the tires out on the surface of the funeral home's back lot, Breakfast grinned and said, "Hoo-wee! Aren't we the wildest, richest, luckiest two people in all creation?"

Olive clapped.

"Now all we need is to find a little river, and have plenty of luck and happiness inside our hearts, and we will get us some fish, or maybe crawdads, or maybe even a turtle so we can fix us some dinner."

Olive bounced, and Breakfast picked his nose.

Although the hearse looked like it might have a siren and flashing lights, it did not. It did have music, though, but as far as Breakfast was concerned, the music it played sounded sad and likely to put him to sleep, so he turned it off.

Breakfast pulled gas from underground tanks at a service station outside Hopeful. They stored four large cans of it in the back of the hearse, which despite also carrying the wild boy's sack of cash, rifle, and collection of tools, still provided plenty of room for Breakfast and Olive to stretch out and sleep if they wanted to.

They drove through the brilliant Tennessee morning, Breakfast scouting for some likely place to fish or hunt, his left foot propped up on the driver's seat so his chin was practically resting atop the wild boy's dirty, knobby knee.

"Me and Joe, we stayed in that smokehouse shed for a week or so, waiting for the storm to die off, just eating ham and pig meat. It wasn't like we were in any hurry to get anywhere, 'cause we didn't have nowhere to get to, anyhow. Ha! Wild! But eventually, all that meat got to poor Joe, who spent about a day and a half squatting and squirting shit in that field. Ha-ha! Poor fucker, out there in the rain, shitting all day long with a cherry cigar in his teeth. And when he got over it, and we finally decided it was time to go, I was considerably fatter, and Joe, who had nearly shit himself hollow, was gun-barrel skinny, like he always was.

"You know what I did? I took one of those hams with us. It was tied on a rope, and I just slung it over my shoulder when we headed out, and Joe told me to stay behind him, on account of he never wanted to look at a ham again for the rest of his life. Ha-ha! Wild!

"Well. Joe was like a father to me, I guess. He taught me all kinds of things, like reading and writing, what all plants we could eat, how to fish with my hands, and how to find stuff; and he told me lots about how things used to be when he was little like me, what he remembered, which wasn't much, and what his own folks told him about what things was like before the damn bugs came. But he never showed me how to drive a car, because I was too little to do it, but I watched him enough to learn. That's how you do it when you're wild, girl—you learn by watching. Wild!

"I suppose we spent until the following spring, when it was starting to get warm, just going from place to place, trying to find people anywhere we could, hiding in big buildings, taking cars. It was Joe who taught me about taking money, too. We were the richest motherfuckers in the world, Joe used to say. But there wasn't nobody anywhere—only those bugs, which we were always lucky enough or fast enough to get away from. They're not very smart, besides, but you already know that, don't you, Olive? Ha-ha!"

Olive bounced up and down.

She loved listening to Breakfast, and she loved their new big black car with the fancy bedroom in the back.

Breakfast slowed the hearse, straining to peer through an opening in the woods to the right of the roadway.

"Does that look like maybe a good spot to you, Olive?"

Olive clapped.

Breakfast nodded and scratched his balls. "Maybe."

Breakfast backed the hearse up and turned onto what had at one time been a dirt road cutting through the woods.

"And that spring, when it was starting to get warm and the bugs were coming back, that was when me and Joe met up with Sergeant Stuart's army, and they took us in at a place we called the farm."

Breakfast parked the hearse beside a small waterfall in the cool shade of a dense Tennessee forest.

"Ain't that pretty, girl? This looks like a wild spot! You know what we are, Olive? Ha-ha! I bet you do, girl! I bet you do!"

Breakfast slapped the steering wheel.

Olive bounced and bounced.

Breakfast and Olive were wild.

The African Queen

Mel said, "This dinner is great."

I agreed. "Yes. This is probably the finest macaroni and cheese I've ever eaten in my entire life."

Mel laughed. Of course, neither one of us had ever eaten macaroni and cheese before that night.

Her eyes became shiny and wet when she laughed. I watched her, and when she saw me, she looked down at her plate.

I was so in love with her, I thought I was going to burst.

You are home to me.

I said, "Did you find a movie for us to watch?"

"I did. It looks exciting."

"I'll be honest, Mel." And then I thought, *No, I won't actually be totally honest with you, because I'm afraid I might be wrong.* But I said, "Everything I've chosen to watch has . . . Well, it's scared the shit out of me."

Mel laughed again. This time she laughed so hard she nearly spat out her food. And I was embarrassed because I'd admitted that

I was frightened by goddamned Bigfoot and stupid blackbirds. But when she laughed . . . those eyes . . . And Mel put her hand on my shoulder, and I wasn't wearing a shirt, and it felt beautiful.

She pulled her hand away and wiped her mouth with a cloth napkin.

Mel said, "Well, this one doesn't look scary. It looks exciting. There's a boat in it."

I was worried the movie might be about the *Titanic*, and I'd be forced to watch that ship sinking, again and again, without end, just as I'd been watching it sink every day of my life in the hole.

"It's called *The African Queen*," she said.

"That doesn't sound scary," I said. "But, then again, you can never tell by the title, can you? What if *The African Queen* is an eighteen-foot-tall, ten-thousand-year-old beast with the face of a rattlesnake, and she bites your eyes and injects them with venom while you're sleeping, and then when you wake up, for all the days throughout the rest of your life the world appears askew, claustrophobic, and horrifying, and it's filled with monsters, like a Max Beckmann painting?"

"I'm pretty sure it's a love story, Arek. There is a man and a woman on the cover. And they have their arms around each other, and they look like they're about to kiss."

"Oh."

She did it.

I knew she would.

Now Amelie Sing Brees, who I was so in love with it was driving me insane, was going to talk about kissing.

I knew she would.

Mel said, "Is something wrong?"

I cleared my throat. "Um. No."

It was suddenly sweltering hot inside the van. I tried to will myself not to sweat or tremble in front of Mel, but will has little to do with these things when you're sixteen years old and a boy, and you're looking at someone like Mel, and you know she's about to talk to you about how you kissed her on the mouth, how you tasted her tongue, just hours earlier.

"Then why don't you say something about it?" Mel asked.

I played stupid, which was not a big stretch. "About what?"

Mel put the fork down and pivoted in her chair. Our knees touched.

She said, "About how I kissed you today."

"Oh. That."

"Yeah. That."

Everything was hot and dizzy.

And Mel said, "I think it is so cute when you turn red, Arek."

"Oh. Um. Thanks."

I pretended to be fascinated by the color of my macaroni and cheese.

I said, "I thought it was good. I thought it was . . . Well, I liked it very much."

"The macaroni and cheese?"

I decided that Amelie Sing Brees probably *did* tease me too much, but I wasn't going to tell her that.

I shook my head, felt the electricity between us, connecting and burning at our knees. It felt the same as when we used to be little, when we'd sit beside each other in the bath.

I cleared my throat. Shakily I said, "No. When you kissed me. It was good. I liked it. A lot."

I swallowed.

For some reason I was thinking about what was going to happen next—how Mel and I might attempt to navigate through the next awkward how many minutes between here and *The African Queen*, and if that movie was going to scare the shit out of me, and where Mel would be, and where I would be when we watched it, and how I would have to try to be strong and not so much as glance over at Mel when whatever man and whatever woman broke down and finally kissed each other.

But Mel said, "Why haven't you ever kissed me?"

I thought about possible answers for her.

I took a deep breath and decided on the truth.

This is how it would be.

I said, "What if I'm the wrong person for you, Mel? We are *not* Adam and Eve. There are going to be other people out here. I know that. Maybe millions of them. Someone like you . . . Well, you shouldn't just settle for me because there are no alternatives."

Mel exhaled a little puff of wind that tickled my bare chest and wordlessly told me that what I'd said angered her a little.

She said, "If there were ten million people out there, and I got to pick the one who I wanted to kiss me, it would be you, Arek."

"Really?"

I still hadn't taken my eyes from the macaroni and cheese. And I decided the color of it was a color I had never seen before, not anywhere.

Mel said, "Really."

Then I looked at her.

"Well, do you suppose we should kiss or something, then?"

Mel straightened her mouth. "You're making me mad, Arek."

"No. I mean . . . I want to kiss you so bad. It's what I've wanted to do since we were maybe eleven years old, but I was too afraid of rules, and of Wendy, and of being wrong. But I want to."

Then I put my hand on top of hers and said, "Can I kiss you, Mel?"

"Yes."

I didn't want to kiss her sitting down. I wanted to kiss her the right way.

I took her hand and pulled her away from the table.

"Here," I said. "Stand up."

We stood in the middle of the floor, at the foot of my bed with the television screen behind us.

Fuck watching a movie, I thought.

I put my hands behind Mel's neck and moved closer to her. Before I kissed her, I pressed my body into hers, and Mel slid her arms around my back. We stayed there, frozen for a few seconds, eyes open, watching each other.

And then I leaned in and put my mouth on Mel's, and I kissed her like I'd wanted to kiss her for as long as I could remember. Our tongues met and played. I combed my fingers through Mel's beautiful black hair, and she moved her hands up and down my back, and around onto my chest and belly. Then she let her hand trail along my body downward, lower, and she began rubbing me softly through those thin pajama bottoms.

Following her, I slid my hands up inside her top, cupping her breasts, and around to the small of her back, lower, slipping my trembling fingers inside the loose waist of her pajamas to feel the smooth curve of her behind, never breaking our kiss.

Mel unbuttoned her shirt—one, two, then all the buttons. She slid the thing down her arms and let it fall to the floor.

I never knew it could feel like this, so perfect, so insanely electric.

You are home to me. I don't care about houses.

And Mel pulled at the waistband of my pajamas, whispering, "Take these off."

"Are you sure?"

"Yes."

"Okay."

In a second, the universe added the most perfect moment of my life.

In a second, Mel and I were both naked, embracing, feeling each other everywhere as we stood, ready to fall, ready to fall, in the middle of the floor of our little lifeboat.

In another second, something began scratching outside.

In that second, something was violently trying to force open the side door.

Larger and larger grew the universe.

The Emperor of Bullshit

Then came the urgent banging on the door.

Knock knock knock knock knock knock knock!

Seven times. I don't know why I counted them.

Mel gasped. "What—"

Knock knock knock knock knock!

Now five times.

"Hello! Is someone in there?"

Knock knock knock knock knock knock knock!

"Hello! I can see your light! Is someone in there?"

There was a person.

I did not want it to be like this. I was not ready to encounter humanity. I selfishly wanted to keep our lifeboat adrift, shoreless, away from anyone else who might be struggling against the wild sea.

There was a person.

It was a man.

I whispered, "Oh my God, Mel!"

We scrambled to pull on our clothes. All I could hear was our urgent breathing, the rustling of our garments, the pounding of my heart. This was something I had never for a moment considered. Of all the possibilities—wolves, Bigfoot, birds—I did not imagine anyone else would ever come to us, assuming, instead, that we would be the discoverers.

"Hello!" The man's voice sounded panicked, maybe angry.

I grabbed the .45 from our pack and put it into Mel's hand, with my lips pressed into her ear, whispering, "You need to hide in the bathroom."

"No."

"Mel. Do it."

I pushed her toward the bathroom and shut her inside, all the while the man in the dark persisted with knocking and calling.

Then I picked up our .22 rifle and switched off the interior lights.

I said, "Who are you?"

And I thought, *I am talking to somebody else.*

Through the door came the man's voice. "I mean you no harm. I'm a friend. Trust me, a friend. I'm a soldier. I represent the governmental authority of the United States of America."

I thought he may as well be representing the Emperor of Bullshit, for all that mattered.

"What do you want from me?"

"I'm alone. I haven't seen another human in two years. Please, just let me see you. Let me talk to you. If I could just see someone else, a human face—"

I didn't know what to do, what I was expected to do. We had traveled all this distance and time, and now that I was faced with the prospect of confronting another real human being, I wasn't sure I wanted to.

I said, "I have a rifle. Go away."

"Please!"

I wished Mel would tell me what to do. I wished this soldier who represented the governmental authority of the United States of America and all the bullshit in the universe would go the hell away and leave us alone, leave us where we were.

The man repeated, "Please. I mean you no harm. Please."

Beside the door was a switch that activated the outside floodlights on the van. I flipped it on. The lights made it like daytime all around our camp.

I said, "Move back ten feet, and I will open the door."

"All right."

"I have a rifle."

"You said that."

"Are you armed?"

The man didn't answer.

He had to have a weapon. Nobody could survive out there alone for years—as he claimed—without some type of weapon. I waited. The silence of the next few seconds told me that whoever was out there was armed; he just didn't know what to say. And now maybe my question had escalated this standoff into something I was not prepared to deal with.

I cupped my hand at the edge of the blinds on the window above Mel's bed and peeked outside.

I saw him.

In the white-hot light cast out from the roofline on the van, he appeared, standing about ten feet away from my door. He was old, maybe nearly as old as Wendy, my grandmother, a soldier in her own right. The man was stocky and had a grizzly-white beard and gray hair that curled around his ears and over his collar. And he wore a cap and uniform—camouflage, like my pajamas, only monochromatic, dusty gray colors, and I thought, *Camouflage clearly doesn't work*. The uniform was a type of jumpsuit—like what we used to be expected to always wear in the hole, but I rarely would—that came all the way up to the man's neck. On one side of his chest there was a cloth strip that said U.S. ARMY, and on the other side, in the same black capital letters, STUART. The only real color on the dusty gray man came from the brilliant United States flags he wore on both of his upper arms. In the center of his chest was a little emblem that looked like this:

And both of his hands rested atop a rifle that was slung across his belly.

So I said, "I'm not going to open the door unless you put your rifle down. Put it over there, behind you, on the bank of the river."

The man—Stuart—glanced behind him, then looked back at the van.

He said, "Fair enough."

I watched as he went to the limit of the floodlights' border and then took a few steps down the bank at the edge of the river in Davy Crockett Campground, which had already proven to be not nearly as fun as the entry signs had promised. Stuart unslung the gun and placed it down in the grass by the river; then, with his hands out, showing he wasn't hiding anything, he carefully walked back into the light near the van.

I opened the door just enough so that Stuart could see the barrel of my rifle. Then I said, "I'm putting mine down too."

I walked over and slid the .22 under the covers on my bed, then stood in the open doorway so we could both see each other. And we just stayed there like that, staring, Stuart with his hands out and me, bare chested in pajama bottoms, saying nothing, for at least a minute.

And I have to say it was an amazing thing to see somebody else who was not a painting or a photograph. The feeling must have been like what humans felt when landing on an island that nobody knew existed, or walking on the moon for the first time.

Finally, Stuart smiled at me and nodded. It was difficult to read, because I had only seen a few other people smile in my entire life.

He said, "Oh my God. I can't believe I found you."

"I wasn't lost."

"Can I come closer?"

"Okay."

Carefully, deliberately, Stuart began to close the distance between us. He stopped about four feet away from the van's doorway and then extended his hand. Although I had never really shaken anyone's hand before—there was no need for it in the hole—I knew what the gesture was supposed to mean.

I took one step down onto the little metal rail beneath the threshold and put my hand in his.

It was the strangest and most frightening touch I'd ever experienced.

I said, "I've not even seen ten other people in my entire life."

"I guess you were born lucky."

"That's what my dad calls me."

"I'm Sergeant Stuart," he said.

"I already saw your name."

"You can read?"

I nodded.

He said, "What are you, thirteen? Fourteen?"

I let go of his hand. "Sixteen."

"Shit. Sixteen years ago, that was when all the shit came down. You really *are* lucky. What's your name?"

"Arek Szczerba," I said.

"Well, then, Arek Szczerba, would it be okay if I came inside?"

I instinctively jerked my head around as though I needed to see what was behind me, if Mel was still hiding.

"I—uh—"

I was definitely not prepared for any kind of civility. Sergeant Stuart could clearly see his request had confused and frightened me. But was it possible to just be out here, adrift like we were, and then simply turn away from another human being?

"I'm not going to hurt you, Arek."

A before-the-hole boy would know what to do, without being indecisive. Before-the-hole boys were probably given lessons in school about what rules applied when a soldier came to your home in the middle of the night and asked to be allowed inside.

A before-the-hole boy would likely have no problem watching a stranger drown.

My heart beat so hard, I felt like I was going to vomit all over Sergeant Stuart's goddamned useless camouflage jumpsuit, and I was pretty sure he could see it.

Then he said, "It's okay. I can see you're scared. I'll go away."

"Uh—"

Sergeant Stuart gave me a kind of apologetic shrug and said, "You wouldn't by any chance happen to have anything to eat, would you? I haven't really had any food in a few days."

I looked back again.

Was he lying? Do people tell lies to get what they want, to trick you?

"Oh. Uh. I could give you something to eat," I said. "Wait here."

And just as I backed my way through the door, Sergeant Stuart smiled broadly and said, "Thank you so much, boy!"

Then he put his boot up on the doorstep and, representing the emperor of bullshit, Sergeant Stuart let himself inside the van. He patted my naked chest and said, "Oh my God, thank you!"

Sergeant Stuart came in and shut the door behind him.

This was worse than the rattlesnake. Because now the snake had come in, presumably welcomed by its victim. I was so frightened I thought I would faint. I steadied myself by holding on to the chair I'd just been sitting in minutes before, thinking, *Why the hell did I choose this place? Why the fuck did Sergeant Stuart have to be here at this moment, in this exact spot, when right now Mel and I should be—*

Mel.

I swallowed, hard. "Mac. Macaroni and cheese," I said.

I grabbed the pot from the stove and poured some of the indefinably colored stuff onto the plate I'd been eating from. There were two plates here, two forks, two napkins. Sergeant Stuart saw them. He looked from Mel's plate to me without saying anything.

Damn our lack of rules. Wendy would have had us clear the table and wash the dishes before we would ever have been allowed to put our tongues in each other's mouths and strip out of our clothing.

"Here." I pushed the plate and my own dirty fork into

Sergeant Stuart's hands and then stupidly slid Mel's plate into the little steel sink, which was just about as effective in making it go away as if I'd covered it with a goddamned camouflaged napkin.

Sergeant Stuart scooped a bite into his mouth. I don't know why I instinctively found him repulsive, like he was violating me, bringing some kind of filth inside what was supposed to be my home with Mel.

Just us.

He chewed and nodded. "This is delicious."

Then Sergeant Stuart's eyes widened as he glanced around and took in the interior of our little hole.

"Man! This is a nice rig! Where'd you get it?"

"I—Iowa. I took it, when I left home."

Sergeant Stuart clinked my fork into the plate. Then he scraped it. I heard the metal tines jangle against his teeth. All the sounds were so nauseating.

He said, "Can I sit down?"

I looked at the chair. I looked at Sergeant Stuart. Some of the macaroni and cheese was stuck in his beard. I never wanted to eat that shit again. I wanted to throw out that plate and fork, too.

He smelled awful.

I said, "Okay."

So Sergeant Stuart sat down, and I sat on my bed with my hand resting on the butt of my rifle, hidden beneath the covers.

Scrape. Clink. Swallow. Grunt.

Stuart cleaned the plate and put it down on the table. He burped.

"That was so good. Thank you again, boy."

He knows my name. Why does he have to call me boy?

"You're welcome."

Maybe he'll leave now.

"You cook like that for yourself every day?"

"When I'm hungry."

"You look like you could stand to eat more now and then, ha-ha!"

Ha-ha. Fuck you.

"Ha-ha," I said.

Then Sergeant Stuart put his hands flat on his knees and leaned toward me. He pointed at Mel's plate in the sink. "But there's someone else here with you. Where's the other guy you're traveling with?"

I took a breath.

"Oh. Um."

"Is it just another little boy? It is, isn't it? You don't need to be scared of me. The army could use boys like you. Survivors. Heck, you're already half dressed for it, with your little camo jammies there, ha-ha!"

"I'm. Um. No, Sergeant Stuart. No." I shook my head.

I wished he would leave.

"Where's the other boy hiding? Is it your dad? No, a grown-up wouldn't leave you to be in charge of dealing with visitors, with representatives of the governmental authority of the United States of America. It's gotta be another little boy. I know these things. One time, I had this little guy in my unit who was completely wild, ran around naked constantly. Refused to wear clothes. For whatever reasons, the little boy was named Breakfast. Tough as nails. He would have been a good soldier. So, where's your buddy at? You boys aren't faggots, are you?"

I'd never heard the word before in my life. But I could tell by the tone of Sergeant Stuart's voice that "faggots" were his enemies.

"No," I said.

"Well, you don't have to be afraid of me, unless maybe if you *are* faggots. Or fucking anarchists. Tell him to come out, so I can see him."

"I—I don't know what that is. Faggots," I said.

"It's boys who diddle with other boys. Haven't you ever heard of faggots?" Sergeant Stuart asked.

"Not until just now."

"Well, I'm not saying you're a faggot, but call your little buddy out. Let's have a look at him."

I couldn't expect Mel to stay in the bathroom forever. Maybe if she came out, and this stupid fucker saw the .45 in her hand, maybe we could get him out of our life and drive away, abandoning him to the elements. I fed him. I let him in. What else could he want from us?

"Mel!" I said.

Sergeant Stuart gave me an approving look. He said, "That's a good boy. You'll see. We're going to be friends."

"Mel?" I spoke to the closed bathroom door. "It's okay, I guess. Come out and meet Sergeant Stuart, and show him how we are not faggots."

Stuart grinned and nodded.

But Mel did not come out of the bathroom.

"Mel?"

I stood and went to the door, listening to see if Mel was on the other side. She had to have heard everything that was going on out here. She had to know what to do. After all, Mel was smarter and braver than I ever was.

Please come out and force this motherfucker out of our home, Mel.

When I opened the door, the bathroom was empty.

Mel was gone.

Part Three

After the Hole

Self-Portrait with Shoreless Man

In 1915, before he could return to painting, Max Beckmann said this: *Whatever would we poor humans do if we did not create some such idea as nation, love, art with which to cover the black hole a little from time to time? This boundless forsaken eternity.*

Like Melville's notion that truth in its highest form is only discernible in landlessness, Beckmann's truth, his boundless eternity, his black hole, presents itself on canvas through the lens of his isolation and loneliness.

This was our life in the hole.

My father sought to construct truth with an assembly of artifacts stolen from the shoreless seas above us and cover our hole a little, from time to time, in trickery.

This is me.

If I could travel back in time and create self-portraits that attempt to strip away the artifice of model, as Beckmann did, mine would appear in two distinct categories: Arek Andrzej Szczerba in the Hole, and Arek Andrzej Szczerba After the Hole.

One of my in-the-hole self-portraits would have been *Self-portrait with Shoreless Man*.

"I can hear the voice of God," Wendy said to me.

My father once told me that when he was alive, Johnny, who had been Wendy's husband, could hear the voice of an actor named James Arness coming from the nonfunctioning old televisions in the hole, so I was not surprised that Wendy could hear God.

I wished I could hear someone who was not there; anyone would be fine.

It's hard to imagine an entire world with only eight voices in it.

"What does he sound like?" I asked.

I was twelve years old. It was Sunday, and Wendy had ordered me out of bed so I could attend church with her. It wasn't like there was an actual show—or whatever they did—going on; it was just Wendy and me, sitting on a cold oak pew and looking at a wood-paneled wall with an empty cross on it that looked like it was made of maple wood. The cross may have been considered Danish Contemporary, which is something I learned about in an art-and-architecture book from our library.

Wendy had fought with me that morning because I refused to put on clothes to come to church with her. My fathers, mother, nobody in the hole, would ever intervene whenever Wendy fought with someone, which was almost always me.

Around the age of twelve, and this may have been entirely in reaction to all the new rules and the forced segregation between the one boy and the solitary girl in the hole, I as much as possible resisted wearing the Eden Project jumpsuit that was the official uniform of the hole.

Although I could not articulate it at the time, this was the beginning of what would become an overwhelming urge on my part to run away from the hole, which, my father explained, was something all boys eventually were driven to do.

One thing I had going for me was endurance.

In the end, Wendy recognized that the only way she was going to get me to go to church with her before Monday came around was to take me in my underwear. So I sat beside her on that pew while she stared at the Danish Contemporary cross and rested her hands on a worn black Gideon's Bible in her lap. And I had absolutely nothing on save for some red-and-white boxer briefs with images of a muscular superhero on them. I was very thin at twelve years because during that year I grew about three inches taller, and all my contents stretched out like bread dough.

The muscular superhero on my boxer briefs wore a skintight blue suit with red briefs on the outside and a red cape. He could fly. He also had a big red *S* inside a yellow diamond in the center of his chest.

While Wendy stared at the cross and the Bible, I looked at the guy on my underwear. I decided that his *S* stood for "shoreless."

Shoreless Man was doomed to fly forever, without ever contacting the ground. As a consequence of this curse, Shoreless Man could always observe the truth but could never touch it— kind of like spending your entire life in a hole. Shoreless Man only needed to find the key that would allow him to be free of the curse of landlessness, so that he might peel himself right off my boxer briefs, fly up to the maple Danish Contemporary cross, and turn himself into Sacrificial Man.

I folded my arms over my chest. "Well? What *does* God's voice sound like, Grandma?"

"It's not a *sound*; it's more of a message that I can feel inside my brain, like a vibration, that only I can understand," Wendy said.

"A message about what?"

"Among other things, he tells me you're a heathen for coming to church in your underwear."

I felt bad about God telling Wendy I was a heathen for coming to church in my Shoreless Man boxer briefs and was afraid Wendy was going to bring up the *among other things* she'd hinted at, which, of course, she did.

Wendy, my grandmother, asked me if I knew what masturbation was.

I told her yes.

"Do you masturbate, Arek?" Wendy asked me.

I thought about all the possible ways I might answer her question. Lying was not something I ever did. In fact, I believe I didn't even know *how* to tell a lie. And I had talked to my fathers about masturbation too, so it wasn't something that, at that point in my life, caused me to feel the kind of inhibition that perhaps a before-the-hole boy might have felt. But I also didn't want to tell Wendy how often I masturbated, because I didn't want to make her madder than she already seemed to be.

So I said, "Sometimes," which could have meant any level of frequency.

"Do you know what God does to boys who masturbate?" Wendy said.

He probably makes them go to church in their underwear, I thought.

"No."

"This is what happens. There was a man in the Bible who did not do what God told him to do. His name was Onan. Onan did something he was not supposed to do with his penis, and, as a result, Onan's semen went on the ground. You know how that happens, right?"

I nodded. I was terrified, because knowing Wendy's Bible stories told me this was not going to end well for the guy whose semen ended up on the ground.

Wendy paused and swallowed; then she bent forward and looked directly into my eyes. "So, do you know what God did to Onan? God killed him."

For just a moment I was relieved that apparently "underground" did not count for God as far as applying the on-the-ground rule about killing a boy for masturbating was concerned.

I said, "Oh."

"That's a true story. It's right here in the Bible."

All stories are true.

"Oh."

"Even Jesus told his followers that if they masturbated with their right hand, they should cut it off, so their right hand wouldn't make them masturbate anymore."

All these amputated body parts, without end.

Wendy patted my knee with her icy hand. "And God also tells me that we need to stay here in Eden, and pray, and wait to be delivered by him, and that you should be baptized in the big sink, as a symbol of our covenant with him, for sparing us." She added, "That's what God says to me."

"Through vibrations," I said.

"Yes," Wendy confirmed.

Then she told me, again, the story of a boy named Ishmael, and about how God had directed the boy's father to circumcise Ishmael on his thirteenth birthday; and after that all boys had to be circumcised so God would be able to sort out good guys from bad guys, like all the boys in her family, who were good, so this was something we all needed to prepare for, since my thirteenth birthday was approaching, and Wendy's brain had been vibrating again, and she wanted me to be brave and show God I was good and thank him for saving us and looking out for us the way he did, and wait to be delivered. Unfortunately, now my brain was vibrating too, but it was not vibrating with what my grandmother's brain had said.

My brain vibrated this to me: *Wendy is fucking crazy.*

But there was never a moment when she had not been crazy for my entire life, so I didn't really have a before-the-hole Wendy to compare this bloodthirsty penis-mutilating one to.

Also, as I sat there, I mathematically calculated the number of days to my thirteenth birthday, because I knew Wendy, our Ahab of the hole, had this serious attachment to ideas and would not easily let them go.

I pointed out, "There's no need to sort out the good guys from the bad guys down here, Grandma, because nobody here is bad."

"I'll tell you what—and it happens time and time again in the Bible, Arek—terrible things happen to people who ignore the vibration in their brain."

I was definitely *not* ignoring the vibration in my brain.

I kept my eyes on Shoreless Man. I traced an index finger around a picture of him flying with one arm outstretched, his red cape billowing behind him.

I said, "But what if the vibration is wrong?"

Toward *Little Grace*

In a deep, clear pool where the river eddied in a slow, counter-clockwise churn at a place in the bank that looked like it had been scooped out in a near-perfect circle, Breakfast caught five bluegills with his wild bare hands. He'd tossed them up onto the shore while Olive jumped up and down in excitement.

Olive was happy.

Olive didn't need anyone else other than Breakfast, and Breakfast was happiest just being with Olive.

Breakfast said, "Days like this are what we live for, girl."

Olive stroked Breakfast's chest. They had finished eating a dinner of grilled bluegill with a chicory and dandelion salad, and were stretched out on the ground, sleepy and full, in the sunlight beside their fire.

Breakfast yawned and scratched his balls, then bent his legs and crossed one foot over his knee as he stared up into the cloudless sky, a twig of chicory pinched between his lips.

"Me and Joe, we stayed on the farm with Sergeant Stuart and his army for a while, I guess, until I was ten years old. In that time, Joe had gone from being a rail-thin boy into a full-grown man with hair on his face and everything. Man! I sure hope I never get hair on my face, Olive. It looks like a curse.

"I was the only one there who wasn't all grown-up, so the others looked after me like I was some kind of special creature, like I was their own child, but of course I wasn't. And that's because I'm wild, Olive. Wild. And I don't belong to nobody, and didn't come from nobody, neither—just like you, girl. The others was four men, counting Joe and Sergeant Stuart, and two women, who were not like the sister ladies from the church since they didn't whisper and sneak. And they all dressed in the same outfits with badges and flags on their chests and arms. Even Joe dressed like an army man and followed orders from the sergeant, always saying 'yes, sir' or 'no, sir' as we moved from place to place, representing what Sergeant Stuart said was the governmental authority of the United States of America, whatever that meant, and how it was us who was in charge of everything.

"Ha! How could anyone claim to be in charge of a place with ten-foot-tall bugs that eat you whole? 'I'm in charge now.' Ha-ha! Have you ever heard such a thing, Olive?"

Of course, Olive had heard such a thing, because Breakfast had told her about it at least a hundred times before.

"Sergeant Stuart even tried to get me to put on some army

clothes and be a soldier with them all, but I wasn't having it. Only in winters when the snow was deep on the ground would I choose to put on anything, and even then it was never army gear, but you already know that about me, don't you?

"The last place on the farm we stayed in was a cellar under an old dairy barn. The dumb motherfuckers already burned down the house and a second building with sleeping quarters too. We kept cows and chickens and always had plenty to eat, but in the following summer, after Joe and I came to the farm, when the weather got warm, well, you know what happened is those bugs would come back, and the army would try to fight them and represent the governmental authority of the United States of America on 'em. Usually they'd set fires to whatever house or building we happened to be hiding in. The bugmen don't like water, but they like fire even less, but I still thought it was dumb to set fire to our own homes, although it wasn't ever my call since I wouldn't put on no clothes with flags on my arms. I don't know what happened to all those monsters by now, though. Maybe they're all starved to death on account of there not being any more people to eat. Who knows? What do you think, girl? Why do you think we ain't seen but a handful of 'em all year long?"

Olive didn't know why they hadn't seen many of the creatures.

Breakfast picked his nose and farted.

Olive tracked her fingers through the wild boy's dreadlocks, looking for ticks and fleas.

"Well, the worst day came during summer that year I was with Joe and the army on the farm. That was the day the place was just covered with those bugs—maybe two hundred of 'em—and everyone tried to hide or escape, but as far as I know, nobody did except for me, and that was only because I jumped into the creek and made a swim for it. Wild!

"I was terribly lonely, and so sorry for Joe and the others, but mostly for Joe, because he had been my only family that I ever knew, and I liked him, despite his attraction to drinking vodka and his always sneaking off alone and playing with himself whenever he found his books with naked people in them. For someone who wore clothes as much as Joe did, he sure did have an attraction to naked people. Joe was wild. Wild and good.

"I miss Joe. I miss ham, too." Then Breakfast scratched his balls and said, "You know what I *don't* miss?"

Olive shook her head and smiled. She knew Breakfast was about to say something really, really good.

"Rebel Land, getting shit on, and Edsel and Mimi. That's what I don't miss. Ha-ha!"

Olive, who had nearly been lulled to sleep by Breakfast's lovely voice, suddenly shot her head up from the boy's chest, nostrils flared. Olive sniffed the air. Her eyes widened.

She saw something out on the river.

Northwest of their little beach—upstream, where the wide river's banks were swallowed beneath an umbrella of overhanging trees—a long blue canal boat drifted lazily into view. Breakfast and Olive had seen boats before, but they were usually small and half-sunk, or massive and completely sunk, like the triple-decker boat with the wheel on its tail end that sat on the bottom mud in the river next to its moorings in St. Louis.

This was different.

The canal boat, narrow and flat topped, appeared to have been well maintained, as though someone may have been living on it. Breakfast's first thought was that there could be people on board, and he did not want to run into anyone like Edsel and Mimi ever again. But the way the stern of the boat swung out in the current also made him think that the thing had simply gotten loose—run away from home, wherever that may have been.

"Hoo-wee, Olive! What do you think about that, girl?"

Olive bounced and waved at the boat, which was spinning in the current, its bow caught up in the low overhang of a hemlock tree.

The boat was called *Little Grace* and was more than thirty feet long. In the front was an open deck area backed by a cabin with double glass doors and unbroken windows all down each side. Unbroken windows were not that common in Breakfast's experience, especially on something so obviously fragile as a canal boat. *Little Grace* had an open deck on top of the cabin with a rail surrounding it and another open area at the back of the boat, where Breakfast saw the ship's wheel and a tiller post. Along the side facing Breakfast and Olive hung two yellow plastic boat fenders.

He didn't know much at all about boats—he'd never even been on one—but Breakfast figured a boat couldn't be more difficult to operate than a shit-pumper truck.

Breakfast scratched his knotted dreadlocks and shaded his eyes with his right hand.

"I'm half-tempted to see what's on that boat," he said.

Olive jumped and clapped, granting her approval.

Breakfast took a few tentative steps toward the river.

He said, "I'm thinking as hard as I can, but I can't come up with no reason a person might fill up a boat with shit."

Olive waved her hands and nodded. She could not think of a reason to fill up a boat with someone else's shit either.

The wild boy waded out to where the water was past his knees.

Breakfast said, "It better not be filled with shit, Olive."

Olive clapped and grinned.

Breakfast scratched his balls and farted. Then he dove into the river, swimming wildly across the current, upstream toward *Little Grace*.

This Is Even Better Than I Thought

Sergeant Stuart looked over my shoulder into our empty bathroom. He stood so close to me his chest pressed against my naked back.

He put a hand on my shoulder. Sergeant Stuart breathed on my neck. I wanted him to go away.

"You have a shitter in here? And a shower, too?" Sergeant Stuart said.

"We. Um. We don't use the toilet part. Only the shower."

"Damn. Is the water hot? Do you think I could take a shower here tonight?" Sergeant Stuart said.

Disgusted, and worried for Mel, I pushed the door shut and tried to squirm around Sergeant Stuart, who was blocking me against the bathroom. He smelled like he had pissed himself.

"So then, where's this buddy of yours?"

I shook my head. "I don't know."

"There's no reason for him to be hiding. We're in this together. We're all friends here. Maybe we should look for him," Sergeant Stuart said.

I did not want to explain to the sergeant that Mel was neither my "buddy" nor was she a "little boy." And I definitely did not want to go searching for her with Sergeant Stuart. All I could think was that Mel must have slipped out the front driver's door while I was talking to Sergeant Stuart outside the van. She had to know what she was doing; Mel was brave like that. And I wanted Sergeant Stuart to decide on his own to leave, but I had the feeling he had already planned to move in to our hole and share our lifeboat with us, no matter what anyone else thought about the idea.

"I don't think we need to look for him," I said.

Stuart moved out of the way and turned toward the front of the van.

He said, "Let's start this thing up and see how she runs. I could help with the driving."

"No! Wait!"

But I couldn't stop him. Sergeant Stuart peered down into

the little washer-dryer below the sink where the clothes Mel and I had worn that day were tumbling around.

"Heh. Is it you boys' laundry day?"

Sergeant Stuart slid into the driver's seat and felt around on the dashboard for the starter.

After a few moments, Stuart sighed, pivoted the seat around, and came back to where I was standing.

"Looks like your little buddy took off with the key, too," he said.

Of course *my little buddy* would do something like that, I thought. My *little buddy* was smarter than Sergeant Stuart and I were.

Sergeant Stuart said, "I guess you wouldn't have made it so long by not being smart like that. Yeah. You boys are good soldier material. We—the United States of America—could use boys like you."

Sergeant Stuart was a delusional idiot.

I pictured myself in the library of the hole, staring at the painting of the sinking ship, the sea, the lifeboats and bodies tossed in the roiling, icy water; imagined rescuing a survivor who proceeded to claim my lifeboat as his own and then ordered me to jump out and swim.

Sergeant Stuart swung one of the dining chairs around. He told me to sit down, that we'd wait for the *other boy* to get tired of hiding outside, alone in the dark. I was defeated. Then Sergeant Stuart put his hand under my chin and squeezed my jaw. He lifted my face so that he could look directly into my eyes.

"Don't fuck with me." He repeated, "Don't fuck with me, boy. Do the right thing by your fellow man. Right? We're in this together now. And it's time for you to suck it up and be a man. We are all going to be friends. Together. It's up to us. If you haven't figured that out by now, it's up to us, and this is our only chance for survival. We need to band together."

Then he let go of my face, and I said nothing, but I did not look away from him either. I could feel where the calloused tips of his dirty fingers had burned into my skin.

One way or another, he was going to have to get out and swim—or drown—on his own.

Sergeant Stuart picked up the pot of macaroni and cheese from the stove and ate out of it with the fork I'd given him. When he was finished, he even took Mel's half-eaten plate from the sink and ate that, too. He burped loudly and said, "I'd really like to take a shower. The problem is what to do with you. You and the other boy wouldn't do anything dangerous if I took a shower, would you?"

I was finished talking to Sergeant Stuart.

I bit the inside of my cheek and folded my arms across my chest.

Sergeant Stuart began searching the van, pulling open drawers and cupboards, dumping out towels, socks, underwear—all our clothes—looking for what, I had no idea. Maybe he was thinking of restraining me somehow, or looking for the starter fob for the van. Maybe he thought *my buddy* was small enough to hide in a cupboard. But at least he didn't notice there were girls' clothes mixed in with mine. Or if he did notice it, his reaction didn't show it.

Sergeant Stuart finally stopped when he opened the cupboard just above my head.

He said, "Whiskey. You boys like to drink whiskey together?"

Stuart waved the bottle in front of my face, tilting it, so he could see how much had been taken from the bottle. Not much.

He put the whiskey on the counter in front of me. I tried not to look at him. I heard the clinking of cups, and then Sergeant Stuart put two coffee mugs beside the bottle of whiskey and sat down next to me, so close that our legs touched.

"This is what we do in the army, boy. It will make us better friends."

Without saying anything, Sergeant Stuart uncapped the bottle and poured whiskey into both cups. Then he spun one around so its handle pointed to me.

"Have a drink, soldier."

I grimaced. "I . . . I don't really drink this stuff, Sergeant Stuart."

"Bullshit. Somebody does. Maybe it's just your little buddy who's been hitting on this? Ha-ha!"

Stuart lifted his cup and took a swallow.

Then he said, "Drink."

I took a sip. It burned inside my nose, but at least it covered the smell coming from Sergeant Stuart's clothes.

Sergeant Stuart emptied his cup and refilled it. He poured more into mine, too.

In ten minutes, we were drunk.

"Drunk" for Sergeant Stuart meant be became a little more emotional and loud, a little more dangerous and stupid.

"Drunk" for me meant the van was spinning, and I was about

to fall out of my chair. I also needed to pee and was extremely stupid.

"What the hell is that?" Sergeant Stuart pointed at the paintball rifle standing in the corner near my bed.

"A paintball gun," I said.

"I know that. I know what paintball guns are, boy. Why do you have a paintball gun?"

I said, "Um. We like to play. Me. And my *little buddy*."

Sergeant Stuart squinted, like he was trying to filter what I'd said, to somehow determine if I was fucking with him or not. He looked back and forth, alternating between the paintball gun and me. Then he got this look of understanding that seemed to say, *Yeah, I bet these two little faggots like to chase each other around and play paintball.*

Sergeant Stuart took another gulp, then nodded his chin at me so I'd at least pretend to take a sip too.

Knock, knock, knock.

The knocking on the door—the second time in all of eternity someone had knocked on the door of our van—came soft and unthreatening. I knew it had to be Mel.

Sergeant Stuart nearly jumped out of his clothes. He jerked his arm across the table, knocking over his cup of whiskey and spilling it onto my lap.

From outside, Mel called, "Arek? Arek? I'm back. Let me in."

I was simultaneously relieved and terrified.

Sergeant Stuart grinned widely and said, "I knew the little feller wouldn't want to stay out there alone for long."

I felt a little sick when Sergeant Stuart got up and went to the door.

He pushed the door open, and then stood there for a moment, staring down at Mel. Then he looked at me. His eyes were dead.

Sergeant Stuart turned back to Mel, smiled, and said, "Well, I'll be. So you're not faggots after all. And aren't you just about the prettiest little Asian girl I ever saw? Come in! Come in! This is even better than I thought!"

The Lifeboat

Sergeant Stuart had no immediate plans to leave Mel and me alone.

He drank whiskey at the small table beside me and stared, unblinking, at Mel, who sat on my bed. The sergeant kept mentioning that he wanted to take a shower, and he even talked about where he would sleep. It was like we were trapped in the Max Beckmann painting *The Night*, and Mel and I could do nothing more than helplessly observe whatever our intruder chose to do to us.

I watched her, too, trying to see if there was any clue Mel tried to give me about where she'd put the pistol, or if she had a plan, but I was too drunk and too confused to figure out anything.

"So, what are you two?" Sergeant Stuart said, waving an index finger between Mel and me, as though it would serve as some sort of divining rod to help him determine the nature of our relationship.

Mel answered, "I don't know what you mean. We came from

a place in Iowa. We got tired of living in a hole, and we wanted to look for his fathers, so we left. That was over a month ago."

Sergeant Stuart smirked.

"Fathers?" Sergeant Stuart asked.

I felt my stomach turn. My dads had told me about how before-the-hole people—men, especially—often disapproved of boys loving boys, or girls loving girls, although they had never told me the kinds of names people like Sergeant Stuart used to describe those commitments.

"I have two fathers," I said.

"Ha! I knew it! I thought you looked like a faggot the first time I saw you," Sergeant Stuart said. He grinned and slapped his knee, proud of himself for figuring out at first glance that I was a faggot.

I looked at Mel, shrugged, and shook my head.

"If you say so," I said.

Sergeant Stuart took his cap off and combed his fingers through his long greasy hair. Shakily he poured himself more whiskey. Sergeant Stuart was confused.

"So, you two—" Sergeant Stuart squinted again, his way of trying to figure out the absolute truth, of receiving the pure data. He asked me, "So you never stuck your dick in her?"

I didn't answer. I said, "I really need to pee. I'm going out."

"Wait, wait, wait," Sergeant Stuart said, waving his arms like he was trying to extinguish invisible flames. Then he turned to Mel and slurred, "It must be pretty sad for you, being out here all alone like this with a faggot."

Mel said, "I don't know what that is."

Sergeant Stuart shook his head. "What's wrong with you people? How could you live this long and not know about faggots? Hasn't anyone taught you anything about right and wrong? About the destruction of our society? About the way the world *is*? A *faggot*. An un-American abomination-of-God faggot. That's a sick motherfucker who only gets hard-ons for other boys."

Mel raised her eyebrows and looked at me. Her eyes were wet. I thought she was almost smiling.

"Arek's not a faggot," she said.

I stood up, and all the blood rushed down from my head. It was like I'd dumped out a full bucket of all my contents onto my feet. I nearly tumbled into Sergeant Stuart. "I need to pee."

I went to the door, fumbled with the safety latch on it, and fell down the steps.

Sergeant Stuart said, "Wait! You can't go out there. Get back in here!"

Sergeant Stuart attempted to stand, then sat back down. Then he pushed himself up again.

By that time, Mel was already in the doorway.

I was on my hands and knees, in the grass at Davy Crockett Campground.

Mel said, "I'll keep an eye on him. It's okay."

"But he's a faggot," Sergeant Stuart, who was not very clever, pointed out.

Mel stepped down and slid her hand under my arm to help me up.

"Are you okay?" she whispered.

I didn't know if I was okay, but I did know how shitty I felt for putting us in this situation. "I'm sorry, Mel. He made me drink."

The knees of my pajama bottoms had holes in them.

Mel said, "It's okay. We'll be okay."

Then she kissed me on the mouth.

Mel guided me along toward the front of the van just as Sergeant Stuart appeared in the open doorway, watching us.

I stumbled forward and peed on the post that held up the Davy Crockett Campground sign, the one that promised all sorts of camping, hiking, boating, swimming, and fishing fun—all with multiple exclamation points, just like the *Last Dance of the Year!* posters at Henry A. Wallace Middle School. And as I peed on the sign, I thought, *Fuck Davy Crockett Campground, and fuck the stupid decision that brought us here. Fuck Sergeant Stuart. Rattlesnakes and monsters are better than Sergeant Stuart.*

I heard the heavy thuds of his boots as Sergeant Stuart stepped down from the trailer.

Sergeant Stuart walked right up behind me, just as I pulled up the front of my pajamas. He put his hand between my shoulder blades. "Don't be afraid. We're all friends now." Then he patted me and said, "Come with me over there, boy, and let's get my gun."

Sergeant Stuart kept his hand on my back and pushed me along with him toward the river's edge. I was dimly aware of Mel following a few paces behind us, but it wasn't because I'd seen her—I could feel Mel was there, that she was looking at me, and Sergeant Stuart, too.

On the bank, Sergeant Stuart tripped in the grass and fell

into me, leaning heavily across my shoulders and nearly toppling both of us.

He laughed. "This is what soldiers do! Ha-ha! That was good whiskey, boy. And, don't worry, it doesn't bother me too much if you're a faggot. But that girl you got with you—she sure is hot. Haven't you ever even wondered—been a little bit curious—about what it would be like to have sex with her? Ha-ha!"

Sergeant Stuart was an idiot.

Also, I had never heard anyone described as "hot," unless it was in reference to the temperature, or a fever or something. But, like Sergeant Stuart's use of the word "faggot," I knew "hot" was something I never wanted to hear him say about Mel.

Finally, Sergeant Stuart took his filthy hand off my back.

He said, "Hey! I could have sworn I laid my rifle down right here."

Sergeant Stuart stamped his feet into the ground, as though making some sort of attempt to force his rifle to materialize.

I turned and glanced back at Mel. She shook her head.

Mel had done something to Sergeant Stuart's gun.

"Maybe it's down that way." I pointed farther out along the bank, nearer the edge of the water, where a low, flat dock extended out over the black surface of the river.

Sergeant Stuart almost fell down the bank. He caught his footing in the soft mud just at the river's edge.

"I don't see it. Where the fuck is my gun?"

"Do you think it could have slipped into the water?" I said.

"No." Sergeant Stuart was angry, breathing hard. "Where the fuck is my gun? See if you can feel it out there in the water."

"I—uh."

"Go on. Feel around and see if it's there."

Sergeant Stuart grabbed my upper arm and pushed me toward the river.

"Just go in a little ways. Feel with your feet."

I tried to resist, but Sergeant Stuart pushed harder. Then my feet slid out from under me in the slick mud, and Sergeant Stuart gave me a final shove forward.

I went face-first into the river. I kicked my feet down below me, but there was no bottom. I heard Mel calling my name from the bank, but there was nothing I could do except struggle to keep my head up and breathe.

"What the fuck are you doing?" Sergeant Stuart shouted at me.

I thought what I was doing was pretty obvious: I was trying not to drown in what turned out to be a very deep, and very determined, river.

The current pulled me out and around the end of the dock. I kicked and thrashed, trying to catch hold of anything I could use to keep my head up. I lost sight of where I'd gone into the river. The lights from the van disappeared behind a curtain of trees. Faintly I heard Sergeant Stuart cursing at me above my splashing and wheezing for air. I tried to kick myself toward the dock, but the river was too thick and strong.

Finally, my straining fingers caught something—an old rotting rope that came from the side of a boat, dangling from the eye of a plastic bumper that hung from the middle of the boat's hull. I grabbed the rope with both hands and tried to pull myself up out of the water, but I slipped back down.

I heard the thuds of Sergeant Stuart's boots drumming across the dock.

"What the fuck are you doing?" he said.

I pulled up again, this time trying to kick my leg over the edge of the boat's hull. My pajamas were down around my knees, so it was like I'd been tied, but I managed to hook my right foot over the gunwale near the end of the boat.

I heaved myself over the edge, then immediately dropped with a painful crash down onto the boat's deck. I coughed and spat, and then vomited a stomach full of river water and whiskey and macaroni and cheese all over the place. I was disoriented and nearly drowned.

"Is that you down in there? You didn't happen to find my gun in the water when you were out there playing around, did you? Ha-ha!" Sergeant Stuart leaned over from the dock and peered down at me on the deck of the boat. "Here, let me help you, boy. Let me help you. Just a minute, here, and I'll fix you up."

I couldn't see Sergeant Stuart, but I suspected he wasn't too concerned with helping me.

I tried to sit up, so I could pull my pajama bottoms back on. I was too dizzy and fell back down onto the deck.

Then Sergeant Stuart threw something into the boat. It landed on top of my chest—the rope that had been securing the boat to the dock. Sergeant Stuart pushed the boat away from the dock with his boot.

He said, "Have a nice journey, boy. She can't really want to be burdened with looking out for a faggot for the rest of her life, now can she? It wouldn't be fair."

The boat spun and drifted in the grasp of the wild river.

And again Sergeant Stuart said, "It wouldn't be fair."

I closed my eyes and blacked out.

On Civilization and Eggs

In the lower right foreground there is a lifeboat lifted on a wave.

The boat sits low in the water. I have counted and recounted all the people in the boat—at times there are thirty, at other times the number is twenty-eight or twenty-nine.

It is almost as though every time I look at it, the painting shows me something different about the world outside the hole. But there are two stories that always fascinate me, trapped in the image. First is the man in the ocean, barely holding his head above water while he desperately clutches an oar with both hands. I can see the strain in his grasp, can sense the cramping of his muscles, because he is only moments away from releasing his hold and succumbing to the frozen sea.

There is a woman leaning over the gunwale, talking to the man in the water. Her expression is enough to convince me she is telling him that everything is going to be good, and he should just hang on until things get better.

The second story belongs to a brown-haired woman seated in the middle of the crowded lifeboat. Her face is turned down, a deliberate effort to blind herself to the images around her— the sea, the sinking ship, the overturned lifeboats, people in the water. She has her hands pressed to her ears.

She is trying to block out the screams and cries.

All stories are true.

I think when Max Beckmann painted it, he had a premonition that he was drifting closer and closer to a hole.

I do not mean to make it sound as though for sixteen years I had never seen the sun or sky.

On the other hand, excursions outside the hole, with the exception of the rule-breaking ice-fishing trip I took with my fathers when I was thirteen, were generally tightly choreographed dances involving our special guns and wild sprinting dashes to the greenhouse, or to the chicken coop, or to pick apples and pears at the end of summer.

But every time I'd go out to help my mother, or sometimes Louis, in the greenhouse or with the chickens, there was always this unexplainable pall of fear that made me feel that I was entering an environment that stubbornly refused to offer any protections.

This was a natural thing for after-the-hole children like me and Mel to conclude, because there was never a day—and hardly a moment in our lives—when someone else, one of our before-the-hole shipmates, did not reaffirm the horrors and dangers of the world above us, without end.

Why would anyone ever want to leave the hole?

Although I could not answer this question, I was lured by the temptation of freedom and escape, by the earthy smell of the damp ground on a sunny and cold autumn morning, to do that thing that boys have forever been driven to do—to go away.

Every day, Louis and one of *the boys* would go up to the surface to gather the eggs from our henhouse. Robby or Dad would stand guard, and Louis would tend to the chickens. Occasionally I would be allowed to help Louis. This started about the time when I was nine years old.

And every time I'd go with Louis to pick up eggs and feed the chickens, he would recite a rhyme to me.

> *Higgledy piggledy my black hen,*
> *She lays eggs for gentlemen.*
> *Sometimes nine and sometimes ten,*
> *Higgledy piggledy my black hen.*

It became an entirely predictable thing, and Louis was a man of few words.

He learned the black hen nursery rhyme in his English class, after he came to America. I don't think he ever stopped to consider what the words meant; as far as I could tell, Louis probably assumed "higgledy" and "piggledy" were real words—models that re-presented something from reality. And who would be able to tell him otherwise?

We had a black hen. She was big and mean, especially when sitting on her nest. I was afraid of her. On one of the first days I was allowed to help Louis with the chickens, he showed me how to use a small hand cultivator to rake out the nests.

But when I ran the tines through the hay, I disturbed a small nest of mice. They ran everywhere, and I was scared because I had never seen a mouse before. This also sent our chickens into a frenzy as they chased down the fleeing mice and pecked at them.

Our big black hen actually ate a mouse, whole. She had to struggle through a few attempts at swallowing the thing, and I watched, horrified, as the mouse's tail wormed into the beak and disappeared down the hen's gullet.

"Higgledy Piggledy!" I said.

"What's that?" Louis asked.

I pointed. "The name of this chicken."

"Oh! I understand!" Louis said. He nodded enthusiastically. Louis was always happy. I liked that about him, and I often wondered why Wendy or my mother couldn't just decide to be happy like Louis could.

We went from nest to nest, picking up eggs. I occasionally dug into the hay with my cultivator, trying to stir up more mice, just so I could watch the carnage.

I said, "But I have a question."

"What is the question, Little Lucky?" Louis, who'd known my fathers since they were boys, liked to call me Little Lucky.

"What is a 'gentleman'?"

Louis shrugged. "A man who is civilized."

"So, there's no such thing as a gentleman anymore, then?"

"Put that back there."

Louis wanted me to put the cultivator down exactly where it had been when we came into the henhouse. Louis was like that. Louis appreciated the idea of order. Louis made life in the hole civilized through the reinforcement of predictability.

Then Louis said, "No. You read; you write; you don't run around naked and spit. You are a gentleman, Little Lucky."

"Sometimes I run around naked and spit," I said.

"That's all," Louis said. All the eggs were gathered in Louis's bucket.

"Not one of these chickens laid nine or ten eggs, though," I said.

Louis shook his head. "No chickens lay nine or ten eggs. One only. No more. One."

I was disappointed in the rhyme. Whoever made it up could have probably figured out something that rhymed with "hen" that wasn't grossly misleading. It bothered me for a long time. Why would Higgledy Piggledy churn out nine or ten eggs for a civilized man who didn't spit or run around naked?

I sighed. "Telling a lie is uncivilized."

Louis patted my shoulder. "That makes you a gentleman."

"Let's see how many eggs she lays for me tomorrow."

The Boy on a Boat Straddles Time

Once I'd read about a morning prayer—a practice in Judaism— that offered thanks to God for restoring one's soul upon awakening from sleep.

It made sense to me.

I often thought you would never know anything, not ever again, if you went to sleep and did not wake up. The enormity of that idea is both frightening and soothing, without end.

When my soul came back to me, I had been drifting in a boat, maybe for hours, maybe for days. Time is irrelevant when your soul checks out.

When my soul came back to me, and I opened my eyes, I was lying on my side. I was shirtless and sunburned, wearing nothing but torn camouflage pajama bottoms that were twisted around my legs.

When my soul came back to me, I was looking directly into the eyes of a brown-skinned little boy with knotted clumps of dripping wet, amber hair that dangled around his face. He was so close to me that it tickled my nose when he exhaled. His cold and wet little fingers were gripping my upper arm, and I was faintly aware that he'd been shaking me.

I remember wondering if I was looking at a human or a something else. The boy seemed to be as wild as anything I'd ever seen outside the hole.

"Hoo-wee! Look at that, Olive! I think he's alive!" the boy announced to someone else I couldn't see.

The boat rocked in the water.

I wasn't fully convinced I was awake.

I raised my hand to my face and rubbed my eyes. Everything seemed to be real, seemed to fit the model I'd constructed in my head. Then I reached across and touched the boy's hair. He was real too. I untangled my pajama bottoms and pulled them higher on my waist. It was all I could do to get into a sitting position. Standing would have been a very bad idea.

I could not remember how I'd ended up here, but when I saw the torn blisters on my palms, I dimly recalled pulling myself up on a rope and struggling to stay afloat in deep and cold water. For just a moment I believed I may have been the drowning man in Max Beckmann's painting.

"Where are we?" I said.

The boy smiled and twisted an index finger up inside his

nose. "Well. We're in your boat, which is named *Little Grace*, on a river that has a name, but I don't know what it is, somewhere in Tennessee, I'm pretty sure."

And Tennessee was inside somewhere else that had a name, which was in another place with a name, and on and on, name after name, word after word, without end.

I closed my eyes and rubbed my face. The connections were all dangling loosely.

"But don't worry. I swum out and tied your boat to shore to stop you from drifting, on account of your being next-to-dead unconscious. Hell! I thought you might have been dead! Didn't I say that, Olive?"

The boy had a little too much energy and spoke a little too loudly for me at that moment. I kept my eyes shut, trying to remember how I'd gotten here.

Then the kid said, "My name's Breakfast, and this is Olive."

I opened my eyes.

And then it hit me that for the first time in my entire life I was in the presence of another young person—a boy who was alive and real and outside of a hole.

I tried to take it all in—coax the pieces to reassemble. The boy who sat in front of me, his knees up in his chin, knuckles braced on the deck of the boat, was completely naked. His lack of clothing wasn't unnerving or stressful, or even odd to me—like it would have been to Wendy or the civilized Louis, or even my mother—because those issues just didn't exist in the after-the-hole world. Behind the boy—Breakfast—were two wood-framed glass doors with windows on either side. I could see inside the boat's cabin, which looked like a house. There was a bed, a kitchen and dining table, and even a woodstove that brought back memories of our last Christmas in the hole, when Wendy had set everything on fire.

And it had all been sealed behind glass—a neatly preserved museum display, like the posters and decorations in Henry A. Wallace Middle School, from a time before I was born.

I said, "What did you say?"

"Breakfast," the boy repeated. "My name is Breakfast."

"I know you," I said. "I've read notes you left behind for us. We've been waiting to find you."

Breakfast rocked enthusiastically and scratched his balls. "Hoo-wee! I knew somebody would find those things, Olive! I knew it!"

Then I looked past Breakfast and for the first time realized the person he'd been talking to—Olive—was not a person at all. Olive was a chimpanzee. She was perched on the edge of the upper deck that sat atop the cabin's flat roof. Although I had never come face to face with an actual chimpanzee in my life, I'd seen enough pictures and videos of them to confirm to me how this one—Olive—fit into my model of the world.

"You— There's a monkey behind you," I said.

Breakfast glanced back at Olive, then, with a little bit of acid in his voice, said, "That's Olive, my best and only friend in the world. Don't call her names."

I shook my head and combed my fingers through my sweaty hair. "I'm sorry. I didn't mean to call her names."

Breakfast nodded. "That's okay, then. I believe you."

Olive bounced up and down.

And Breakfast said, "Are you hurt or something?"

I shook my head. "No. I don't think so. I'm really thirsty."

Breakfast stood up and pointed over the top of the bow. "We have water. And food, too. Are you hungry?"

I said, "Yes."

"Well? Do you have a name, or are you just the boy we found on a boat?"

"Arek."

"Nice to meet you, Arek!" Breakfast rubbed the back of my neck and added, "And I'll be honest—I'd have left you out on the water if you was old, and not just a boy, because, you know, old people who's been around since the other times, well, you just can't trust 'em, can you?"

"No. You can't."

"Well, let's get you out of the sun. You look like you're as burnt as you could ever be!"

Breakfast flattened his hand to shade my eyes. Then he grabbed my hand and pulled me up to my feet. I saw how he'd taken a line from the bow and secured it to a tree along the shore, right by where a fire burned inside a ring of stones.

And, straddling time, that was exactly the moment when I remembered about Mel, and how I'd left her behind at Davy Crockett Campground, alone with that insane old Sergeant Stuart.

I had to get back to Mel.

Keeping My Eyes Out for Hungry Leopards

"Dang if driving a boat ain't about ten times simpler than driving a car," Breakfast said. "And there's less to crash into, too."

The boat—*Little Grace*—chugged slowly against the current, heading upstream.

The wild boy was a kind of miracle. He sat with one leg over the rail of the stern, his armpit hugging the tiller as he focused on the wide path of the river ahead of us.

He said, "Maybe me and Olive might look into getting a boat like this."

"Well, if I get back to my van, you can have this one," I said.

Olive clapped and patted my knee.

Breakfast and Olive had fed me fish and wild greens, and I'd sat with them in the shade of their little camp, where we exchanged stories about our lives as after-the-hole kids. While I had the strongest feelings of mistrust for Sergeant Stuart, Breakfast, who was born from the same time as me and Mel, made me feel as though I somehow belonged in his community—that we understood each other in a way that I hadn't experienced with anyone in my life, with the exception of Mel.

And it was easy to see how Breakfast fully regarded Olive as just another person—albeit one who did not speak. I found myself completely taking for granted the notion that Olive knew just as much about what was going on, if not more, than either Breakfast or I did.

And while I'd finished eating what they'd given me, Breakfast had scrambled between shore and boat, over and over, lugging heavy gas cans and tools and canvas bags, and in very little time the wild boy had the engine running on *my* boat, promising he and Olive would help me get back upriver to Mel and our van.

Breakfast took a deep breath and chewed on the end of a stalk from one of the plants he'd used to prepare the meal we had eaten.

"Damn," he said. "Sergeant Stuart. I could have swore he got eaten at the farm when we were completely overrun by those goddamned bugmen two summers ago. Do you know I wasn't even ten years old, and he wanted me to join the army?"

"He wanted to get me to join too," I said.

"I never said yes or no about it. I wouldn't even talk to him. But I refused to put on clothes, especially ones with all those symbols and flags on them. He did get Joe to join, though. Poor Joe. He was probably the same age as you when we first met Sergeant Stuart." Breakfast picked his nose and flicked a little scab of mucus into the river. "How old are you, anyway?"

"Sixteen. Same as Mel."

"I only seen a handful of girls in my entire life, besides Olive. And most of them were old enough to be my mother's mother."

"I've only seen four in my entire life," I said.

"Besides Olive," Breakfast added.

"Yes. Besides Olive," I agreed.

Breakfast nudged the tiller out a few inches and pushed forward on the boat's throttle with one of his bare feet.

"It's so hot," he said. "I have half a mind to just jump out into the water."

"I can't swim."

Breakfast was shocked. He couldn't understand how there would ever be such a boy who did not swim, nor catch things with his bare, wild hands.

"No wonder you wear britches, then. You ain't even a bit wild."

"I suppose not," I said. "I was raised in a hole."

"I lived in plenty of holes," Breakfast said. "That never stopped me from *living*."

"There were lots of rules in the hole."

"Well, I could show you how to swim. There's not much more to it than knowing not to breathe in water. That's the main rule of swimming: Don't breathe water."

"Thank you."

"You have any money?" Breakfast asked.

"What?"

"Money. Don't you know what money is?"

"I guess I do. But I don't have any."

"Well, you should look into getting some. Me and Olive have lots of it. We're rich. We need to find more people with money, though. Otherwise it's not worth much."

"I guess that's true of most things."

Breakfast scratched his balls.

"How many bugs you seen since you left your hole?" Breakfast, who knew all too well what living inside holes was like, asked.

"Only two, and they're both dead now," I said.

"This year, we ain't hardly seen none of 'em either. They're dying all over the place," Breakfast said.

I nodded. I thought something was wrong. Nothing came close to the model that had been built for us inside the hole. The world was different, changed from how my parents believed they'd left it.

Olive bounced contentedly. She rubbed my back and combed her fingers through my hair.

Maybe the hole was closing, I thought. Maybe it was all over, everywhere, and now people could finally come out from their holes and reestablish all the magnificent things that made us human—hatred, war, competition, betrayal, thievery, selfishness, sinking ships, rules—the things that drove men like Max Beckmann to paint.

It's no wonder cicadas live so briefly after they come out; cicadas probably did really shitty things to one another, given enough time.

"We killed one the other day, and it was all full of worms inside," I said.

"Yep," Breakfast said. He held up a hand and wriggled his rough little fingers. "I seen that before too. White worms, as big as your fingers. Yep, I think they're dying off. Good for us, right?"

The afternoon cooled into evening. I had no idea how far down the river had carried me, or how long I'd been sleeping on the deck of the *Little Grace* when Breakfast found me. I didn't want my mind to start imagining all the terrible things that might have happened to Mel since the night we separated. Those things were too frightening to put into words, and putting them into words would help to make them real. I tried to only think about the perfect last moments Mel and I had been together and alone, before Sergeant Stuart showed up, pounding on our door, tricking us, invading our hole.

In my mind, I made up a story about *The African Queen*— about the boat in the movie, if it was anything like this one, and if the man and the woman on the cover's picture actually ended up kissing, or maybe doing a lot more than just kissing in the movie. I decided the man would be named Arek, and the woman would be named Mel. And, in the movie, Arek and Mel are on this boat together, but they don't know where they're heading. The movie Arek and the movie Mel love each other very much, but they both want the other to be free and wild, so neither of them admits how they feel. In his defense, the movie Arek had been hit in the balls with a bag of rocks and was forever cautious about relationships after that; and, in her defense, the movie Mel was very patient and hopeful that the movie Arek would believe in himself and stop being afraid of things that would never happen, like Bigfoot attacks and murderous blackbirds. Then movie Arek and movie Mel get separated, and they both become very lonely and realize how badly they'd squandered their opportunity to find the only thing that truly matters.

Then movie Arek gets eaten by leopards and dies a frustrated virgin.

The end.

That was my movie, and all stories are true.

I hoped I'd be able to watch it with Mel, even if movie me did end up being eaten.

I hoped Mel and I could crawl back inside our little hole in that black Mercedes van and shut everything else in the universe out, without end.

And as the *Little Grace* trudged along, I kept my eyes out for hungry leopards hiding in the trees along the darkening shore.

An Optimist for a Librarian

Fathers are required to reveal frightening truths to their sons.

Sometimes those truths are after-the-fact explanations, like when my dad, Austin, told me the truth about why getting hit in the balls with a bag of rocks hurt as bad as it did.

Sometimes those truths are inaccurate but elaborate models of reality. All the colors are dulled, all the edges made safe to touch.

And sometimes those truths make you think about things you never want to deal with. They keep you from sleeping at night. They make sons wish they could take on all their father's hurt.

Maybe all boys have to confront their terrible truths at the age of thirteen.

Robby, my other father, told me this: "When I was in seventh grade, just after I turned thirteen years old, my father went away. And even though everyone expected him to come back, he never did."

I wanted to ask Robby what that was like for him, but it was all too much. I had no construct for knowing what school or seventh grade would have been like, or how that was also the year that Robby fell in love with Dad. On top of everything, I did not want to think about either of my fathers going away and then not returning to me, to the hole.

And I don't know why Robby told me about his father at that particular moment.

This happened just after the imposition of Wendy's bath-segregating rule. I was only eleven years old, and I was in the shower room, drying myself off like a good banished and segregated boy was supposed to do. It was morning, Wendy's official *boys' time* to take showers, and I was watching Robby shave.

Matching him, I wrapped a towel around my waist and stood next to Robby at the sink.

I was fascinated by shaving, watching my fathers do it as often as I had. With each stroke Robby made with the razor, I mirrored the same sweeping movements on my own face, using my first two fingers as my pretend razor.

"How long were you sad for?" I asked.

Robby stopped shaving and looked at me. Robby was always so good at looking at people when he talked to them.

He said, "Forever, Arek."

"Oh."

"At first, nobody knew he was not going to come back. But when it became obvious, I almost couldn't deal with it. I thought it was about me. I think all kids have a tendency to do that, to believe that whatever happens is always directed at us personally, no matter what. I thought my father left us because he didn't like me."

"But that wasn't true, right? Who would ever not like you?" I said.

Robby tilted his chin up and shaved his neck.

I did the same thing with my fingers.

Robby said, "There were a lot of people in the world then. It was natural, and practical, to be picky."

"But not with your own son."

I could not believe such things ever happened, despite the enormity of the before-the-hole population above, and Robby, sensing this, was kind enough to offer, "You're right. Nobody would ever do such a thing to their sons. But it was hard for me not to blame myself. It was hard for me to blame him."

Robby rinsed off his razor in the sink.

I rinsed off my first two fingers.

Robby wiped his face with his towel.

I did the same thing.

"Well, if you and Dad ever went away and did not come back, I'd come look for you," I said.

"It's a really big world out there."

"Then why are there so many more books and stories about people finding each other than there are about people losing each other?"

Robby said, "Eden has an optimist for a librarian."

"Just don't ever go away, okay?"

Robby hugged me and told me that he loved me, and that he would never go away.

Jumping on the Bed While the Ship Goes Down

When Breakfast asked me if I'd seen the man in the sky, at first I thought he was talking about God.

I thought this was going to end up being some kind of conversation like those I'd had while sitting in my underwear beside Wendy on a cold pew, staring at a plain Danish Modern crucifix, even though I'd quite obviously already ruled out the possibility the wild boy would throw in Wendy's admonitions regarding circumcision and cutting off your right hand.

"I seen him three times now, all in different places, flying by, overhead, in that noisy airplane of his," Breakfast said. "I'm not sure if he's ever seen me and Olive or not."

"We saw the plane . . . I don't know, maybe a couple days ago. I think the people flying it are my fathers," I said.

Breakfast frowned, and his little eyebrows came together. "How many fathers do you have?"

"Two," I said.

328 • ANDREW SMITH

"Damn. I don't even have one. How many mothers do you have?"

"One. And one grandmother. That's my entire family. My grandmother makes me go to church. It's scary."

"Damn. Well, you have a lot of people, that's for sure. All I got's Olive. But I did live in a church at one time. I used to pee on its colored glass window."

Olive, completely understanding Breakfast, bounced and clapped, perched above us on the edge of the upper deck.

And Breakfast said, "Why'd you run away from 'em?"

I had to consciously stop myself from saying *I don't know*.

I said, "I need to find my fathers. I need to let them know that it's okay for me to be out here on my own now, even if I don't live long, because I am not going back to live in a hole for the rest of my life."

The wild boy shook his head. "Nothing's worse than being in a cage."

In the dark trees rising like canyon walls on either side of the river, insects buzzed and sang.

Breakfast chewed his lip thoughtfully and picked wax from his ear. He stood up on the back rail of the boat and peed over the side into the river.

Breakfast said, "Well. If we don't find the place where you parked your vehicle soon, we're probably going to have to tie the boat up for the night. It's soon going to be too dark to see where we're going."

"Let me see if I can get some lights on. There's got to be lights on this boat somewhere," I said.

Olive followed me inside the cabin. The place smelled like the inside of the boys' locker room at Henry A. Wallace Middle School, like the little hole Mel and I had found in Rome. There's something about air that has not been breathed by any living thing for decades that gives it a kind of dry and peculiar staleness. I went along both sides of the cabin and opened every window I could. Olive, fascinated, stayed right beside me.

At the bow end of the cabin, just on the other side of the woodstove's chimney pipe, I found a bank of smudged plastic light switches. I began flicking them up, and soon lights came on everywhere inside the cabin, as well as out on top of the deck, where floodlights aimed down at the river to the front and rear of the *Little Grace*.

Olive jumped on the bed.

I used to jump on the beds in the hole. Sometimes I did it with Mel, and sometimes my dads would do it too. I never saw Wendy or my mom jump on beds, but I can't believe they never did it. Maybe jumping on beds was a secret thing for Wendy and Mom. I think human beings are inescapably driven to jump on beds. Because there is something about jumping on beds that acts as an eraser to everything else on a canvas. Unfortunately for me, when I got up on the bed with Olive, if I stood, my head hit the cabin's ceiling, so I had to jump on the bed on my knees, which were scuffed up from falling down in the dirt outside the van on the night of Mel's birthday.

When I started jumping on the bed with her, Olive clapped and wriggled.

Breakfast yelled through the cabin's door, "What are you doing in there?"

I said, "Jumping on the bed with Olive."

"Not without me, you ain't!" Breakfast said.

Then Breakfast released the tiller, set the boat in neutral, and came into the cabin and started jumping on the bed with me and Olive.

Olive was very happy.

There was a terrible grating crash, and then the boat pitched forward and tipped sideways.

The *Little Grace* ran into a rock before Breakfast got four jumps in, and we all spilled off the bed and onto the floor of the cabin.

And for just an instant inside the cabin of the *Little Grace* it was 1912, and I was being tossed on the wild frozen sea. And I thought, given human nature and the size of the *Titanic*, there had to have been at least one or two people jumping on their beds when the ship hit the iceberg. Maybe even the captain himself was.

"Motherfucker!" Breakfast said. "Ha-ha! I hope you can learn how to swim real fast!"

Unlike the *Titanic*, the *Little Grace* did not sink, however.

Olive and I followed Breakfast out to the boat's stern deck. The *Little Grace* had come around in the current and was drifting downstream again. Once Breakfast engaged the engine and corrected the boat's course, I could see from the lights cast ahead of us that we had come back to Davy Crockett Campground. The dock where the *Little Grace* had been tied up when Sergeant Stuart pushed me into the river lay on the left bank just ahead of us.

A Shot in the Dark

I had never been away from home to the degree that I would know what a homecoming might feel like.

In all my years growing up in the hole, I never thought about what finding myself disconnected from what the others called Eden would really feel like, despite the fact that there were very few things I wished for more than leaving the hole.

I think the feeling of coming back home is something beyond our conscious control—as though each individual cell in our bodies gets a kind of magnetic programming about returning to a place of sanctuary and stability. That was the incomprehensible feeling I had that night when I came up the river's bank and saw our black Mercedes van parked exactly where I'd left it at Davy Crockett Campground.

There was no sign of anyone there.

The Mercedes was dark. Either someone had turned off the lights after I left, or the van's batteries had died.

We stood back at the crest of the bank and watched the quiet vehicle for several minutes.

Olive held Breakfast's hand.

The wild boy said, "Dang. You live in that?"

"Yes," I said.

Satisfied that there was nobody awake and moving around

inside the van, I walked across a narrow strip of grass, past the sign promising all the fun imaginable at Davy Crockett Campground, up to the Mercedes's door.

When the door opened for me and I realized Mel—or whoever—had left it unlocked, I knew it was a bad sign. I stuck my head inside, unable to see in the darkness, listening, even trying to smell, to find out if anyone was still here.

I stepped up into the van and felt for the interior light switch.

The lights came on. The first thing I noticed was the open bottle of whiskey on the table and the chairs where Sergeant Stuart and I had been sitting, still pulled out as we'd left them. Everything was exactly as it had been the night I went away from this place. The paintball gun was propped untouched in the corner; even my .22 was still under the covers on my bed.

Mel and Sergeant Stuart were both gone.

As far as I could tell, neither one of them had stayed in the van at all after I went into the river. I checked the bathroom.

"Mel?"

Nobody.

"Are they gone?" Breakfast stood at the van's open door.

"Yeah."

For the first time since opening my eyes on the sunburned deck of the *Little Grace*, I felt overwhelmed by fear, and I began imagining all the worst, most terrible things that might have happened to Mel.

I pushed my way past Breakfast and Olive and ran out to the little rise above the dock, screaming and screaming Mel's name, over and over, out into the darkness of the night.

"Mel! Mel!"

Breakfast and Olive stayed beside me. Then the wild boy told me, "You may want to plug up your ears, because I'm about to give a whistle, and it's pretty loud at times."

I had no idea.

Breakfast's whistle was so painfully loud it nearly knocked the teeth out of my mouth.

Olive apparently liked it. She jumped and clapped and hugged Breakfast.

In the dark surrounding us, I could hear sounds like thrashing in the trees and along the river's edge as animals ran from the noise of Breakfast's whistle or dropped dead in their tracks from fear.

I was stricken deaf. My ears rang so badly it felt like my head would split down the middle.

And despite not hearing him, I could tell by the grin on his face that the wild boy had said something to me like, "That was a good one, wasn't it?"

Olive jumped up and down and patted Breakfast's bony shoulders.

I rubbed my ears. I never wanted to hear that sound again.

But through the audible mud of the horns blaring in my head, seconds later we heard two gunshots coming from somewhere in the woods to the south of us.

"Motherfucker!" Breakfast said. "There's someone out there. Wild!"

I froze, unable to decide what to do. Gunfire is probably not something you'd want to run *toward* through dark woods in the middle of the night. On the other hand, the only person around here who'd likely have a gun was Mel. Sergeant Stuart had lost his somehow; I was certain of that.

Breakfast was watching me, waiting to see what I'd do.

He said, "Well? Don't you think we should go see if that's your girlfriend out there?"

What was he doing? Nobody had ever called Mel my *girlfriend* before. Where did Breakfast get that idea? I was confused, I could barely hear, but I also needed to find Mel.

"I—uh—"

"Well, come on, Olive! Let's get our rifle and see for ourselves who heard us."

Breakfast padded across the dock, back toward the *Little Grace*, with Olive right behind.

I shook my head in an attempt to clear it, but it didn't work too well.

"Okay," I said. "Wait. Just give me a second."

I went back to the van and grabbed some shoes and the paintball rifle from its resting place beside my bed.

We stumbled through the twisted undergrowth along the riverbank for at least half an hour, trying to find whoever it was who'd fired the gunshots we'd heard. Olive, who was patient with the lack of agility on the part of Breakfast and me, led the way. She occasionally stopped to sniff at the air or some brush, and as we looked, I'd call out for Mel every few minutes. Eventually, we came to the edge of an opening in the woods at the base of a rocky escarpment of hills that rose up toward the west. Breakfast and I stopped right behind Olive, who tensed up when she heard movement—a sort of scraping noise—coming from the other side of the clearing.

"Mel?" I called.

"Arek? Arek?" Mel's voice was muddled, like she was underneath something.

"Are you okay?"

"Well, I'm kind of stuck."

Just Like a Scene from a Love Story

It turned out that it was Amelie Sing Brees who'd fired the shots we'd heard.

There was no sign of Sergeant Stuart anywhere, and Mel was, as she pointed out, kind of stuck.

She was pinned down inside a low, narrow tunnel at the base of a hill. The opening of the shaft looked as though it may at one time have led to a mine, or possibly an ancient storage place of some kind. And Mel wasn't alone in being stuck inside the tunnel. A large mottled Unstoppable Soldier was halfway buried in the opening, stuck up to the middle of its abdomen and unable to move forward or back as it continued to dig and struggle in an attempt to get to Mel.

So I said the stupidest thing that anyone could possibly say at that moment—I told Mel not to move, and to stay where she was.

Breakfast turned his face toward me. His knotted dreadlocks twirled like tassels.

He said, "She probably figured that out on her own, don't you think?"

But the creature was hopelessly stuck and had obviously weakened. It was impossible to say how long Mel had been pinned down as she was—it may have been a couple of days, for all I knew.

Cautiously, Breakfast, Olive, and I moved into the clearing to get a better look at how the monster had trapped itself. The creature's four hind legs kicked and scraped against the rocky ground. The footpads on them had all been damaged—toes were broken, and the legs were oozing the foul-smelling goop that circulated within the Unstoppable Soldiers' bodies.

After all this time out of the hole, I realized that Unstoppable Soldiers were not very smart at all. It must have been sheer numbers and little else that had allowed them to overrun all the before-the-hole humans and that drove the handful of us to condemn ourselves willingly to Eden.

Breakfast, fearless, stepped right up to the thrashing monster. He scratched his balls. Then Breakfast raised his hand and slapped the thing—*whack!*—right in the center of its back.

"Ha-ha!" The wild boy laughed. "I never touched a living one before!"

"What the fuck are you doing?" I said.

Breakfast smiled and raised his hand in preparation to slap it again.

Olive jumped and clapped.

The Unstoppable Soldier flailed with rage. It raised its bruised carapace and fluttered its shredded wings wildly as Breakfast laughed and hopped from foot to foot. The wild boy slapped it again, and, infuriated, the creature thrashed and kicked while Breakfast peed on it.

I repeated my very non-rhetorical question: "What the fuck are you doing?"

Then Breakfast caught hold of one of the monster's back legs and began pulling on it.

"I'm wild! Come on, little peckerhead. Come out and play! I'm wild!"

He was fucking insane, is what he was, I thought.

Breakfast spat and cheered. "Hoo-wee! Lookit this, wouldja? Ha-ha! I'm wild! Wild and rich! That's how come I can live like this! Hoo-wee!"

I screamed at him, "Let go of it!"

Breakfast waved me off. "You watch, britch-wearing boy. If this thing comes around and gets a look at Olive, it'll kill itself just trying to get away from us! And you want to know why? Because it knows we're wild!"

Olive knew why.

The Unstoppable Soldier thrashed, buzzed its useless wings, and kicked its wounded legs, angrily curling its pillowed abdomen, shitting and pissing in rage.

Olive clapped. She scooted past the wild boy, climbed up the face of the hill, and perched herself above the blocked doorway.

Mel called out from the tunnel, "Arek? Is that you? What are you doing?"

Breakfast pulled fiercely on the monster's leg, laughing and whooping.

Watching Breakfast play with the creature was frustrating. I was sure I was about to see this little wild punk, who I liked for unexplainable reasons, get shredded by the thing's spikes and barbs.

I said, "Fuckbucket."

Then I raised the paintball rifle, unhitched the safety mechanism, aimed, and fired two shots that struck the monster's quivering abdomen just beneath its damaged, pulsating wings.

The Unstoppable Soldier exploded in an eruption of unfertilized eggs, steaming ropes of white goo, and wriggling maggotlike parasites that were as big as cucumbers. The hot fountain of slime sprayed all over the little wild naked boy who'd been jerking the monster's leg to torment it.

"Aah! Motherfucker!" Breakfast screamed. "It's full of shit!"

The wild boy was very, very mad. He'd never expected to be hopelessly covered with incomprehensible shit and slime for a second time in his life, not to mention the gigantic maggots.

Then the Unstoppable Soldier's leg—the one Breakfast was tugging on—came off in the boy's goopy grasp, and Breakfast slid backward in the writhing stew of innards, falling hard onto his back.

"Gah! Fuck! Fuck this!" Breakfast squirmed and kicked, trying to regain his feet in the wriggling gelatinous slop. More and more of the creature's acidic bowels emptied, hosing all over the protesting Breakfast, into his mouth and nostrils. About a half dozen of the cucumber-size maggots slithered up the wild boy's legs and across his belly. Breakfast slapped at them, then took off running like the wild boy he was, crashing and snapping through the brush, down toward the river, swearing and howling, with the unquestionably loyal Olive happily following behind.

The Unstoppable Soldier, emptied out, slumped motionless and deflated, broken into oozing segments in the noxious and steaming lake of its innards that boiled with hundreds of glistening worms.

In the distance, at the river, Breakfast cursed and wailed.

I stepped around the burbling puddle that had formed beneath the carcass of the monster, in order to peer into the tunnel where Mel was trapped.

"Mel?"

Mel's voice came out of the darkness of the little shaft. "Oh my God, Arek. I was so scared."

"It's all right now. The thing's—well, it's kind of rearranged now," I said.

"Where were you? What happened to you?"

"I don't really know. I woke up and I was on a boat, and I'd been found by this crazy little naked kid and a monkey named Olive, but don't call her a monkey, or the naked kid will get mad at you."

Mel didn't say anything for a few seconds. I was reasonably sure my explanation was a lot for her to take in, all things considered.

Then she said, "Are you okay?"

It sounded like she maybe thought I was crazy, or possibly drunk.

"I'm okay, Mel. Are you okay?"

Mel said, "I'm tired of being in here. I've been stuck like this here for two days."

"Well, it's time to get you out, then, I guess."

I could almost hear both of us sighing with the same breath.

"Thank you," Mel said.

"Mel?"

"What?"

"I'm stupid."

"Are you drunk, Arek?"

"No." I swallowed. "I'm stupid because I should have told you a long time ago how goddamned much I'm in love with you, Amelie Sing Brees."

"Oh," Mel said. "This is just like a scene from a love story: You, me, and a giant fucking dead bug in between us."

"And there's maggots as big as my forearm," I added.

"Of course. And there's maggots," Mel said.

"Sorry."

"Arek?"

"What?"

"You made me so happy right now."

"With the maggots?"

Way back there, in the cave, Mel laughed. I could almost imagine seeing her eyes.

Mel said, "I love you so much, Arek."

"Well, good. Let's try to not get any of that bug pus on our faces, then, so when you come out of there we can kiss like people in love with each other are supposed to kiss. I mean, this being a love story and all."

Journey on the Fish

Max Beckmann said, *What matters is real love for things of the world outside us and for the deep secrets within us.*

All these things of the world and all our secrets had been hidden too long.

I thought I'd been looking my entire life to find what mattered—Max Beckmann's notion of *real love*—only to come to realize after leaving the hole that, like a shoreless sea, real love was everywhere around me, tossing and churning, and I was helpless to its wildness.

The year the Nazis came to power in Germany, when Max Beckmann had been labeled "degenerate," he started a piece of twinned images he called *Journey on the Fish*. It is a painting about uncertainty and love.

In it we see a man and a woman who appear to be flying above the curved horizon of the planet, over the sea. The man and woman are riding atop two fish, descending toward the uncertain world. The man is lying on his belly, naked, hiding his eyes in fright, his feet bound with a black rope around the tail of one of the fish; and the woman, who is sitting on the man's back, looks over her shoulder, downward and unafraid, to the rapidly approaching dark shape below. Her dress enfolds the man's body.

Like so many of Max Beckmann's paintings, *Journey on the Fish* displays what I think was Beckmann's recognition of the strength and bravery of the women he knew. The woman on the fish is a likeness of Beckmann's wife, after all.

And I always knew Mel was much braver than me, too.

On the curve of the blue sea is a solitary boat, its pregnant white sail supported by an unmistakable blackened crucifix. It is unclear whether the pair are plummeting toward an empty abyss or a dark shoreline—misfortune or sanctuary. In the man's hand is a mask—the silhouette of his lover's face—and in the woman's hand is the mask of the man.

The lovers on the fish, falling rapidly toward an uncertain fate, had removed each other's masks to allow the deep secrets beneath them to be revealed.

Falling and falling and falling, without end.

This is me.

Mel was still wearing the same pajamas she'd had on the night Sergeant Stuart showed up pounding on our door.

We were both dirty and tired, but I knew when I saw her crawl from the tunnel's opening that Mel was the most perfectly beautiful thing in the world outside the hole.

She dropped the .45 she'd been carrying, and we fell into each other's arms.

I said, "This is how it was always supposed to be."

"Yes."

"Even if I'm wrong."

Mel said, "You're not."

"Let's get away from here," I said.

Mel picked up the gun and took my hand, and we walked across the clearing into the woods. She looked around as though something were missing, or perhaps to be certain we were alone. And Mel asked, "Didn't you say there was someone else?"

I nodded. "A little boy named Breakfast."

Mel stopped. "The same kid you and your dad have been talking about?"

"Yes. He found me. And his friend—he has this friend named Olive, and she's a chimpanzee, but Breakfast thinks she's just a wild person."

"And you're not drunk?" Mel said.

I shook my head and called out, "Breakfast! Olive! I'm coming back to the van! Breakfast!"

Then came the inevitable whistle, and I was very happy that we were perhaps a quarter mile from where the wild boy had gone down to the river.

And through the dark of the woods came Breakfast's voice. "Hoo-wee! I ain't never going to let one of those peckerheads blow up all over me again! Wild!"

The night Sergeant Stuart shoved me into the water, Mel had, as I'd suspected, left the van through the driver's door while I talked the sergeant into leaving his rifle on the riverbank. And it was Mel who'd thrown the man's gun off the dock before she came back to the van.

"What happened to Sergeant Stuart?" I asked.

"I'm not sure," Mel said. "He was crazy. He was furious because he knew I'd done something with his gun. He told me he was going to make me a soldier, that he was going to show me what you never would be able to. I pulled the gun on him and told him to stay away from us, or I'd shoot him."

"Would you have done that?"

Mel said, "I don't think so. He didn't believe me either, so I ran into the woods, and he chased after me. That's when the bug came out. I think Sergeant Stuart fell down or something. I heard him cussing and yelling. He was really mad about what we'd done, Arek."

"Oh."

"And two days later, you came back."

We emerged from the woods near the dock. In the light cast out through the van's windows, I could see the forms of Breakfast and Olive, waiting for me to come back.

Mel said, "Looks like your friends are here."

"They're good . . . um . . . people," I said.

Then I grabbed Mel's hand and made her stop so we could kiss one more time before going back to the van.

Home to Me

I drove that night until I began falling asleep at the wheel.

When I knew it was too much and I had to rest, I parked the van in the middle of the roadway and went back to take a shower and to throw out my torn and filthy pajama bottoms.

I came out dressed in the boxers Mel had washed for me. Mel sat, wearing my number 42 basketball jersey as a nightshirt, talking and laughing with Breakfast. It was a scene definitely worthy of committing to canvas: Mel in my tank top, sitting on the edge of my bed, in deep conversation with a naked wild boy and a chimpanzee, while I stood observing from the bathroom doorway, dressed in boxers with John Deere tractors on them.

This was the world after the hole.

And the four of us climbed onto my bed and watched *The African Queen* together, which was the first thing I'd seen on television that did not scare the shit out of me. It was also the first movie Breakfast had seen in his entire life. I'm not sure about Olive, but I'm guessing she'd never seen one either.

But we did all start to cry at the end when Charlie, who was not named Arek and did not get eaten by leopards, and Rose, who was not named Mel and who was not at all patient with Charlie because she was much more like a movie version of Wendy than she was like Mel, got married just before they were about to be executed by German soldiers during World War I, which was exactly the same hole that D. H. Lawrence and Max Beckmann had gone through.

Even Breakfast and Olive cried at the end of the movie.

Olive wiped Breakfast's red face.

The wild boy's nose ran a steady stream of cry snot.

And Breakfast said, "I'm madder than a shiny treasure chest full of hornets. I ain't ever cried in my entire life, and now I feel like this is going to turn my guts inside out. Motherfucker!"

Then we laughed, and we cried some more too, because this was the first time, maybe on all the planet, that after-the-hole kids found after-the-hole kids.

We said our good-nights. Breakfast and Olive went to sleep on Mel's little bed, and, for the first time since we were just small children, Mel and I went to sleep together in mine. We held on to each other, and I pressed my face into the side of her neck so I could breathe Mel into me.

And I whispered to her, "You are home to me. I don't care about houses."

"I love you so much, Arek."

"Thank you, Mel. Nothing else matters."

Dobey's Corners

My hair grew long.

The skin on our shoulders and arms turned brown from sunlight.

We were joined to the world outside, not as pieces of a model, but as the *thing* itself.

We straddled time, and in doing so, changed. I can see the Arek and Mel who were born and lived in a hole as images on a canvas observed by the Arek and Mel after the hole.

One day I will paint that.

There were no secrets within us.

All our stories, exposed, were true.

Months after the hole, we found ourselves in the dead middle of a brutal summer.

We drove through a wasteland of felled trees, washed-out bridges, and highways reclaimed to wildness by woods; and although we'd seen two more sick and dying monsters, we found no more humans. At times I wanted to quit looking for my fathers—to find a home and stay there for a while with Mel—but she would not allow me to give up.

Mel was like that.

She would always remind me of that one line from Lawrence, because we didn't need a house if we had already found our home.

Once, in the hole, I'd asked my second father, Robby, why

there were more stories about people finding each other than there were about people losing each other.

Robby was never one to give answers merely to soften the impact of all those unexpected things that scrape boys' knees. That was another thing about Robby that I realized was part of his plan to prepare me to get out of the hole, like the fishing trip we took when I was thirteen.

We came to a small town that was little more than the intersection of two straight roads. The town was called Dobey's Corners.

Before we'd left that morning, the four of us—Mel, Breakfast, Olive, and me—played Yahtzee. Olive won. She was very good at Yahtzee.

Breakfast and I drew gas up from an underground tank at a service station. Diagonally across the intersection from us stood a three-story brick building with a rusted sign hanging vertically along one corner that said CHICO'S.

On the windowless side of Chico's was a sign that had been painted directly onto the bricks. The sign was blue with a red-and-white checkerboard pattern on its border, an advertisement for Purina Chows, whatever that may have been.

I had no idea what Chico's used to be either. Most of the front wall of the building had collapsed, and loose bricks were scattered everywhere in the street. Mel and Olive hunted inside Chico's and the other three buildings that established the entire town of Dobey's Corners. They were looking for anything that might be useful to us.

"What do you think that was?" the wild boy asked.

I said, "Purina Chows was the name of Chico's father. He disappeared when Chico was just a boy, so Chico painted the sign on the side of his building as a reminder to everyone in Dobey's Corners to keep looking for his father."

"How old was the boy when his daddy vanished?" Breakfast asked.

"Twelve, just like you," I said.

The wild boy always liked it when I made my stories about someone exactly like him.

Breakfast picked his nose and scratched his balls. "Did he wear clothes?"

"Never. Chico was wild."

"Ha-ha! Wild! That's how come I knew it, just from his name. Nobody would ever be named Chico unless he was wild."

"Or Breakfast," I said.

"Hell yes. Wild."

Breakfast walked to the edge of the station lot and peed on an old rusted sign that had numbers and the names of different kinds of fuel on it. He said, "Well, why did Purina Chows disappear?"

I shook my head. "It was a great mystery, because Purina Chows loved his son Chico, and Chico's mother, whose name was Willa, very much. Most people think that Purina Chows was attacked by an enormous flock of ravenous blackbirds, who disassembled him in their beaks, piece by tiny little piece, and then put him back together again, up in the clouds."

"Is that true?" Breakfast asked.

"Of course it is," I said.

"Can blackbirds really do that?"

"Yes."

"Well, cover me up with a truckload of somebody else's goddamned shit if I don't have another thing I got to look out for now. Fucking birds!" Breakfast said.

"Yes. Fucking birds," I agreed.

Breakfast spat.

And as though cued by some hand marking the canvas that contained our world, a plane, rumbling, flying low in the sky out of the north, came nearer and nearer to the brick-strewn spot called Dobey's Corners, where the wild boy and I stood.

Enough People for a Real Basketball Team

This time, they saw us.

The plane circled overhead, so low at times we could see hands waving at us in the windows.

Mel and Olive came out into the street to watch with us, and the plane, coming lower and lower, flew out directly over Route 854, which was one of Dobey's Corners' only two streets.

And a mile away from us, the plane touched down, turned around, and came to a stop on the surface of the road.

"Is it them?" Mel asked.

"I think so," I said.

It was the same plane from the manuals Robby had kept in the library of the hole.

The strange thing to me was, in that moment, I felt confused, almost as though I didn't honestly want to find my fathers. It was as though looking for them had been enough to keep us from returning to the hole, but now the end of their flight was perhaps the end of our journey. I imagined going back to Iowa with them, seeing Mel, re-dressed in a white Eden Project jumpsuit, while, without end, I endured Wendy's rules, went to church with her, witnessed the annual setting of flames to Christmas, and arrived at last on some final and resolute shore.

Maybe that was why the man on the fish in Max Beckmann's painting covered his eyes: He didn't want the journey with his lover, as uncertain as it was, to come to an end.

That's why all boys go away: to chase endlessness.

Ahead of us, the door on the plane opened. One person got out and stepped down onto the road, followed by another.

"Hoo-wee! It's the man in the sky!" Breakfast said. "I knew it was only a matter of time before he came down here and showed himself. Wild! Let me grab some money for him!"

The wild boy and Olive ran back to the van to retrieve some of Breakfast's treasure.

Mel took my hand, and we started walking toward the plane and the people standing in the roadway.

"Is it really them?" Mel asked.

"Regardless, I think we now have enough people for a real basketball team," I said.

I Am Shoreless Man

Dad grabbed me and cried.

It was only the second time in my life I had seen my father cry.

Robby, my other dad, hugged Mel and then kissed me on my ear.

Robby said, "Your hair is long, Arek."

And Dad told me, "Wendy would not approve of your outfit, son."

I was only wearing boxers.

I was half-wild, at least.

I said, "It's a superhero outfit. I am Shoreless Man. Besides, wait till you see our friend with all the money." And I hitched my thumb over my shoulder to point down the road behind me, where a chimpanzee and a wild naked boy with shoulder-length dreadlocks, carrying handfuls of cash, came walking toward us.

Dad wiped his face.

"Your eyes look different," he said.

"They're after-the-hole eyes, Dad," I explained.

Dad nodded.

He understood.

After all, my father could straddle time too.

My father looked at Mel's hand in mine and said, "When you were thirteen, you told us that you never wanted to go back to Eden. Remember?"

I squeezed Mel's hand.

"But we're not a very good version of Adam and Eve, Dad."

Dad shrugged. "Who could know? It's only a story."

"All stories are true."

Dad smiled and nodded. "How do you like it out here?"

"Well. There are no rules," I said. "There are no rules, and it's wild."

Acknowledgments

Before writing this book, I had a dream about a wild boy named Breakfast. I never questioned the name, and I knew he had to be in this book, because like Arek, Mel, and Olive, he was part of what would happen next.

I went through a hole before I wrote this book.

The thing about holes is that when you're in one, you can't imagine being out of it. And then one day it just happens, and you realize you're once again aboveground.

I wrote a few books while I was in that hole, and they are all to some degree self-examinations of what being in (and out) of holes is like.

Most of this book was written at my home in Southern California.

I wrote an awful lot of it in airports, some of it in San Francisco and St. Paul, and some of the final pages in Denver.

People don't often talk about the *place* where a particular book was written.

I wrote about half of it on my laptop and half on my desktop computer.

They are both Macs.

I've done some edits here and there on a PC. It messes up the fonts and page numbers, which can be confusing when you go back and forth, but most of the time I have no choice about when and where I can work.

Like Max Beckmann, I have always been fascinated by the idea of the self-portrait.

This is my thirteenth self-portrait.

I am also fascinated with the number 13. (I prefer odd numbers to even, by the way.) I was staying with my aunt, Fernanda Tinti, in Trieste, Italy, on my eighteenth birthday. She gave me a silver key chain with the number 13 on it that day. She told me that for her, thirteen was a very lucky number, and I've never had any reason to disbelieve anything she ever told me. She was like my second mother, and I miss her (and Trieste) very much.

I think Beckmann painted himself in so many different ways because he was endlessly trying to strip away exterior and arrive at truth—what he called the deep secrets within. I don't know whether or not any of us is capable or brave enough to expose all those truths. Max Beckmann tried more than eighty times, so I've got dozens of future attempted self-portraits ahead of me, at a minimum.

In 1947, Max Beckmann came to America to teach at Washington University in St. Louis. Today, the St. Louis Art Museum hosts one of the finest collections of Beckmann's work, including *The Sinking of the* Titanic and his *Self-Portrait* (1950), which was one of the artist's final works. He died in New York in 1950.

I remember it was quite an interesting cab ride the day I went to the St. Louis Art Museum with my great friend A. S. King to look at the Beckmann collection there. It moved me so much I had to explore what he saw and try to put some of it—however flawed my interpretations are—in a book. This one.

• • •

There are so many people I knew before the hole who supported me and helped me through the time that I wrote my lost and introspective in-the-hole books, and who remained my friends during the time that I assembled this after-the-hole self-portrait.

I have endless thanks, appreciation, and gratitude for them. First, my inspirational writing partners, A. S. King and Z. Brewer. You are beautiful, and I love you both. You help me be a better person and, hopefully, a better writer. It's nice to know people who you can confidently say make the world a kinder place. Thank you, Jandy Nelson, for being the person you are and a writer whose words are brave and beautiful. And great thanks to Anthony Breznican, Mahvesh Murad, Yvonne Prinz, Alex Green, Jason Piccioni, Christa Desir, Michael Grant, Will Walton, and Tommy Wallach. Thank you, Matthew MacNish (Rush) and Jonathon Arntson. I love you guys.

Thank you, thank you, thank you, Matt Faulkner and Kris Remenar, and also Brendan Heffernan. You make the world more beautiful.

And I have to give tremendous thanks to all the readers, especially the kids, all over the world who send me notes expressing positive things my books have done for them. There is no greater reward in life than hearing from you, and so much of this can only be facilitated because of mentors—teachers, librarians, parents, and friends—who help build those connections between words and their readers.

To my family: Jocelyn, Trevin, and Chiara, I love you very much, without end. And much love to Peggy, Gene, Rosemary, Aunt Kim, Cousin Kim, James, Dan, Matt, Amy, Al, Christie,

Donny, Rachael, their swarming masses of children, Flora, Kim, Renata, Cindy, Patrick and Debbie, Steve and Linda, and all the ghosts who follow me everywhere.

Thanks to my editor, David Gale, and all the talented, enthusiastic people at Simon & Schuster: Justin Chanda, Lucy Ruth Cummins, Amanda Ramirez; and to my agent, Michael Bourret, and everyone at Dystel, Goderich & Bourret literary management; to Dana Spector at CAA; to Scott Rosenberg, who wrote one hell of a screen adaptation for *Grasshopper Jungle*; and to Edgar Wright, who, after reading *Grasshopper Jungle*, asked if I wanted to go to dinner and talk about that particular self-portrait.

One final note about Max Beckmann: He was once asked why he put fish in so many of his paintings, and what did the fish symbolize. Beckmann, who claimed he had never cried, and who never liked talking about what his paintings *re-presented*, said the fish symbolized whatever people thought they symbolized, and he included them in his works because he thought they were beautiful, and he also liked to eat them.

Sometimes thinking about fish makes me sad.

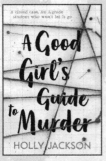
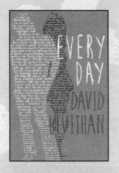